Buried
DREAMS

BOOKS BY NATASHA MADISON

STANDALONE NOVELS

Mixed Up Love

Faux Pas

Holiday Unscripted

THE SOMETHING SO SERIES

Something So Right

Something So Perfect

Something So Irresistible

Something So Unscripted

THE HEAVEN AND HELL SERIES

Hell and Back

Pieces of Heaven

THE TEMPT SERIES

Tempt the Boss

Tempt the Playboy

Tempt the Ex

Tempt the Hookup

THE LOVE SERIES

Perfect Love Story

Unexpected Love Story

Broken Love Story

THE HOLLYWOOD ROYALTY SERIES

Hollywood Playboy

Hollywood Princess

Hollywood Prince

THE THIS IS SERIES

This Is Crazy

This Is Wild

This Is Love

This Is Forever

THE SOUTHERN SERIES

Southern Chance

Southern Comfort

Southern Storm

Southern Sunrise

Southern Heart

Southern Heat

Southern Secrets

Southern Sunshine

THE ONLY ONE SERIES

Only One Kiss

Only One Chance

Only One Night

Only One Touch

Only One Regret

Only One Mistake

Only One Love

Only One Forever

THE SOUTHERN WEDDING SERIES

Mine to Kiss

Mine to Have

Mine to Hold

Mine to Cherish

Mine to Love

Mine to Take

Mine to Promise

Mine to Honor

Mine to Keep

THE MADE FOR SERIES

Made for Me

Made for You

Made for Us

Made for Romeo

THE MEANT FOR SERIES

Meant for Stone

Meant for Her

Meant for Love

Meant for Gabriel

THE DREAM SERIES

Shattered Dreams

Forbidden Dreams

Buried Dreams

Stolen Dreams

Forgotten Dreams

THE ONLY FOR SERIES

Only for Tonight

Only for Love

Only for Him

Only for Her

Buried DREAMS

DREAM SERIES

NATASHA
MADISON

BLACK STONE PUBLISHING

Published in 2026 by Blackstone Publishing
Cover design by Jay Aheer

Printed in the United States of America

ISBN 979-8-228-62954-7
Fiction / Romance / Contemporary

Version 1

Blackstone Publishing
31 Mistletoe Rd.
Ashland, OR 97520

www.BlackstonePublishing.com

One

EVERLEIGH

THE SOFT MUSIC PLAYS in the background as I twist open the mascara and look in the mirror, leaning forward to apply it. My long black hair is freshly blow-dried and pushed to one side, and my white robe is open down the front and loosely tied.

"Baby." Brock walks into the bathroom, wearing his weekend mechanic's uniform for when he goes to help his father. "I was calling you." He places his hands on the counter beside my hips. Fitting himself behind me, he pushes his chest up against my back. I feel the hardness of him all over, and I can't help but try not to smile at him.

"Brock, you are filthy." His face is streaked with a little bit of grease as he watches me move the makeup wand up and through my lashes. I look into his dark brown almost black eyes through the mirror. His hand goes around my waist, pulling me closer to him. "Your hands are covered in oil." I laugh at him as he leans down to kiss my neck, ignoring what I just said.

"Why did you take a shower without me?" he mumbles as I turn my head to the side. He doesn't wait for me to answer him. Instead, his lips come down to mine, kissing me softly before his tongue invades my mouth. I turn in his arms, not caring he's still dirty from work. My arms wrap around his neck as his hands grip my hips. "If you continue like this, we aren't going out tonight." His voice comes out hard and sexy as his hand moves from my hip and his finger trails down the edge of the opening of the robe. He pushes it to the side as my nipple, pebbled by his touch, stops the silk material from opening fully. His finger trails the little love bite he has been leaving me since we started sleeping together some six years ago. Right near my nipple, I wear his teeth marks or a little love bite. Either way, it's always there. He loves it. I'm not going to lie—I feel naked now without it on me.

His eyes always fixate on that mark as he licks his lips. "If you continue this . . ." I push him back, stepping away from him. He puts his hip against the counter, taking one more look at me as I make my way to the door.

He pushes off, removing his shirt and tossing it to the side, my eyes roaming him up and down. "And if you keep looking at me like that—"

"I'm leaving." I turn and walk out of the bathroom with a backward glance at him as he's unbuttoning his jeans, leading to one of my favorite parts of him. I close the door to make sure I don't turn around and join him, leading to us having sex in the shower. Instead, I run around picking up things to put in the dishwasher. Between the two of us working full-time, him helping his father on the weekends, and me helping my mom, the house could use a good cleaning. I load the dishwasher before heading to the bedroom and grabbing a pair of jean shorts and a tank top. The bathroom door opens, and the steam from the shower follows him as he walks out with a towel around his waist instead of naked like he always is.

His hand holds the towel closed at the side of his hip. "They will be downstairs in five minutes," he mumbles as he grabs a pair of boxers from his drawer by the bed, then drops the towel, showing me all of him. He's been my only boyfriend, and I thought once we moved in with each other, I would get used to seeing him naked all the time, but I haven't. Our sex life also hasn't died down. If anything, we're having more sex than ever. Before, we were having sex all the time, and we've also had sex all over the place: in his truck, by the creek, and in the bathroom at the bar. I smile at the memory, then shake my head. If we have an itch, we scratch it.

"I'm ready," I say. I walk back into the bathroom and apply lip gloss before watching him saunter back in wearing jeans and a T-shirt. He runs his hands through his jet-black wet hair a couple of times before turning to me and kissing my neck.

He's tying his sneakers at the same time the buzzer rings, and I look at him. "Don't make any plans for tomorrow," I inform him. "We are going to spend the day deep cleaning this place."

"Can't," he says, opening the door and pushing me out of it, "I plan on spending it naked and having you on every single surface I can have you on." He slaps my ass, pushing open the glass door to the apartment building. "I'm planning on wearing myself out." He grabs the white cooler I prepared before he got home. We usually take turns bringing a couple of bottles of beer. I can't help but laugh at him as we spot Waylon's pickup at the curb. The music blasts at full volume.

"Hey," I greet, holding up my hand and seeing Autumn smile at me as Brock opens the back door of Waylon's truck. "How is everyone doing?" I ask, getting into the truck and scooting to the middle of the seat.

"Good," Autumn answers with a smile over her shoulder. I can see she's been crying, but I don't ask her about it. We make eye contact, but she just shakes her head and looks over at Waylon. I can see this is another fight the two of them have had. The two of them spend ninety-five percent of their relationship fighting. The other five percent is Autumn tolerating what a dick Waylon is. If it wasn't for Autumn, I don't know if any of us would be friends with him.

"Hey," Brock says, slapping Waylon on the shoulder, "how are you doing?"

"Could be better," he replies, pulling away from the curb and almost peeling out of the parking lot. I put my hand on Brock's knee and squeeze it. I look over at him and raise my eyebrows, sharing with him that we should have just stayed home and had pizza.

The windows are down, so my hair flies all around my face as I turn to look out the window. The green trees line both sides of the road as we make our way over to pick up Charlie and Jennifer.

No one even tries to make any conversation as we pull up to their house. The two of them recently moved in together. "I am going to go in and pee," Autumn announces from the front seat of the truck.

"Jesus, again?" Waylon glares over at her, and the look isn't a friendly one. Instead, he's looking at her like he hates her. "You pee every ten seconds," he says, honking the horn to let Jennifer and Charlie know we are here.

I lean over, putting my hand on Brock's leg. His arm's across the back seat, around my shoulders. "If you ever looked at me like that," I whisper into his ear, "I would stab your big toe with a fork."

He chuckles and kisses the side of my head. "Why a fork?"

"It has more entry wounds." I look up at him as the passenger door closes. "So it means you'll be in more pain, which would make me the happiest."

The front door opens, and Autumn runs into the house. "She gets on my last nerve sometimes," Waylon mumbles, and I bite my tongue to tell him she's not the one who gets on our last nerve. I think Brock knows I'm about to say something because he picks up the hand that is on his knee and brings it to his lips and squeezes it.

The front door opens, and a second later, Jennifer is coming out, wearing white jeans and a turquoise top, her hair flying with the light wind. "Hey," she says, opening the door closest to me, and I squish over to Brock. She gets in the truck and leans over to kiss my cheek. "How are you?" she asks with a smile on her face before looking over at Brock and saying hello. She then turns and says hello to Waylon, who just mumbles while he texts something on his phone before tossing it to the side. He puts his hand in a fist and pushes the steering wheel so the horn honks again.

This time, the front door opens, and Autumn walks out in front of Charlie, who follows her to the truck. "Took you long enough," Waylon snaps when Autumn opens the passenger door and then looks over at Charlie.

"You sit up front." Autumn tries to hide she's pissed off at him and his words, but she fails miserably as she walks to the back door and opens it, sliding in and slamming the door, not giving Charlie an option. The four of us squish into the back seat. Jennifer moves closer to me, and I move closer to Brock, my ass practically in his lap. His arms wrap around my waist to make sure I don't fly anywhere.

"Hey." Charlie gets in the front seat, greeting us and trying to avoid the awkwardness of how quiet the truck is. He looks over at Brock, sharing a look. "How's everyone doing?" Charlie barely has his seat belt on before Waylon drives off, making Brock shake his head. "Good times," he says, looking at Jennifer, the two of them sharing an inside look. My eyes go to Autumn. She's looking out the window and not talking to them. Her finger pulls the side of her eye to stop the tear from coming out. I shake my head and look at Brock, who just shakes his head, telling me not to.

We head over to Waylon's family's hunting cabin some fifteen minutes on the outskirts of town. The log cabin is painted red, with a wraparound porch and four rocking chairs. We've been hanging around at the cabin since we were all sixteen, going up there with a couple of cases of beer that Waylon would get using his older brother, Winston, to buy it for us. We all went to high school together, all except Charlie, who just moved to town a couple of years ago.

Even after high school, we all stayed local while going to school. I attended to get my marketing degree, while Brock just got his bachelor's degree in architecture and will now be doing a complete internship for Waylon's family's construction company. Waylon's family has been around this town dating back to the nineteen twenties, when his great-grandfather started a construction company and went into lumber trading or something like that. Now they just do construction. If a building goes up in town, it's always with the Cartwright family building it. Brock will be helping them with the new development they plan on building. It's going to be one of their biggest projects ever, and he's helping develop the look of it.

As soon as Waylon turns the truck off, the doors open, and everyone jumps down. Brock goes to the back of the truck bed and grabs the cooler. He comes back to me and slides his hand in mine, as always, and we walk to the side of the house where eight big logs lie in an octagon shape around a firepit. We are here almost every single weekend just to sit and shoot the shit, or even during the week, we can go and eat and then just come here and chill.

The sun slowly goes down as Waylon returns with some wood and starts the fire while I sit on a log. Brock lets my hand go, kissing me quickly before walking over to stand with Charlie. They both watch Waylon as they chitchat.

"I am exhausted," Autumn states, sitting down on the log next to me. "I want to sleep for twenty-four hours straight." I sit next to Autumn, and then Jennifer sits next to me. "Like a whole twenty-four hours. Is that possible?" I laugh at her question and so does Jennifer.

"I don't know. The last time I slept really long, I was hungover after Brock's graduation. I swear to God, I think I slept half on the bed and half on the floor. I have a vague memory of that. I even fell asleep standing in the kitchen, waiting for the coffee to come out, but instead, I sat down on the kitchen floor and totally fell asleep." Jennifer leans in to me, laughing as I tell the story. The three of us have been friends since kindergarten and have literally gone through everything together. I'm an only child, but with the two of them, I feel like I have two sisters. Even when we were in high school, we spent every single weekend at one of our houses.

The sound of crackling from the fire fills the night air as we all talk about little things here and there, with us laughing and giggling at something one of us would say. When Waylon gets up and goes to his truck, all eyes go to watch him, wondering what the hell he's doing. When he opens the driver's side door, he turns the truck on and blasts the radio. The sound of a country song now replaces the sound of the snapping firewood. He holds one hand up in the air as he sways his hips. "Autumn, get your ass over here and dance with me." He grabs a bottle of water from the truck. Autumn groans from beside me but gets up as Jennifer also gets up. Autumn walks over to Waylon, who lunges for her, grabbing her arm and pulling her to him. She holds up her hands, pushing his chest as she tries to get away from him. "Baby," Brock says, and I look up at him, "will you dance with me?" He holds out his hand for me.

"Oh, yeah." I just smile at him, getting up and wrapping my arms around him, rising on my tippy-toes and waiting for him to kiss my lips. "Anything to be in your arms," I say as he rubs his nose with mine. I hear Autumn and Waylon arguing from beside me, but my eyes are locked on my man.

His hands move from my waist to my ass as he cups it. "You know what's better than this?" I ask him as we sway to the music. "Being naked in your arms."

He hums as he bends his head to kiss me at the same time Waylon shouts, "We should get the fuck out of here!" His voice is almost a scream as he tries to be louder than the music. "Hit up the bar in town, and see what's going on there." Brock's hands drop from my ass as I turn in his arms, wrapping my arms around his waist as he drapes one around my shoulders.

"We shouldn't do that," Autumn quickly says. He looks at her, and it's a look between a glare and a sneer. Either way, it's horrible, and I hate him even more for treating her like this.

"No one asked you, Autumn," he retorts, shaking his head and turning toward the four of us. "Who is with me?" He looks at the four of us. "Should we take off or what?"

"We can't leave until the fire is out." Charlie motions with his head toward the fire that is still going strong. No doubt trying to calm the situation.

"No problem." Waylon storms to the side of the porch where they keep the hose. Dragging it to the firepit, he puts out the fire in no time. "There, now let's get the fuck out of here."

"I think we're going to go home," I state, not wanting to be around him when he's in this kind of mood. "I have an early morning," I lie, and I know the girls know I'm lying since I told them I had nothing planned.

"Fuck that," Waylon spits out, going back over to the truck, "get your ass in the truck." My back goes up, and I'm about to say something, but I don't have a chance to because Brock does.

"Watch the tone, man," Brock warns him, and he just laughs it off, as he does with everything.

"It's all good, man," Waylon assures him. "Let's just get out of here and get to the bar. Then if you guys want to leave, I'll drive you home." He looks back at me. "There, happy?"

Brock and I share a look, and then we glance over at Jennifer and Charlie. I'm not sure what to do, but I know I don't want to go anywhere with him when he's in this mood. "Let's go, people." Waylon swings his arm around and around to get us moving toward the truck.

The four of us start walking to the truck. "I'll drive," Autumn offers. "I can drive." She walks over to Waylon, who just glares at her. She ignores his glare and smiles at him. "I can drive you around for once." Her voice goes soft as she holds on to his hips, but he shakes off her hands.

"No way." He shakes his head. "My truck, I drive."

"Waylon," she murmurs in a plea.

"Get in the truck," he orders her, his tone tight like he's losing his patience with her, his teeth clenched together, "or fucking walk home."

"Relax," Charlie finally jumps in, trying to break up the drama with the two of them, "we're supposed to be having fun."

"I'd be having more fun if we could get the fuck out of here," Waylon almost snarls, stomping over to the truck. "Now get the fuck in the truck, or else I'll leave you all here."

"I don't know if that would be a bad thing," I finally mumble as Brock chuckles beside me, pulling me to him and kissing my temple.

"I'm not sitting in the front. That's for sure," Autumn says, and I look at Brock, who just shakes his head.

"I'll sit in the front," Jennifer offers. "That way, the two of them will be happy at least."

"No way." Charlie shakes his head. "You sit in the back. I'll sit with him up front."

"Fine," Jennifer relents, watching Autumn get into the back seat, leaving the back door open for Jennifer to get in after her. I follow her and get on my side as much as possible so Brock can get in and shut the door.

The driver's window is open, and I see Waylon finish his water bottle and tossing it out the window. "Let's go, bro." He smirks at me and then at Charlie, who shakes his head but gets into the truck.

Waylon turns his truck around and speeds up at the same time. He puts the music on a bit louder. "Love this song!" he shouts, turning down the long stretch of road lined with trees on each side.

"He's being more reckless than normal," I whisper to Brock, who tightens his hold on me even more.

"Can you focus on the road, please?" Autumn asks what everyone is thinking.

"Can *you* focus on the road?" Waylon mimics her as he picks up his speed and goes even faster. "Pain in my ass," he grumbles and then turns his head around to talk to Autumn, taking his eyes completely off the road. "You're a pain in my ass. You focus on the fucking road." My eyes go from watching Waylon shout at Autumn to the flash of light that looks like it is coming straight for us.

"Watch out!" I shout to Waylon, who stops looking at

Autumn and looks ahead. "Oh my God, we're going to hit him." My eyes are on the road in front of me as the headlights look like they are getting closer and closer to us. It feels as if the car is heading straight toward us. The sound of honking now fills the outside noise.

He jerks the truck right, going off onto the gravel and then quickly turns the wheel to the other side. The sound of metal scraping now fills the truck. I don't know who yells first, me or Jennifer beside me. I'm now completely on Brock's lap, holding on to his arms around me as Jennifer slides to the middle of the bench. It takes a second, or maybe even less, for us to feel like we are flying through the air. I look at Brock, the fear in his face. "I love you," I whisper before my eyes shut, and I hear the crunching of metal. The blackness hits me as I feel like I'm being shoved forward.

Two

EVERLEIGH

Nine years later

I PICK UP MY GLASS of water while reading the email that just came in at the same time as my phone rings from beside my keyboard. Looking down, I see it's my mother. My eyes immediately go to the lower corner of the screen, noticing it's just after seven in the evening. It's like clockwork. There are certain things I can count on in my life, and my mother is one of them. Just like these nightly calls are. I slide the arrow to the side, accepting the FaceTime and seeing her face fill the screen. "Hey, Momma." I smile at her.

"Hey, baby girl," she replies, sitting in the reading chair in the living room that isn't facing the television but instead the street. I've been trying to get her to turn it around since I was fourteen, but she says looking outside and seeing her neighbors is more entertaining. I mean, sometimes it really is, especially when cranky old Mr. Ferrucci next door was caught having an affair with one of his coworkers. Mrs. Ferrucci threw all of his stuff out onto the lawn. It was raining clothes for a good hour, and just when you thought it would end, there would be another stream of clothing falling from the window. "Whatcha doing?" I see her with her feet curled up under her.

"Nothing much," I say, "just answering an email."

"You are always working," she replies, shaking her head. "When are you going to get out and find some friends?" I roll my eyes at her.

"I have friends," I assure her. "It's a Wednesday night," I lie to her. I've been living in this city for the past seven years, and truth be told, I don't really have any friends like I did before. I have my guard up all the time. I don't know why, but it's hard for me to make friends, and again, truth be told, I don't want to make friends.

"When you lived here, you were out every night," she reminds me, and I roll my eyes. "It was hard keeping you home."

"Is that what you called me for, to ask me why I'm home?" I ask, leaning back in the chair and listening to the little wind chimes I brought from home that I put up by the window. "Why are you home?"

"It's seven at night, and I wake up at five to go to work," she snaps.

"But you finish work at five, so you could get yourself a man and be busy by seven," I goad her. Her eyes go big, and she gasps.

"You watch that mouth, young lady," she scolds. "You don't need to worry about my needs. They are well taken care of."

My face grimaces. "I just threw up." It's been Mom and me since I was born. My father decided a child wasn't on his bingo card, so he dipped as soon as she told him she was pregnant with me. She worked two jobs to make sure I had everything I needed. She worked her ass tirelessly to make sure I never missed anything, and to this day, there is nothing I wouldn't do for her. Well, at least one thing I won't do for her, but she's never really asked me. She's never been with another man after my father, or none I was aware of. There have been occasions when I thought she went out with a man a couple of times.

She laughs at my face. "How was your day?"

"It was okay. I have this new nightclub I am working on. It will be a restaurant until ten p.m., and then it'll turn into a club. What about you? How are things?"

"Same old, same old," she reports. I see her face go weird, and she stops talking.

"Mom." I sit up in my chair. "Mom, are you okay?" I ask as the back of my neck gets warm.

"I don't feel well," she admits, and then the phone falls to the floor. The image on the screen is now of the ceiling in the living room, and my heart sinks as I spring out of my chair. "Mom!" I scream her name. "Mom," I say again as my heart sinks to my feet and panic rushes through me. "Mom!" I yell again, hoping the phone is picked up, and she tells me she's fine. I wait one second, literally one, before I hang up on her and call the neighbor who lives across from her.

"Hello," Mrs. Gregory answers her phone while I tear through my one-bedroom apartment going to my bedroom, feeling that my heart is going to come out of my chest.

"Mrs. Gregory," I quickly say, taking my bag out from the closet and tossing it on the bed. "My mom—" I try to calm myself down. "My mom, I was talking to her, and then something happened. She said she didn't feel well, and then the phone fell out of her hands."

"Oh my," she replies, and I can hear her moving and then walking.

"She said she didn't feel well. I can't call 911 from here." I take the phone off my ear and then open the browsing app and type in the emergency number for Montgavin. My hands are shaking so much it's a miracle I can even type. "She needs help." I sob out the last words, feeling more helpless than I've ever felt in my life.

"On it," Mrs. Gregory confirms. My head spins as I run around my bedroom, throwing things in a bag. I look down at the phone and see she's hung up on me. The tears pour down my cheeks, and I feel like I'm going to be sick. The idea of not knowing what is going on with my mother while I'm so far from her is killing me. I zip up the bag, running around to my office and unplugging my laptop, putting it in my backpack along with all the papers on my desk.

I'm out of the house ten minutes later, knowing I forgot something but also not giving a shit. I'm in my car and rushing out of the parking garage when my phone rings. "Hello."

"Sweetie." Mrs. Gregory's voice is soft and low. "Honey," she says. I can hear her sniffling from her side of the phone, and all the blood from my body feels like it's being drained out. My hands grip the steering wheel as the tears pour down my face like the rushing of a stream down a hill. "They just took her," she chokes out as she silently cries. "They think it was a heart attack." I close my eyes. "They got her heart started again right before they left."

"I'm on my way," I say. "I should be there in about nine hours."

"I'm going to the hospital right now," she declares.

"Can you call me," I whisper, "and give me updates?"

"I will call you on the hour every single hour, even if there isn't anything to report."

"Thank you," I reply, grateful she was there to help me and save my mom. "Did she regain consciousness?"

"No, sweetie," she reports. I put my head back, and my bottom lip quivers. "She didn't."

"Okay, I'll speak to you in an hour."

"Yes." She disconnects the phone, and I put the hospital address in my phone and head on my way, going way over the speed limit. I just hope that if I get pulled over, they will have a little bit of sympathy for me.

Every single hour, Mrs. Gregory calls me to tell me the latest news. Mom was rushed into surgery for a blockage in her heart. For the past six hours, I've been on autopilot as I wait for her to tell me she is out of surgery. I spent the past six hours talking to her about how much I missed her. About how much my life would never be the same without her in it. About how she is the only person in my life who has never let me down.

I drive into town after eight hours. The town name lights up, and if you didn't know any better, you would think this is a peaceful town. A town where everyone is friendly, and I have to say when I was growing up, it's where I knew I wanted to live forever. But now, now it's the place I want to run away from. It's as if my body knows I'm back because the minute I cross that threshold, the memories come back with a vengeance, and I can't stop them no matter how much I've locked Pandora's box.

"Baby." I hear the soft voice in my ear, and I want to open my eyes, I really do, but I can't. My eyes are just too heavy. "Baby, please," Brock pleads with me, but then I hear more voices all around me.

Voices that seem far away but in abundance. "Holy fuck," a man says right before I'm sucked back in. "We're going to need the Jaws of Life."

The shouting makes me try to open my eyes again. "Jennifer!" Charlie calls her name frantically. The approaching sirens make me want to force my eyes open, but they feel like they are sealed shut. Someone says something as my eyes flicker open and the buzzing starts in my ears right away. I try to lick my lips, but the taste of metal is on them, and I feel like I've been punched in the face. I wiggle my fingers and try to move my hand up to my face, but it's stuck under something. "Brock," I whisper. "Brock." I try to move my head, but it's lodged against Jennifer's.

My eyes shut on their own as the darkness takes me away again. The sound of crunching metal drags me back from the darkness. I try to say something, but everything hurts. My face feels like it's on fire. "How the fuck did this end up upside down?" someone asks once the crunching metal stops.

I try to move off Jennifer, but my body feels like it's dead weight, and I hear Brock. "Baby, are you okay?"

After trying to answer him with words and forcing my eyes to open, I groan. "Everleigh," he sobs, "please answer me."

My left side feels like it is being crushed as I try to take a deep breath, but the pain rips through me. I groan softly, trying to push away the pain, "We got this door open!" I hear someone shouting, but I'm not sure if it's right beside me or far away.

"Fuck," another voice yells, "let's get him out!"

"Everleigh?" Brock mumbles from beside me, or at least I think he's beside me. "Everleigh, are you okay?"

"Hmm," I hear mumbled, "my head." I finally pant out, "It hurts."

"Guys, how is Jennifer?" Charlie asks from the front seat.

"I think she's on top of me," Autumn says. "I can't move."

"Brock, are you okay?" Charlie asks as I blink my eyes more and more to make sure I don't close them for too long. I try to turn my head, but I'm not able to.

"Foot is stuck. It feels like something is in my leg." His voice is pained, and I want to touch him, but I feel squished on both sides.

It sounds like a saw is working near us, and then the sounds of crunching metal make me wince again. I want to lift my hands to my ears to stop the pain. "We got a door off!" someone shouts. "Fuck, I think he's DOA." DOA, *my head screams. Does that mean someone is dead? "We need more hands." I can hear more and more people's voices as I try to look around, and finally, my eyes spot Brock, who is the one pushing me into Jennifer.*

"Brock," I say, and his head turns to mine. Blood is running down his face. The bright light now feels like it's being shined into my face, so I close my eyes.

"Everleigh," Brock says to the man.

"We have to get you out first and then get her," the man states, and then I hear him roar out in pain from beside me, and I want to help him. It's a howling sound I don't think I will ever forget. "We need a paramedic here."

"His foot is jammed," someone announces. "If we pull him out, it'll rip through his whole thigh."

"We need to get the driver out." I hear more footsteps from the other side of the truck.

"What a fucking mess," another voice adds. "Three-car accident. One man struck on the side of the road."

"How many in this car?" a woman asks as I hear shouting coming from far away, and then the sound of more sirens fills the night. Red lights flashing cut into the darkness of the truck for a couple of seconds, but I don't have time to look around before it's dark again.

"We have three in the back and two in the front." That doesn't sound right. How are there three in the back? I wonder if Jennifer or Autumn fell onto the floorboard.

The sound of metal clunking feels like it's right outside my door. I wince as my head throbs. "We got you," I hear right after the sound of clunking is done. The weight on my side is gone, and when I open my eyes, I see they got Brock out. "We got him out."

I feel hands touching me. "We're going to get you out." I hear the soft voice and look at the man dressed in a firefighter uniform. "We got you."

"I don't think I can move," I say as he puts a white plastic thing around my neck.

"I'll carry you." He puts one hand under my knees as he tries and pulls me away from Jennifer.

"My friend Jennifer. She must be stuck somewhere," I say as he moves an inch at a time. My leg suddenly cries out in pain, but I push it away from me. "She's in here. We are six people in the truck." My eyes get heavy as the light shines on my face, making me close them as I feel like I'm floating on air now.

"She said there were six in the truck," the man reports, and I try to open my eyes. "Where is the other person?"

"There are only three people back here," a man says softly, and I want to open my eyes to tell him it's a mistake, but right before the darkness takes me away again, the man says, "Unless she's under . . ."

"Turn left at the stop sign," the GPS tells me, and I come out of the memory of the night that changed not only my life but everyone's life irrevocably. It's not that I need the GPS at this point, but it's been on since I started driving, just to tell me how far away I was.

I don't even notice my face is wet with tears as I pull up to the hospital parking lot. I grab my phone and my keys before rushing into the emergency room, where I find Mrs. Gregory sitting with a coffee in her hand. "Oh, thank goodness you got here. She just woke up."

I put my hand to my chest. I've never heard sweeter words before in my life. I mean, only three other ones have been sweeter. "Can I see her?" I ask, and she gets up, nodding.

She walks with me to the nurses' desk. "This is Ms. Maddie's daughter," she informs them, and the woman smiles at me.

"Can I see her?" I ask, my hands shaking. "Please, just for a minute."

"You can." She gets up and motions with her head to follow her. I follow her to the back, past two swinging doors. The only lights on are the lights at the nurses' station in the middle of the corridor. Most of the doors to the rooms are open, and you can see in each of them with the big windows giving you access.

She stops beside a door, and I look in and see my mother lying in the middle of the bed with her head elevated. My feet move before my head can even wrap around that she looks like she's sleeping. I pick up her hand gently, feeling her warmth seep through me, and bring it to my lips. "I love you, Momma," I sob out.

I hear her head move on the pillow, and her eyes open. "Everleigh?" she says, confused I'm here. "What on earth are you doing here?"

I can't help but smile through the tears. "Mom, you had a heart attack," I inform her.

"I'm fine," she huffs. "I need to get out of this bed and get to work." She looks like she's about to get up when I shake my head.

"She's a stubborn one," the doctor says, walking into the room. He's wearing scrubs and a surgical hat on his head. "She's lucky we found her in time." He stands in front of the bed with his hands on his hips.

"What does he know?" My mother looks at me. "I'm telling you I'm okay. I feel fine." She fights to keep her eyes open.

"How long does she have to stay here?" I know my mother has probably asked this question already.

"I can tell you she won't be able to open the shop in three hours." He glares at her, and my mother refuses to even look in his direction.

"Everleigh, can you get my purse?" My mother ignores him. "Harmony is going to be there with the cakes, and I have to start getting the donuts ready."

"I'll go," I offer, knowing if I don't go, she won't rest. "I'll go and get everything sorted today, and you can rest and go in tomorrow," I bargain, looking at the doctor when he looks like he's about to say something.

"Fine," she relents. I know by her giving in without even fighting with me, she really doesn't feel well, but she won't let me know. "But you need to leave now."

I look over at the doctor, who I motion with my head to the side, hoping he understands what I'm trying to say, and he looks at my mother. "I'm going to be back in a bit to check on you."

"Wasting your time, Oliver. I said I'm fine." I look at both of them as my mother closes her eyes. "Now, I'm going to rest, and you're bothering me." She looks back at me. "You, get going."

"Will do," I agree. Walking out, I stop by her door and let out a huge sigh of relief. "I guess she's fine."

"She is not fine," the doctor corrects me. "I'm Dr. Cardinal, but you can call me Oliver. I've been telling her for years that she's burning the candle at both ends." He looks at me and then through the window. "If you weren't on the phone with her, we would have lost her." His voice trails off. "She needs to be off her feet for at least six weeks."

"You think you'll stop her from doing things for six weeks?" I ask, trying not to laugh.

"I'm hoping you can help me with that," he says, and I want to ask him so many questions, but his phone buzzes. "We are going to run tests today, and depending on the results, she could be here for a week. I have to go, but I'll see you later."

"Oh, I'll see you all right," I assure him, watching him walk away. Instead of leaving, I walk back into the room and go to my mother and bend to kiss her cheek. "I love you, Momma," I say softly, but for once, she doesn't answer me.

I walk out with my head hanging, spotting Mrs. Gregory

waiting for me. She holds her arms open for me, and I give her a hug. "I don't know how to thank you," I say. "If you weren't there . . ."

"Hush yourself," she scolds, letting me go. "I'm going to go home and get some sleep and come back later."

I nod at her as we walk out together, but she goes one way while I go the other. I get into my car and head down Main Street. My eyes roam down the empty street as I park and let myself into the little bakery store my mother used to work at and then bought from the old owner when he retired.

I turn the lights on and head to the fridge to take the big bowl out. I ignore the burning of my eyes as I start doing all the things I need to do. I'm taking the last batch of donuts out of the oil when I hear the bells for the front door jingle. I look over, seeing it's just after seven. Wiping my hands, I walk out of the back, seeing a brown box on the counter.

"Hi," the woman says, smiling at me.

"Hey," I greet her as I walk over and look into the box to see there are cellophane-wrapped cakes.

"Are you okay?" she asks with worry in her voice, and I can't even imagine how I feel.

"You must be Harmony, the girl who bakes the cakes," I say, totally ignoring the question of if I'm okay. I'm not okay, but I know if I stop, I'll collapse in a puddle in the middle of the floor.

"I am." She nods at me.

"I'm Everleigh," I introduce myself, "Ms. Maddie's daughter." Saying my mother's name breaks me a little as I blink away the tears that are threatening to come back. "She had a heart attack last night." Harmony's hand goes to her mouth to stop the gasp. "Luckily, I was on the phone with her when it happened, and I was able to get her neighbor to help her, so the ambulance got there in time."

"Oh my." Her own tears now run down her cheeks. "Is she okay?"

"She was resting this morning when I left the hospital," I say. "Doctor says she needs to stay off her feet and rest." I exhale, trying to control my breathing and making sure I don't sob. "But she's stubborn, and unless I'm going to stay here and watch her—" I shake my head. "So now, here I am for the next little while." I decided it as soon as I saw her lying in that bed.

"Is there anything I can do to help?" she asks, and I just shake my head. "I have another one in the truck." She points at the box on the counter before turning and walking out of the store. When I look up, my eyes go to the mechanic shop smack in the middle of the block, facing Main Street. You can't miss it once you get to the intersection. You either have to turn right or left or drive right into it. My chest contracts as I look over at the windows. Seeing a couple of men arriving, I scan to see if I'm able to see him.

The door opens again, forcing my eyes to go back to see Harmony place another box on the counter. "Do you have my number?" she asks. "If you want to take my number down, let me know if you need anything."

I pull my phone out of my back pocket when she gives me her number, and I text her.

561-277-6498: It's Everleigh.

"That's my number in case you need to get in touch with me about the deliveries," I say as she does something on her phone.

"Do you know when they are discharging her from the hospital?" she asks, and I take a big inhale, thinking back at the scene that happened this morning.

"I might have to get cuffs and cuff her to the bed," I mumble. "From what the doctor said, depending on the results of her tests today, it could be up to five days."

"I'll let you get back to work," she says as the door opens, and I see a couple of customers come in. "I'll see you tomorrow."

I smile at her. "I'll be here," I confirm. My eyes go to the mechanic shop, wishing like hell I wasn't here in the town where I lost two of my best friends and the man I thought I would love for the rest of my life. A man I thought I would marry and have children with. A man who shattered my heart, and it's never, ever been the same since. I don't think it ever will be. "For however long I need to be here."

Three

BROCK

THE CHIMES START RINGING, and I absentmindedly throw my hand on the side table and hit the phone. My eyes open, and I wince at the bright sunlight coming into the room. It was a long-ass night, and for whatever reason, I couldn't fall asleep for anything. I tossed and turned from when I got into bed at nine o'clock until the last time I checked the clock, which was after three in the morning. My chest was all tight, the nervousness was all over me, and I had no idea why. I'm going to be hurting today. I rub my face with my hands before tossing the covers off me.

Getting out of bed and shuffling my feet toward the bathroom, I shut the door before walking over to the toilet. Something I started doing when Saige turned six, two years ago, and she had more questions about why "my thing" was big in the morning. When she's here with me, I make sure the door is closed. I grab a pair of shorts before I walk over to the sink and turn on the cold water. Cupping my hands under it, I bend at the waist to splash water on my face. The coldness isn't fucking doing anything to wake me up. I grab a towel and dab it on my face before I walk out and hear the alarm again.

Picking up my phone, I see I have ten minutes before I have to get Saige up and ready for school. I walk out of my bedroom and into the kitchen, then go around the island and straight to the coffee machine. Pressing the button on top of it to start it, I go over to the drawer beside the stove and grab a pan. The smell of coffee fills the room as I open the stainless-steel fridge, remove two eggs from the tray, then open the drawer on the bottom and grab the bag of frozen sausage patties. I put it all on the counter beside the stove before pulling open the cabinet and grabbing a mug. I take a sip and then make my way over to the other side of the house to wake up Saige.

I walk past the family room and toward the three bedrooms on the other side of the house. When I inherited this house from my father, it stayed almost the same until two years ago when I finally had enough money to renovate the whole thing, adding in my bedroom over the back of the two-car garage. I gutted the kitchen that must have been at least fifty years old. I grew up in this house but moved out for college, then got my own place when I was done. After the accident that single-handedly ruined my life, I moved back in with Pops. It was supposed to be temporary, but my father passed away about eight months later, leaving me the house. My mother has never really been in my life. She left us when I was six to be free. She used to come by a couple of times a year, but then that stopped. The last time I saw her, I was seventeen years old. I don't even know if she is alive. It's not like she ever checked in with me.

Walking down the hall to the room that was the primary bedroom before I moved it to the other side of the house, I push open the door and see Saige is lying on her side in the middle of her double bed. The pinks and purples in the room let you know a little girl lives here. At least every other week.

My feet sink into the plush carpet as I bend to look at my

girl with jet-black hair, my chest filling with pride as I bend and kiss her. "Wake up, baby girl," I say softly, and she mumbles before she brings the cover over her shoulder, making me laugh. She loves to sleep—well, during the week, she loves to sleep, always did. "I'm making you an egg and sausage breakfast sandwich." I sit on the side of the bed, draping my arm around her. "Do you want it in a croissant, muffin, or toast?"

"Croissant," she answers me, her dark blue eyes remaining shut, "and can you add cheese?"

"What kind?" I ask. I learned the hard way she has different tastes for different days. The meltdown she had when I put American cheese instead of Swiss on it, you would've thought I had sold the state secrets. It was bad. She pouted and refused to eat it. I offered to make her another one, but she said her heart was just too broken to eat.

"Swiss," she replies, and I nod.

"Okay, I'll go get started on that, but you need to get up." I move her hips back and forth and then bend my head to blow bubbles in her neck until she is giggling and I know she's awake.

"Get dressed." I get up and head back to the kitchen, grabbing my mug of coffee before turning on the stove. I add butter to the pan before tossing two sausage patties to the side and then cracking open the eggs. Walking to the pantry, I grab two croissants and cut them, putting them in the toaster before grabbing the cheese. I wouldn't have gone with Swiss, but I always have what she has. That way, if she wants more, she can have mine.

I'm flipping over the eggs and sausage when she comes out of her side of the house, and it really is hers. One room is my office, which never gets used, and now that she's eight and her homework is more computer stuff, she has taken over that room. The other one sits empty. I thought I would make it a guest room but the only ones who sleep over are friends of Saige's, and they usually end up crashing in her bed. Maybe when she gets older, we'll knock down the wall and make it a bigger room for her.

"Dad," Saige calls my name before walking to the fridge and grabbing orange juice, "can you braid my hair?"

"Sure," I agree, plating her sandwich and then mine.

She sits on her stool. "And next time, can we have a pizza night?" I nod, thinking about how empty the house will be with her gone for the next week.

I take a bite of my sandwich. "I'm going to go shower and get dressed," I say. "Eat, and if you want more, take mine." I point at my plate. She nods as she walks over to the family room, just off the kitchen, grabbing the remote and putting on her show.

It takes me twenty minutes to shower and slide on my black work pants, with the black shirt with the Jessie and Son Mechanic Shop logo on the right. Jessie is my dad's name, and when I started working with him, he added in the son.

"Dad," she calls, coming into the bedroom. "Can you braid my hair now?"

"Yeah." I motion with my head for her to come to the bathroom with me. She stands in front of me, and I grab the brush from her hand, combing through her hair.

"I want a ponytail and then a braid." I nod and finish her hair. When she turned four and started wanting all these things, I went to the hairdresser with her, and the girl was kind enough to teach me how to do it. She also gave the best head, and she was fucking wild in bed. She came over to give me one-on-one lessons, which always ended up with us in bed. It fizzled out, like it always does, because I have nothing to give, and I'm not making anyone besides Saige promises. We still hook up occasionally when we run into each other, which isn't that often since I am either at work or with Saige. On the weeks I don't have her, I'm in the shop for fourteen hours a day, getting ahead for when I do have her.

"There," I say when I finish, bending to kiss her head. "Get your stuff, or we'll be late."

"Okay." She turns and walks out of the bedroom. Ten minutes later, I have a thermos of coffee in my hand, and she's holding my other one while we get her in the truck before going on with our day.

I pull up to the school and get out first before opening the back door and watching her get out. "You call me tonight," I say, and she nods gently. "Give me a kiss." I squat in front of her, and she hugs me around my neck.

"I'm going to miss you," she says softly.

"Me too, baby girl, but you can call me, and maybe we can have dinner during the week," I suggest hopefully, even knowing her mother probably isn't going to agree.

"Yeah." Her eyes light up, and the bell rings. She kisses me and runs into the schoolyard, stopping and waving before walking in.

I get into the truck and hear the phone beep with a message from Karla.

Karla: How was drop-off?

I look down at the message from my ex-wife and Saige's mother.

Me: Everything was good. I was thinking maybe I could pick her up on Wednesday and take her to dinner.

We knew each other in high school. She was always sniffing around me if I'm being completely honest. Then like a very bad cliché, one drunken night and a broken condom bonded us for fucking life. Well, at least until Saige is old enough to decide on her own. We got married a month after she told me she was pregnant. Instead of being happy I was starting my life, it was one of the most dreadful days of my life. There was a pressure in the middle of my chest that just tightened as the minutes ticked by. It was just the two of us at city hall, and the minute I slipped the ring on her finger, I knew it wouldn't last. We lasted one year until we, or better yet I, told her I was done. I couldn't do it. It wasn't healthy for us to live together and not like each other, at least not for Saige. Co-parenting could be going so much better if Karla wasn't as bitter as she was, but I put my head down and do what she says so I don't get on her bad side.

Karla: Maybe, we'll see.

I roll my eyes, tossing my phone to the side and pulling out of the parking lot. I make my way over to the shop, passing by the big Cartwright development I had started working on ten years ago when I thought I was at the top of my world, but the saying is always right. The higher you go, the harder the fall, and fuck, did I fall hard. I was terminated six months after the accident when I couldn't do anything they wanted me to do. They literally had my future in their hands, but when the truth came out, they didn't have anything they needed from me. So I was discarded. Now, from talk around the town, there is major structural damage in buildings because of the way the drawings were done. It was what I told them would happen from the get-go, but I was an intern, so no one was going to listen to me.

The second I pass the development, my phone rings, and I look down to see Winston Cartwright is calling me. He's been trying to reach me for the past week, and just like all the other times, I declined the call. I pull into the side of the parking lot of the mechanic shop, where my father always parked. It's not something I ever thought I would be doing, but sometimes those dreams you have for yourself get buried.

With the thermos in my hand, I walk into the front of the

shop, seeing the desk empty and paper all over it. Before walking to the back where my office is, another desk is filled with paper that needs to be filed. I toss my keys on the desk before heading into the garage. I have five mechanics who work for my shop even though there is room for ten. Not everyone wants to live in a small town fixing cars. I know this isn't what I wanted my future to be. The last thing I wanted was to follow in my father's footsteps, but here I am. I mean, I'm surprised I have even five guys. Four of them come into the garage with coffee from the bakery.

"Morning, boys," I greet as they stop talking to each other and look at me.

"Hey, boss," Eddie says.

"Did you hear about Ms. Maddie?" Tony asks, and I just look at him. "Had a heart attack last night." My chest seizes when I hear the news.

"Is she okay?" I look over at the bakery, and everything in my body freezes. It feels like time stands still when I see what is in front of my eyes. Surely, it can't be, but I'd know that body anywhere. I'd know that black hair anywhere. I'd know that face anywhere. I'm pretty sure I could be blindfolded, and they could place ten women in front of me, and I would be able to pick her out. She rushes to her car, her hair even longer than the last time I saw her, blowing in the wind, grabbing something before she turns her head to the side, and I see her for the first time in almost nine years.

"That's Ms. Maddie's daughter," Tony informs me. He's new in town, so he has no idea the connection I have with her. "She's taking over for Ms. Maddie."

"She's smoking hot," Ryan observes. "I'm going to wait a couple of days and see if she'll go out with me."

I take one look back at the shop, seeing her disappear. I

shake my head, and the rage works its way up my spine, and hatred pours into my heart. "Get the fuck to work," I all but roar out, the four of them jumping and giving me a look before heading to their stations. "Do yourselves a favor and stay away from her. She's poison."

Four

EVERLEIGH

THE ELEVATOR DOORS OPEN, and I step in, pressing the button for the fourth floor as the door closes. I look, seeing the numbers fly by until the doors open again.

The white wall with the number four painted on it greets me as I turn to my left and walk past the two open brown doors. Hospital rooms on both sides line up until you get to the nurses' station, which is in the middle of the floor with more rooms after it.

I smile at the nurse typing something on the computer in front of her. "Good afternoon." She nods to me. "She'll be happy to see you."

"I bet she won't," I joke. It's been four days since my mother had her heart attack. Four days she's been trying to get herself out of this hospital but has been blocked by the doctor not discharging her, and the fact I won't let her discharge herself. She's still the stubborn woman she has been, but she is more tired than she is used to. I think even she is freaked out about it.

"Hey, Momma," I greet her, walking into her hospital room and seeing her sitting in the chair in the corner of the room. Her eyes come up from the book in front of her to me. Her long brown hair pulled back and tied in a bun at the nape of her neck.

Her face immediately transforms into a scowl. "What are you doing here?" she asks, then picks up her phone. "It's not even three."

"I'm doing amazing, Mom." I ignore her snark. "How are you doing on this fabulous day?"

"Everleigh Ann Bishops"—she uses my full name—"do not sass me."

"I'm not sassing anything." I put my purse down on the hospital tray table before walking to her and kissing her cheek.

"Why are you here?" my mother asks again.

"Because my shift is over. May showed up for her shift from two to six, so why would I still be there?"

"To make sure she doesn't need anything." My mother closes the book she was reading and puts it on her lap.

"Mom, all the donuts have been made and placed out. Worst case, she has to make a fresh pot of coffee. I'm sure she can handle that."

"An owner never leaves," she tries, and I hold up my hand.

"She's fine. She's worked for you for the past four years," I point out and raise my eyebrows. "You hired her and trained her."

"You have to keep on top of them." She starts in on me, then stops when Oliver comes into the room. He's dressed in blue slacks and a white button-down shirt with his sleeves rolled up, and you can see some ink on his forearm.

"Hello, ladies," he says, nodding at me and then looking over at my mother. "Maddie, how are we doing?"

"I told you before I'm fine, and I'll tell you again. I'm fine." She turns to stare at him.

"Well, the results of all your tests have come back," he says. I can tell my mother is about to say something else, so he puts his hand up to stop her from talking. "I didn't say it was all normal." She rolls her eyes. "But nothing has changed since you've been here. So I'm going to go ahead and discharge you tomorrow."

"Oh, come on," my mother groans, "my ass is getting numb from sitting in this chair."

"And then it comes to the next part," he continues, and even I know she won't like this. "Six weeks, no work. I want you up and walking a couple of times a day, and then we can see how that goes."

"No." My mother shakes her head, but I do notice she hasn't jumped out of her chair, something she would have done if she was actually feeling one hundred percent. "Absolutely not."

"Madeline." He says her full name and if my mother's head could spin around, it would. "I don't think you understand what just happened. You could have died." He takes a minute. "How would you feel if you left Everleigh?" He uses me as a secret weapon, and if I could high-five him, I think I would. "Now, think of that when you are arguing with me." The glare is on point. "I know how hard this will be for you, but you have to fucking rest." His voice gets tight. "Excuse my language." He looks over at me, and I just shake my head, trying not to laugh. "Now, you are going to listen to me and do everything I tell you to do because no one wants to lose you, no matter how stubborn you are." He about hisses out the last part. "I'll be back later if you have any questions." He looks at her one more time before turning and practically storming out of the room.

I wait to make sure he's gone before I turn to look at my mother, her eyes staring at the empty doorway. "What was that all about?"

"He's being dramatic." She plays it off. "He's always been like that."

"How do you know him so"—I fold my arms over my chest—"well?"

"We knew each other in high school," my mother relays softly, and my mouth hangs open. "He left to go to medical school. He's been in and out of town since then. A couple of years ago, he decided he wanted to come back to town."

"Are you two"—I point at her, then point at the door—"like, a thing?" I'm still confused at the scene that just played out, and I wonder if I should have disappeared when they were having their discussion.

"Don't be silly." She avoids looking at me. "How is the bakery?"

"Deflection at its finest," I retort, and instead of pressing her further, I tell her about the bakery. I stay until it's after dinnertime, only leaving when she is getting into bed. "See you tomorrow." I kiss her cheek before walking out and toward the elevator.

Oliver steps out when I'm about to step in, and he holds the door open with his arm for me to enter. "How is she?" he asks.

"She was just getting into bed," I say, and he nods.

"Did she plan my death yet?" His voice is soft and full of worry.

"Oh, yeah." I laugh when I say it and see the anguish on his face. "But if it makes you feel better, she's also planning mine. Guess we are going down together."

He shakes his head. "Impossible. You are what she lives for." I swallow the lump that suddenly rushes up to my throat. "Have a good night, Everleigh."

I step into the elevator and wait for the doors to close before I let out my breath. I make it back to my mother's house, grabbing a sandwich and then heading off to bed. Luckily, I'm so exhausted that sleep takes me right away. But my dreams, my dreams never allow me to let go of the past.

When the alarm buzzes the following morning, my eyes flutter open, and it takes me a second to remember where I am. I'm in my childhood home in the single bed I've always had, in the room where I haven't slept for the past eleven years. I turn on my back, get out of bed, and make my way to the bathroom. Twenty minutes later, I'm opening the front door and stepping out into the warm breeze. The sun is just coming up, and birds are chirping as I walk down the steps, past my car, and toward the street. It feels like it's been forever since I've done this, but then again, it seems like I was walking out of the front door and heading to school just yesterday. It suddenly seems like I never left this town, and I don't know how I feel about that.

I head down the street and around the corner. Most of the houses are quiet. A couple of people are outside grabbing their paper, which has become almost nonexistent in the city, but not here. One of the older men is watering their flowers as I walk by, and like always, they look over, and I get a surprised look. They aren't the only one who's surprised I'm back.

"Hey, Everleigh," Mr. Hank says, turning off his hose, "how is your mom doing?"

The news of her heart attack flew through town like wildfire. "She's coming home today," I say happily.

"I'll tell Mrs. Hank, and we'll bring over some food," he informs me, and I just smile at him before walking to the bakery. It takes fifteen minutes for me to walk to the bakery as I pass things that automatically make the memories come back. Memories simmering at the edge, but I'm keeping them at bay. My head is not ready to go through them all right now. One thing at a time, I guess. Right now, my main focus is getting my mother better and trying to keep her from getting all fired up. I know the next six weeks will be hell for both of us. More for her than for me, but still.

I pass by the mechanic shop, and I know the minute I do because, even if I wasn't looking up, my chest always tightens as I pass by it. Like my heart knows that half of its missing piece is lingering somewhere on his property. I breathe in and out as I make my way past the shop, my chest loosening as I do it.

I open the bakery and head to the back to start the donuts, and Harmony comes in, dropping off the cakes. I'm almost done filling the front when the door opens, and I look up.

My face looks like it's seen a ghost because it feels like it. She walks in pushing a baby stroller in front of her, and I look at her and then the child, who is sitting up with his straps over his chest. One of his chubby legs is on the handle while he looks around, babbling. His soft black hair is combed to the side. "Hi," Autumn says softly when she gets to the counter, and I look back at her. "I heard you were back in town." The last time I spoke to her, I told her I never wanted to see her again. I also told her she was the world's shittiest friend. Through the years, I've regretted saying those words because, in the end, I was the one who became the shittiest friend. When she needed me the most, I turned my back on her, but I was going through so much that all I could see was my hurt and pain and not hers.

"Hi," I reply, my heart beating so hard in my chest it's making it hard for me to breathe. "I am."

"I heard about your mom," she starts, and I just nod as the little boy twists in his seat to look back at her, making sure she knows he wants out. "I'm so sorry," she says and all of the words I've wanted to say to her over the years disappear when I see her lean down and unbuckle her son and then pick him up, kissing his head. "Hey, Mr. Big Man," she coos softly, "this is Everleigh." She tells him my name. "This is my son, Landon William, but we call him Wills." I don't say anything. "I wanted you to meet him." She has tears in her eyes. "I was hoping that maybe . . .

perhaps, if you had time, you would want to sit down and talk." All I can do is stare at the little boy in her arms, and it dawns on me how much I missed. How much I've locked myself away from everyone and everything.

"You have a baby," I finally am able to say, "like a real baby." She laughs through her tears.

"Trust me, he's as real as it gets." He slaps her chest.

"I had no idea. Mom never mentioned anything." I trail off, not really sure I should tell her I forbade Mom to even bring her up. After what she did, I wanted nothing to do with her. I didn't want to speak to her.

"I would love to catch up," she states, her voice hopeful, "but I understand if you still—"

"I would like that." I think even I'm shocked when I say the words. "Are you working at the bar?" I ask, and she nods.

"I'm going to be on Thursday night since the bartender who is usually on has a family thing," she answers. "So I'll be working, but you could drop by."

"I think I will." She just smiles at me, the big smile I've loved since we were kids.

The smile she would give when she was really, really happy. "Perfect," she says as she wipes away her tears. "I'll see you then." I nod as she turns the stroller and heads to the door. "It's good to have you home, Everleigh."

Five

BROCK

I LOOK UP from the transmission part I'm putting back together while sitting down on the stool. The sun wasn't even up when I walked into the shop this morning, but I knew I had a few more days until Saige returned home. Last night, I was able to pick her up after work and take her out for ice cream, which was not what I asked for, but it was also better than nothing. So I didn't make a big deal out of it. However, I am getting a bit pissed, and I know I will eventually have to go to the lawyer to have Karla take me seriously. I just wish we could figure it out like mature adults.

The music plays in the background so softly I don't even know it's playing. I stop what I'm doing to look out the window, and everything halts when I do. Everleigh is walking by the shop again, something she's done for the past few days. It started three days ago when I was working, and it was as if a magnetic force made me stop what I was doing and look up, and that was when I saw her. The pit of my stomach burned, and that feeling moved up through my body, and I wanted to scream out my rage. But she didn't deserve my rage. She deserves nothing from me. She did what she needed to do, and I did what I needed to do. I never thought she would leave me the way she did. Never thought she wouldn't understand why I did it. I watch her pass with her head down, heading to the bakery and walking in the door. Only when she's inside do I turn back and focus on the parts in front of me.

Now here I am, working in my father's garage and keeping up with the legacy of it. It was not what I ever wanted to be doing. I thought I would have my own architecture firm at this point. My goal was always to do my internship and then just start small at first and build it up, but fate had other plans for me. Plans I said I would never make, but when everything went to shit, I knew I had no choice but to try to save the only thing I could, and that was my father's shop. He taught me everything I knew, and when I was ten, I would come out on the weekends and help him out until I turned thirteen, when he saw I could do an oil change and not fuck things up. But when I turned fifteen, I started tinkering with transmissions.

I was also really good at designing car details, which is why I went into architecture. I loved drawing and designing things and then seeing them all come together. After drawing, building things was always my favorite part. I'm the transmission specialist in the area, obviously, but more than that. A couple of us focus solely on transmissions, and I'm one of them. Something the Cartwrights couldn't bury was my name in other counties. I have a waiting list of people to work with me, all of which are old cars that need rebuilding. This list has grown even more in the past couple of years.

The phone rings beside me, and I look down to see it's Saige. I press the FaceTime button and wait for her face to fill the screen.

"Good morning, baby girl." I smile at her face and see that it looks like she just got up. "How did you sleep?"

"Good," she mumbles as she rubs her eye with her palm.

"That's good." I grab the cup of coffee that has grown cold since I got here. "Did you have good dreams?"

"Yeah, I dreamed of the beach," she says, as if her hints are subtle, and I laugh. "You know, like the one we went to the last time."

"I remember," I say of the trip we took this year on her spring break when it was my week. We spent a week in St. Thomas, and she loved every single second of being on the beach. She would wake up and be ready. She even learned how to surf and then wanted to go scuba diving, but I drew the line at that and instead just let her snorkel.

"Can we go there again?" she asks.

"I think I can maybe see if we can go when I get you at Christmas," I say, and her face lights up.

"Saige, let's go," Karla says in the background, and my dick cringes. "I've called you three times already."

"I'm talking to Dad." She looks over at her.

"Your breakfast is on the table, and it's getting cold," she scolds, and Saige sighs.

"Okay, Daddy, I love you." She puts her whole face on the camera and gives me a kiss.

"Love you too, baby girl," I say. "You have a good day at school and then call me later, yeah?"

"Okay," she agrees and disconnects with me. I finish the cold coffee when the front door opens, and I hear the sound of the bells.

"Morning," Ryan says from the front as he walks into the garage on his way to the break room, his cooler in his hand. "What time did you get here?"

"About five," I mumble as I take my tools out.

He doesn't say anything until he returns from the break room. "You almost finished with that?" he asks, and I nod.

"I'm almost done with the paint job also," he informs me. I hired him when he came to town a couple of years ago. He didn't know how to fix anything but could do a mean paint job on a car. He is also great at design, which is something he's getting more and more comfortable doing.

"Once we get this in and Eddie finishes the engine, it'll be done," I say of the Camaro someone brought to us a couple of months ago. It was literally just a shell of a car; weeds were growing between the steering wheel and the front window.

"When are the seats coming in?" Ryan asks as the bells ring again, letting us know someone has come in.

"I have to check," I reply, and he leans against the table.

"You need to hire someone to do paperwork," he reminds me. "It's a shit show out there."

"Why do I need to hire someone?" I ask. "You are all grown-ass men. Can't you put things away neatly?"

"You just answered your own question. We are grown-ass men. We don't do any of that shit."

He laughs as Eddie comes in. "I need a coffee and a donut, bad."

Ryan laughs at him, and the hair on the back of my neck stands up. "You mean you need to go and make sure Everleigh remembers your name."

The minute they say her name, the tool falls from my hand onto the metal table, the sound making the two sets of eyes come to me. I don't say anything because the bell rings again, and we hear two more voices as they walk to the back, only one of them has their lunch box.

"Are we going for coffee?" Eddie asks once the other two walk in.

"Let's go, lover boy." Ryan pushes off and looks at Tony. "He apparently needs a coffee so bad."

Tony just laughs at him. "I'm going to need you three to stop fucking around and get to work."

"It's not even eight yet," Tony reminds me. "I'll get you a coffee and a donut." He slaps my shoulder. "That should get you in a better mood."

"What will get me in a better mood is moving cars faster." I look at the three cars that are up on lifts. "That is going to make me feel so much better."

"On it, boss," Eddie assures me. "Just after we get coffee."

I grunt at them and ignore the urge to slam my hand on the table in front of me for two reasons. One, all the small parts will probably go flying, and finding them will be a pain in my fucking ass, and two, I am trying to tell myself that I don't give a shit what she does or who she does, but I'm also failing at that miserably.

I look down at the parts in front of me. I haven't thought about Everleigh for the past eight years. I pushed her to the back of my mind and refused to give her any more headspace. That doesn't mean it worked the whole time. Sometimes she would sneak into my mind, regardless of how much I didn't want her to. Like on her birthday. Even though I forced myself not to, I would wonder what she was doing. On the day when we started dating is another one, and the day she walked away from me. That day I'm usually my most angry—unless Saige is with me, then the anger simmers at the edge until I can give in to it. The first year after she left me was the worst. She was the only thing I thought about morning, noon, and night. When I was awake, I wanted to call her, and in my dreams, I wanted to call her back to me. Both of them had the same results. I was left without her, and as the days turned into months and then turned into years, the longing for her turned into hatred.

The boys return ten minutes later, laughing at something Eddie told her. Ryan puts the cup of coffee on my table with a donut on a paper towel beside it. "Let's get the doors open," I mumble, ignoring how good the donut smells.

If it was Ms. Maddie who made them, I would, without a second thought, take a bite of it, but knowing her hands made them, there is no way in fuck I'm touching it.

We work the whole day. I get up to stretch my legs after three, once I'm done with the transmission, before I walk into the office and decide to clean it up a bit. Grabbing all the papers on the desk, I put them in order in front of me. I'm getting up out of my chair and walking to the front of the shop when I see her again. This time, she's walking toward me, looking straight ahead. She hasn't changed one bit since I last saw her. Her hips sway side to side as the wind blows through her black hair.

She looks over at the garage when she gets closer and smiles at one of the guys, waving at whoever the fuck is talking to her. My hand goes into a fist, and the paper in it is crushed and crumpled.

"Do you love me, Brock?" I hear her voice in my head. *"Do you really, really love me?"*

"I love you more than life itself, Ever," I said as I kiss her neck after, feeling her heart beating under my lips. "More than life itself, baby," I repeat, and I always, always get the smile. The smile that made my day. The smile that would make my pulse pick up. The smile that I would wake up to and go to bed to. The smile I thought I would be able to see every single day of my life. Until the smile was ripped away from me, and I yearned for it.

The side door to the garage opens, and Ryan comes in with a paper in his hand. "This job is done on my part." He hands me the paper, his eyes going to my hand that is still gripping the other papers. His eyes go from me to the window as he watches Everleigh walk by it. "You good?"

"I'd be better if everyone fucking stopped giving that—" I try to calm myself down. "That woman more attention than she needs."

"What's the story with her?" he asks, his interest piqued.

"There is no fucking story," I snap. "I need you guys to focus on what needs to be focused on. You want to chase her pussy, do it on your own time." The thought of one of them actually chasing her pussy almost pushes me over the edge. Before I say something I know I'm going to regret, I swipe the paper out of his hand and storm back again to my office; the windows face the back, so there is no way I'd even be tempted to look out and see her walk by. It's a good thing I don't venture out of my circle because there is no way I'd ever let Everleigh back into it. Not in this lifetime.

Six

EVERLEIGH

I WALK OUT OF THE BATHROOM in the bathrobe I've had since I was seventeen. It's white and plush with blue, red, and yellow hearts all over it. I got it for Christmas one year, I think, or maybe it was my birthday. My hair is wrapped up in a white towel as I walk down the steps to go find my mother.

I'm halfway down when I call her name, "Momma." I look at the chair in the living room that faces the front window, seeing it empty. My eyes go to the kitchen right off the living room, and it is empty, with dinner dishes already dried and put away. I get to the bottom of the steps and look out of the side door that leads to the covered porch area. "Momma." I stick my head out the screen door, seeing the two rocking chairs empty. "Momma." I start to make my way to her bedroom when the bathroom door opens.

"What are you hooting and hollering about?" she scoffs. "Can't a woman go to the bathroom?"

"I wasn't hooting and hollering. I was wondering where you were."

"We don't live in Buckingham Palace"—she walks over to her chair—"so I couldn't really go far."

I point at her. "With you, you never know. You could have escaped and gone to the bakery."

"I should have." She sits down in her chair and grabs her glass of water from the side table. "It would serve you right for hiding my car keys."

"I didn't hide them," I remind her. "I put them in a safe place that was not near you or where you could find them." Walking over to the fridge, I pull it open. "Are you hungry?"

"Oh, good Lord." She throws her hands up. "Will you stop hovering over me?"

"This isn't hovering." I grab the sweet tea pitcher out of the fridge. "This is being thoughtful and wondering if my mother is hungry."

"We ate dinner not too long ago," she snaps, "so I'm fine."

"What do you want to do tonight?" I ask, and she just looks at me.

"Why don't you get out of my hair?" she asks. "Go out and maybe leave me alone for a bit." She's been home from the hospital for two days. It's been two days of her being, as she calls it, cooped up. Two days of her telling me she's fine and it's all hogwash.

"But then what fun will you have?" I pour the sweet tea in a glass as I stare at her, and she glares at me. I'm about to fire back at her when the doorbell rings. "I wonder who that could be." I walk around the island and toward the front door.

"Tell whoever it is I'm not here," she whisper-hisses. I just roll my eyes as I pull open the door. For the past two days, we've gotten visits from practically everyone in the neighborhood, trying to see my mother and wish her well. She was very polite to their face, but once the door was closed, she would bitch at me for letting them in. I pull open the front door, expecting to be greeted by one of the neighbors again, but I don't know why I'm shocked when I see Dr. Oliver. Instead of his regular doctor attire, he's wearing jeans and a white button-down with a leather jacket, and I think my jaw hits the floor. Right behind him is a motorcycle that has to be his. "Dr. Oliver," I finally mumble and unlock the screen door.

"Don't let him in here," my mother hisses from the side as I push the screen door open, and he walks up the two steps to come into the house.

"Hey, Everleigh," he greets me quietly, coming in and then looking at my mother. "Madeline."

"Oliver," she grumbles with her teeth clenched together, "what are you doing here?" Her eyes are big, and she goes from looking at him to looking at me. I have to roll my lips. She looks like I did when I was caught making out with Brock on the couch once when she was at the store. Of course, I was seventeen and not in my fifties.

"I came to see how you were doing." He shrugs off his jacket and hangs it over the banister before walking over and bending to kiss her cheek. I have seen my mother look at me with murder in her eyes, but I've never seen this type of murder. "What have you been doing?" He ignores her look as he sits down on the couch next to the chair.

"I'm going to go"—I point up toward the stairs—"and get dressed, and then I think I'm going to go see Autumn."

"That sounds like fun," Oliver says. "I can watch over your mother."

"You won't be watching over anything," my mother snaps at him, "because you'll be leaving." She looks at him, then me. "And you should go out, and then I'm going to go and lie down and rest." I nod at her as I see Oliver grin.

Walking up the steps to my bedroom, I close the door and silently giggle at them before I take off my robe. Grabbing my matching lace white bra and thong panties set, I slip on my long, flowy, pink-flowered skirt that lands down to my ankles before I put on a short white T-shirt that sits right at the waist of the skirt. I walk out of my bedroom to go to the bathroom and hear their voices. Closing the door behind me, I pull off the towel from my hair as I comb through it before putting spray in and fluffing it with my hands. I apply just a light coat of mascara, then make my way downstairs.

"Okay," I say, seeing Oliver and Mom in exactly the same spot they were when I went upstairs, but now the television is on. "I'm going to head out." I put on my flip-flops. "I won't be late." I stop beside my mother's chair and bend to kiss her cheek. "Love you, Momma."

"Have fun," she replies. I look over at Oliver and nod. He returns the gesture.

"I'll see you around?" I say, not sure if it's a question or not.

"You will." He smiles and then looks at my mother. "For sure."

"Don't do anything I wouldn't do," I mumble at them before walking out and closing the door behind me. I hold my phone in my hand as I walk toward the bar. The sun is setting, and the stars are starting to twinkle in the sky. Walking down Main Street, I pass the diner that looks like it's almost done with the dinner rush.

I hear music coming out of the bar, and when I turn the corner, I'm surprised to see it almost jam-packed. Except no one is here who I recognize. It's all fresh new faces, which means no one will be gawking at me the whole time. I look around, seeing Autumn behind the bar with another bartender beside her. The two of them work on filling drinks as four servers work the floor.

I zigzag toward the bar and stop in my tracks when I see Charlie sitting on the stool in the corner of the bar. His eyes meet mine, and he smiles at me and gets up from his stool. My feet move on their own toward him. "Everleigh," he says, then hugs me big, "it's good to see you." Once he lets go of me, I have to blink quickly to get the tears to go away.

"Charlie, I—" I shake my head. "It's so good to see you here." I look at him and then at Autumn, who has stopped doing what she is doing and is just staring at us.

"Autumn said you might be coming by." He sits back down on his stool, and I pull out the stool beside him and sit down. "Thought I would . . ." He shrugs, and I look at him and then at Autumn. The last time I heard, he had shown up at her house, drunk off his ass, and told her he wished she was dead.

"Ignore him," Autumn advises, putting down a coaster in front of me. "I told him not to come but"—she shakes her head—"he came instead of staying home with our child."

"I'm sorry, what?" I slap the bar, and two things happen. One, her face pales, and two, Charlie about jumps out of his chair to step in front of her. I lift my hand right away. "No, no, I don't." I start to think of words. "It's just a—" I put my hand on my head. "You two have a baby?" My eyes shuffle back from Autumn to Charlie, who looks at Autumn with a look of love I've never seen on his face before. A look that is returned by Autumn. "Landon is his?"

"He's mine." Charlie sits back down on his stool. "All twenty pounds of him," he states proudly, picking up his bottle of beer and putting it to his lips, taking a pull.

"I just, I had no idea you two were together," I reply, shocked.

"We got married two years ago," Autumn explains, putting a glass in front of me with light amber liquid inside.

"This is wild." My head is spinning. "I had no idea."

"I thought for sure your mother would have mentioned

something to you," Charlie adds, and I just shake my head, looking down at the glass in front of me.

I turn the glass around in my hand before picking it up. "I didn't really want to know what was going on in town." I leave it open-ended, hoping they both get what I'm saying. My stomach aches from admitting it, but I push it aside and put a smile on my face. "To catching up"—I hold the glass up—"and healing old wounds." I bring the glass to my lips as the stool beside me is pulled out, and someone sits down next to me. I feel his heat beside me as my heart catches in my throat. I look to the side, seeing him there. Brock. The man who shattered my heart and single-handedly buried all of my dreams in one single move. Holding the shovel in his own hands as he picked up the dirt and piled it on. His face covered with a little beard, like he hasn't shaved in over a week, something he did all the time back then. His hair is even longer than it was the last time I saw him. A memory that I buried and refused to think about, until fucking now.

"Hey, Autumn," he says, and I can hear Autumn gasp as I ignore him beside me. Which is really fucking hard when all I want to do is turn and look at him. I want to see if he looks the same. I want to see if you can see the small golden specks in his right eye if he's looking into the light. I want to see if, in one look, he can calm all my fears. But I'm not taking what I want. I'm doing what I need to do, and that is ignoring the fuck out of him. "Charlie." He looks right past me, or at least I think he does because I'm staring straight ahead. "Can I get a shot of the new blend?"

"Brock," she replies to him as she walks to the end of the bar, grabs a glass, and fills it with the same liquid that is in my glass. He doesn't say a word to anyone as he takes his glass and brings it to his lips, downing it all. My body feels like my skin is going to crawl off my bones. My heart is soaring through my chest, and I'm pretty sure if they stopped the music, you would be able to hear it beating quickly. My breathing is coming in short bursts as I try not to have a full-blown panic attack in front of him. I close my eyes as I hear him put the glass back down and then his heat moves away from me as he gets off the stool, and then tucks it back in as if he was never there. He puts money on the bar before turning and walking out.

I close my eyes, the scent of him lingering in the air. "Are you okay?" Autumn asks softly, and I open my eyes, trying to play it off. "Drink that." She motions with her chin to my glass, as my hand brings it to my lips, and I take a deep pull. I hiss at the burn when it goes down my throat. "That was intense," she declares, her eyes about to bulge out of her head.

"That was something," I state, my heart beating back in a normal way. "It was something, all right." I look at Charlie. "I take it you two aren't as close as you were?"

"You can say that," he responds, his jaw tight. "He's not close to anyone. Stays mainly to himself." The statement shocks me even more because Brock had friends everywhere he went. He was always friends with someone, and that was because he had different friend groups and would be active in each of them.

"That makes no sense." I finally give in to his statement.

"A lot has happened over the years," Charlie notes. "People change. Some for the better, some for the worse."

I nod, picking up my glass again and putting it to my lips. "Some we just don't even care about," I reply right before I finish the whiskey in my glass, ignoring all the questions now screaming at me. "Some we just need to walk away from and never look back."

Seven

BROCK

I WALK OUT OF THE BAR; my whole body feels like it's being lit on fire. The back of my neck feels like you've stuck a million needles in it and have drained all of the blood out. I walk toward the shop, forcing my feet to go one in front of the other instead of turning around and going back into the bar.

When I walked out of the shop ten minutes ago, I was on my way to the truck when I decided to go and get a quick drink. Never in my wildest dreams did I imagine I would find her sitting on a stool next to Charlie. I ignored her like she didn't even exist. Like she wasn't sitting two feet away, and I could smell her perfume wafting through the air. My cock woke up as if he's been in hibernation for the winter, while my heart feels like it started working again after being stuck on pause. I hate that she has this effect on me. I hate that I still let her get to me. In the past eight years, I haven't allowed myself to admit how much I missed her because I knew if I did, it would be so overwhelming that I would be buried in the feeling, and I had Saige to think about. It wasn't just me anymore. I had to be strong for my daughter. But now I admit how much I fucking miss her.

The ache is so sharp it's like a knife slicing into my heart and slowly being pulled out.

Slamming the truck door behind me harder than I should, the anger from letting her get to me pours over. I pull out, my eyes going to the road in front of me until the end of the street. Instead of turning right and going home, I make a left twice and then park my truck off to the side before getting out.

As I walk toward the creek, I can hear the water trickling down to the rocks toward the stream. The sound is supposed to be relaxing, but it makes me even angrier after what just happened. Why I even came here is beyond me, I wonder as I walk down to the small clearing hidden behind dense trees.

The minute I do, the memory comes back as if it's finally being let out of the vault.

"The water is cold, baby," I said from the blanket where I was lying down on my side, my feet crossed at the ankles as I watched her roll up her jeans and step into the little stream, "and some of the rocks might be slimy."

"I'll be fine," she replied, looking over her shoulder as she stepped into it. The moonlight bounced off the top of the water as I watched her. "Fuck, it's like ice," she hissed as she took another step.

"Baby." I finally sat up with my feet on the cover, the picnic basket beside me. I placed my elbows on my knees, watching her round ass take another step. "You are going to be cold for the rest of the night."

She turned around with her ankles in the water. "Would you stop bothering me?" she retorted. With a twinkle in her eye, she lifted one leg and flicked water on me. The drops landed on me like big drops of rain. "See, it's not that cold."

"Don't you dare," I told her. She lifted her foot and splashed me again. "Someone is looking for a fight."

"Who, me?" she asked innocently, yet there was nothing innocent about Everleigh. We had been dating for about a year, and I knew her inside and out. I knew her better than she probably knew herself. She had consumed me, body and fucking soul.

"Yeah, you." I nodded my head and got up to stand on the blanket before I took two steps toward her. "Only you, Everleigh," I said softly, watching her walk in the water for a bit before she finally gave up and walked out toward me.

She stood there in front of me, and my hands came up to hold the side of her neck. "I love you, baby." The words just came out without giving me a chance to stop them.

Her face went from shock to a smile. "Is that so?" she quizzed as she stepped closer to me, putting her hands on my hips. "Took you long enough."

I chuckled. "Is that so?" I used her words against her. "I didn't see you dying to profess your love for me."

"I know how macho you are"—she tried not to laugh but failed—"and big and strong. How are you going to tell everyone else I said I loved you first?" she taunted, and she only stopped talking when I slammed my mouth down on hers.

The memory kicks me in the stomach, and I have to put my hand out to stop myself from falling to my knees. The cold bark on my fingers stings as I try to steady my breathing, feeling as if I just ran here from my house instead of driving here.

The sound of twigs breaking makes me look to the side, and I think my eyes are playing tricks on me. I blink a couple of times to make sure I'm not dreaming, or I'm having another memory I don't want to have. Her head is down as she walks through the trees right to me. I push off from the tree and turn to face her.

"You've got to be fucking kidding me," I hiss, scaring her because she stops in her tracks, looking up at me. One of her hands goes to the middle of her chest, the other to her stomach as she looks up at me.

"Brock." The minute she says my name, it's as if she puts her hand into my chest and rips my heart out, squeezing it in the palm of her hand until the blood seeps out of her fingers, and the heart stops beating in her hand, rendering it useless.

"Don't say my fucking name," I hiss at her. She takes a step back, and I see her shoulders get tight, and I know she's going to come back and fight with me.

"Trust me, I don't want to say your fucking name," she snaps and continues her steps toward the creek. "If I never say your name again for the rest of my life, I'll be happy."

"I bet you fucking will." I stand here as she comes toe to toe with me. I can smell her perfume lingering in the air. My fingers beside my leg start to tingle to come up and touch her. "Surprised you remember this place."

"Yeah"—she folds her arms over her chest, pushing up her tits even more—"and why the fuck is that?"

"I thought you would have forgotten this place," I bark, "just like you forgot me." I hate myself for saying the words, but they come out so fast I can't take them back.

"Funny coming from you," she says. "I wasn't the one who forgot about the other person. You sure as fuck forgot about me the minute I left town." She unfolds her hand and points it at me. "I was just a fucking memory to you." She leans into me, and I move back so she's not too close. "Since you were wearing someone else's ring less than two months after I fucking left." Her words feel like they're pulled from the depths of her soul. The hurt there is so evident, but she doesn't let her guard down. "So don't fucking pretend my leaving hurt you."

"Way I remember it, you left me. Cut me off." The venom in my tone isn't falling on deaf ears. Her eyes go to slits.

"Of course, you would remember it that way." She shakes her head and turns to leave, when my hand comes out and grasps her wrist. The heat warms the coldness that's been in my bones since she walked away from me. I yank her to me, her other palm flat against my chest.

We stare at each other for a full minute before it happens. I don't know if I'm the one who bends my head or she lifts on her tippy-toes, but our mouths meet, and the kiss is as angry as it could ever be. Our tongues touch for a second before she bites my lower lip. My hand drops her wrist, and I wrap it around her waist and pull her to me. Lifting her off her feet, I turn her back to the tree. "I wish I never saw your face again." Our noses are touching, and again, it's that tug-of-war.

Her mouth opens at the same time my tongue slides in. My eyes close, and it's as if I've reached euphoria. It's better than any high I've ever had. It's better than any buzz I've ever had. It's fucking heaven and hell all at the same time. I hate she still has this effect on me. I turn my head to the side, the kiss not gentle at all. Instead, it's a kiss filled with rage and anger. I push her deeper into the tree, her hands gripping my shirt in her fingers, pushing it up before scoring me with her nails all the way down my chest. The sting of it goes straight to my cock, which is pushed deeper into her. She lifts her leg to hook over my hip as I push my cock into her even more, and I swallow her moan. My hand goes to her leg, around my hip, finding it bare. The softness from it makes me move my hand up her leg until my hand is cupping her bare ass. I squeeze my hand so hard, I'm sure she'll have my fingerprints as a bruise, but I don't fucking care. Let her have it, let her fucking be reminded of me every single fucking day. Just like I'm sure to have the taste of her on my tongue. The more I kiss her, the more I can admit I missed her. The more I admit that, the angrier the kiss gets. "I hate you." She leans her head back on the tree, her fingers gripping my sides so hard her nails are cutting into my skin.

"Yeah." I press deeper into her. "I don't think you hate me more than I hate you," I hiss at her. "I hate you to the depth of my soul."

"I hate that I loved you for as long as I did." The pain of her words makes my head feel like it's exploded. "I hate I loved you at all," she repeats the words in a whisper. "I will always hate you."

"Good. So you'll still hate me after tonight."

"I'll hate you for the rest of my life." That is the last thing she says before I cover the gasp that comes out of her mouth with mine. Her legs wrap around my hips as she pushes herself into me. It's my turn to moan as her hands move to the waist of my jeans. Her hands are frantic on the button while my hand moves from her ass around to her hip, moving her thong to the side, the smoothness of her like satin under my fingertips. I let go of her mouth so I can open my eyes and watch her face. Her eyes flutter open, and our pants drown out the sound of crickets. Our eyes look at each other as I slide my fingers into her. Her wetness and heat make me almost come in my fucking pants. Her eyes flutter closed as she puts her leg down and opens them even more.

I was wrong before. This, this right here might be my very own kryptonite. Her hands unbutton my jeans and then the zipper echoes in the darkness. "This changes nothing," she declares when she pushes the jeans and the boxers off my hips, my cock springing free. Her hand grips my cock, and I about hiss and come in her hand. I thrust my hips into her hands, feeling her softness on me.

"This changes nothing," I repeat the words with tightness in my stomach, moving her skirt up to her waist and then sliding my fingers out of her. "It might make me hate you more," I admit to her, picking her leg up and throwing it over my arm. "Or at least I fucking hope it will," I growl right before I bend my knees and slam into her.

Eight

EVERLEIGH

"THIS CHANGES NOTHING," he repeats my words. My skirt moves up my leg as he slides his fingers out of me. I want to grab his wrist and pull him back, but my hands are busy pushing his jeans over his hips. My head is yelling *this is a bad idea*. My heart is telling me *we might not be able to survive this*. But my body, my body feels like it's been awakened from a deep sleep and is finally able to feel. "It might make me hate you more," he growls. I want his words not to hurt me, but I've learned over the years that you sometimes don't always get what you want. "Or at least I fucking hope it will."

I'm about to tell him I'll hate him just as much, but all words are lost when I feel him slam into me. My back pushes deeper into the bark of the tree. "Fuck," he hisses as he stays rooted inside me for a minute. My hands go to his bare arms and roam up while he takes his hand at my hip and moves it up, pulling my T-shirt up. His fingertips feel like they're waking up every single cell in my body. He pulls down the cup of my lace bra and bends his head to bite my nipple, making me arch my back. I want to moan his name, but instead, I stay silent. "I fucking hate you." He pulls out and then slams into me, filling me.

"I hate you more," I pant out. "I hate you so fucking much more." I have to close my eyes so I don't watch him bend and suck my nipple into his mouth before biting it again. "I fucking hate you more," I declare as he ravishes me. Over and over again, he pulls out and slams into me. He moves his head up so his forehead touches mine, and I move my face to the side so I don't have to look at him. He could be another faceless man to me, except my body knows him. My body comes alive with him like it's been the missing piece to make me whole. He buries his face in my neck at the same time I feel myself coming on his cock. He picks up his speed, and it feels like he's going to fuck me in half. His cock is thicker than my body remembers, his thrusts slamming over and over again, grunting each time his cock is buried all the way. I can't catch my breath when one orgasm rolls into another one before he bites my neck, plants himself to the root, and moans out his own release.

My eyes close even tighter as I try to steady my breathing, but his chest collapses on me. The bite of the bark sears into my back, and I'm sure it's cut me at this point. But I don't really care. His heat warms me like a cozy blanket after a bitter, cold day. I inhale deeply, and he finally dislodges his face from my neck.

Neither of us says anything when he pulls out of me. His arm moves, and my foot drops to the ground. My skirt slips down, and I right my bra, pulling down my T-shirt while watching him tuck himself in and then zip his pants up. He looks up at me as he buttons his jeans, but I'm not going to give him the time of day. Instead of saying anything to him, I move past him and away from him. I have to get away from him before I cave and ask him why he did what he did to us.

Why he chose everyone else before he chose us. Why? That is the only thing I want to know. Why? But instead, I walk away from him. Or better yet, I run away from him. My body aches for his heat. My mind replays every single second we were together. My fingers come up to touch my lips that are still tingling from his touch. No one has ever had this effect on me but Brock. No one has ever had me like he has. No one will ever have me again because I'm not giving myself to anyone like I gave myself to him.

I turn the corner and walk toward my house, seeing the bike is gone from the street. The house is dark as I walk up the steps. I turn the handle and step in, finding it quiet in the night. I tiptoe to the end of the hall, pushing open the slightly closed door to see my mother on her side, sleeping.

I'm about to pull the door closed when she speaks, "You're home later than I thought you would be." She looks down her legs toward the door at me.

"Yeah, Autumn and I were talking," I lie just a little. I mean, Autumn and I did talk. Except I would have been home earlier. It was better than saying, *"Sorry I'm late because I was fucking Brock against a tree. Or better yet, Brock was fucking me against a tree."*

"That's good." She turns on her back. "It's about time the two of you let bygones be bygones."

"I think so too," I admit. "I can't believe her and Charlie." I shake my head. "And they have a baby"—my voice goes up—"together."

"You aren't the only one." She laughs. "Ruffled lots of feathers, that pairing. No one saw it coming."

"He loves her," I say softly. My mind goes back to tonight when he got up to go and whispered something in her ear and then kissed her lips. But it was more than that. It was the way his eyes followed her the whole night. The way, if she was down the bar at our end, she had to be touching him, even if it was her pinky with his. You could feel how much they loved each other.

"He loves her fiercely," my mother confirms. "Only one other person I saw in my life love someone like that." She closes her eyes as her voice trails off. "Get some rest." It's her way of letting me know the conversation is over.

"What's going on with you and Dr. Oliver?" The question comes out to change the conversation over from whatever I was going to say to her.

"Good night." She ignores that I even spoke, and I smile in the darkness before turning and walking to the stairs. I walk into the bathroom, turning on the light and pulling my shirt off me, before turning and looking at my back in the mirror. There are red lines all down my back. Gasping out when I see something I haven't seen in nine years. Something I thought I would never see again. Something I vowed to make sure was never on my body. Not by him and not by another man. My fingers come up, but my eyes are fixated on the mark he left and not the fact my hands are shaking when I touch it. "That motherfucker."

I shake my head and walk over to the shower, turning on the water as hot as my body can take it, before stripping down and getting under the spray. The water is hot enough to almost burn me as I wash his scent off my body. I ignore looking at his mark and know it'll be gone in seven to nine days. That was how long it took for the last mark he put on me to disappear. I know because the last time he left a mark on me, I watched it fade away, just like I did.

I wrap myself in a towel before walking to my bedroom and sliding into the bed, naked. Too tired to even dress, I turn on my side and close my eyes. I tuck myself under the blankets, and my head immediately goes back to Brock. I can hear him as if he's right in front of me.

"I swear, baby, sometimes I think you do things to piss me off just so we can get my cock in you." The smile I used to love filled his face. "If you want me, baby, all you have to do is tell me."

"Brock, just admit you do things on purpose to piss me off so we fight, and then we fuck."

"The only thing I'll admit is that I'll love you until I'm dead and gone."

My eyes fly open to make the memory go away. "He's a liar," I remind myself. "He has no idea what it means to love anyone." I don't know if I'm saying the words out loud in order to convince myself or not. Finally, turning on my back, I look at the stars until my eyes won't open anymore.

The following morning, I'm walking down the steps quietly, getting ready to head to the bakery, when I hear movement coming from the side and look over to see my mother coming out of her bedroom. "Where do you think you're going?" I put my hands on my hips and stare at her.

"I'm going to the kitchen to make myself a coffee," she snaps, "or am I not allowed to walk in my own house?" She's wearing beige linen pants, a white tank top, and a long peach sweater that hangs to her knees. Her hair is pinned on the top of her head. "Someone is crabby this morning."

"I'm not crabby." I slip my feet in my sneakers. "I just thought you were going to make a run for it."

"You're safe for today," she assures me, pouring coffee in a mug and then putting some in a stainless-steel cup. "Now, tomorrow is another story." She hands me the to-go cup.

"We'll see." I grab the cup from her. "I'll see you later." I kiss her cheek before I walk out of the house.

The walk to the bakery takes even less time today since I'm

speed walking, especially in front of the garage. I don't even look to see if his truck is there. Last night was one of the biggest mistakes I've made, and it's not going to happen again.

I'm almost at the bakery when I notice two guys hanging around out front. One of them tries to open the door, while the other one looks in the window. They are both dressed in jeans, T-shirts, and baseball caps low on their heads to hide their faces. I wait a second to see one of them tell the other to go to the back. He takes a couple of steps toward the back when he looks up and notices me.

The scar on his left cheek makes shivers run down my spine; his blue eyes almost look like he is looking right through you. "Can I help you?" I ask them when I'm standing in the parking lot.

"Um." The one at the door fumbles with his words, and I look at him. He's shorter than the other guy, but not by much. The man at the door has brown eyes, and when he smiles, there is nothing friendly about it. "We heard this is the place to get some coffee and donuts."

"It is." I look around, wondering if anyone is going to see if something happens to me. The street is pretty much empty with just the three of us. "But we open in about an hour," I tell them. "You are more than welcome to wait."

They share a look. "We'll be back," the man who was going to walk in the back says, nodding at the other man, who shares a nod with him, and the two of them walk over to a black car. I watch them get in and drive down the street. My eyes go to the license plate as I take my phone out and take a picture.

"You are being paranoid," I tell myself, putting my phone into my back pocket before I open the front door. The sound of a car approaching has me looking up to see if they have returned, but instead, it's Harmony, who is parking right in front.

"Morning," she greets when she gets out of the truck. "How are you?"

"Good," I reply. "What kind of cakes do you have for me today?" I put the two men in the back of my mind and go on with my day.

Nine

BROCK

I GRAB MY CUP OF COFFEE at the same time as the phone starts ringing with a FaceTime call from Saige. Propping it against one of the walls in front of me, I slide it to the right and wait for her face to fill the screen. The smile on my face goes even bigger when I see she's waiting for me. "Good morning," I say when we connect.

"Morning, Daddy." Her voice is so chipper today; it usually is when it's at the end of her week at her mother's place, and she knows that at the end of the day, we are going to be seeing each other. I can see she's not in bed this morning, but instead, she's sitting at the island in her mother's house, eating or just finished eating.

"How are we doing?" I ask and see Karla in the background going back and forth.

"Good," she replies. "I'm going to school now. Are we having pizza tonight?"

"We can," I answer her, "but if we have pizza tonight, then we have to cook tomorrow."

She groans, thinking she would have gotten pizza tonight

and then also tomorrow since Saturday was declared pizza night since she was five. "We can have it two nights."

"We can," I agree with her, "but we won't." She throws her head back and almost snorts while she rolls her eyes. "So you let me know tonight."

"Fine," she pouts. "I have to go brush my teeth."

"Okay, baby girl, love you, and I'll see you tonight, yeah."

"Bye, Daddy." She waves at the phone while I blow her a kiss, and she disconnects.

The guys start to trickle in one at a time today. It's always slower on Fridays because they usually have drinks at the bar on Thursday night. "Hey," they say when they walk past me.

I wait until they are all in before turning on my stool. "Happy Friday." I take a sip of my now cold coffee. "We have a busy day. We have fifteen oil changes. All of the slips are already done and hanging on the board." I point over at the board. "Switch them up. I don't give a shit."

"You did all the slips?" Tony asks me with his feet spread, his arms over his chest, and his eyebrows pinched together in confusion. It's no secret I hate paperwork. I just don't give a shit, and I know I need to keep up to date on it if I'm going to pay my mechanics, which is why I make a point to make sure everything is up to date every second Friday before Saige comes home for the week. "For the oil changes?"

"Yeah." I nod. "Got in early today and did some paperwork." I look over at Ryan. "Mr. Bills is coming in to get his Camaro today. I assume it's all ready."

"Yup," he confirms, "we finished installing the dashboard yesterday after you gave us the transmission."

"Good. Let's get today over so we can have a nice weekend. Who is on call this weekend?" I look at everyone, and they all point at Eddie, who holds up his hand.

"Don't forget to transfer the line," I remind him. "We forgot to do it last week. Got a knock on the door at eight a.m. on a Sunday to check Mr. Mendelson's car." As the only mechanic shop in town, we used to be open seven days a week, but I changed that when I took over. We work Monday to Friday, and on weekends, we only come in if there is an emergency. Every weekend, we take turns being on call. I do it only when I don't have Saige, but then again, when I don't have her, I'm usually in the garage both days anyway.

The bell rings over the door, and I look out. "Let's get moving." I get up and walk out to the front and see Brady standing there in the waiting area. He's Autumn's brother, and the two of them run the bar and the whiskey distillery. "Hey," I greet him, and he looks up from his phone.

"Hey," he returns, "I'm bringing in the truck to get looked at." He hands me the keys to his red truck. "It pulls to the left. I think Harmony hit a curb, but she's refusing to admit it."

I chuckle. "We'll get it looked at, and I'll call you when it's done."

I walk over to the desk and pull out a work order, writing his name on top and then the issues. "Anything else we should check while we have it?" I look at him, and he shrugs, making me laugh before walking out and making his way over to the bakery. I watch as he pulls open the door, my eyes looking inside to see if I can see her. But the way the sun hits the door is like a mirror, so I see nothing. Which is just as good. The last thing I want to see is her.

Turning and walking to the back, I place the work order with the keys on the board under Tony's name. I walk over to my bench and sit down to continue taking apart the transmission I started working on this morning when I showed up at the ass crack of dawn. Or even before that, fuck, the sun wasn't even up when I came in. Picking up the screwdriver to start taking it apart, I allow my mind to drift back to last night even though I have forced myself not to think about it.

I fucked her against a fucking tree. The thought makes my cock stir in my pants. I don't even know what came over me. One second, I was telling her how much I hated her. The next, I was fucking her into the goddamn tree. I don't think I've come as hard in my life as I did when I came in her. Another fucking mistake since I wasn't wearing a fucking condom. She's the only one I've ever not worn protection with. Even with Karla, I was wearing a condom, but it broke, and then my life changed in more ways than one. Even when we were married, we never, ever did it without. I think it's one of the reasons she hates me. She knew I would never fully give myself to her. I wasn't a hypocrite about it. She knew going in I had zero feelings for her, and she also knew I didn't know if I ever would. I had to be honest with her, and I was, but she refused to listen to me, thinking she could change me. Thinking eventually she would get in there, but we both knew she wouldn't.

I work through lunch, and I only look up when the bell sounds over the door, and I hear Saige's voice. "Daddy!" she shouts, and I smile as I turn on my stool, seeing her stick her head in the garage. "Can I come in?" She looks around to see if she can come in, something I taught her when she was five to make sure she didn't get hurt.

I get off my stool and walk toward her, and she bounces on her feet as I get closer to her. She lunges herself into my arms when I'm close enough, and I wrap my arms around her as she wraps her arms around my neck. "Daddy." She giggles when I kiss her neck and tickle her with my beard as she tries to lift her shoulder to stop me.

"Hey, baby girl." I walk into the waiting area, where Karla walks in with Saige's bags in her hand. Her long brown hair flows in the wind as she pulls open the door.

"Hey," she mumbles to me as I put Saige down. "Here are your bags, Saige." She's holding out her backpack from school and then the little travel case she likes to take between houses.

Saige walks over to her, grabbing the bags. "Give me a kiss." She bends, and Saige gives her a hug. "I'll call you later," she tells her, and Saige just nods. "I want to talk to Daddy for a second. Go wait in his office."

I wait for her to walk by me as she leaves the bags there by the desk and goes to my office. I wait until she is out of earshot before I turn back to Karla. "I don't think it's a good idea having dinner with her in the middle of the week."

It takes everything I have in me not to roll my eyes at her. "Why is that?"

"It throws her routine off," she tries to say, "confuses her."

"She's almost nine. She knows the days of the week, and she knows when we do the exchanges."

"I still don't like it." There it is. She doesn't like it, so we can't do it.

"If you like, I could go to my lawyer and ask to have the custody decree revised to include one visit during the week. If you want, I'm more than happy for you to do the same during my week."

"Why do you have to be like that?" she asks. "It was working until now."

"I'm not saying it's not working well. I'm just saying I would like to have dinner with her during the week when she isn't with me. Why are you busting my balls about this?"

"Trust me, the last thing I want to do is bust anything when it comes to you," she hisses. "Been there, done that, over it."

"Glad to know." I shake my head. "She's going to be old enough to decide where she wants to go when she wants to go. Wouldn't it be better if we weren't at each other's throats?"

"Whatever, Brock," she says, walking past me and sticking her head into the office. "Bye, baby, I'll call you tonight."

"Bye, Mom," she replies, and I hear the squeak of the chair she's sitting in before her mother storms out without saying goodbye to me.

I put my hands on my hips and look up at the ceiling before walking into my office. I see Saige sitting in my chair, going around and around in a circle while she watches something on the iPad I keep here for her. "I'm going to close up, and then we can head out," I say, and she nods, continuing to spin.

I clean up my hands and check in with everyone before I walk back to get her. "Let's go," I urge her. She puts her iPad in the drawer and then skips over to me. I pick up her bags before placing them in the truck and opening the back door. "Get in."

"Dad, cupcake." She points at the bakery.

"It's Friday," she reminds me. "We get cupcakes on Friday." She puts her hand in mine and pulls me toward the bakery.

"Um, how about we go for ice cream instead?" I offer, hoping she changes her mind but knowing she won't. It's the first time I hate that she's stubborn like me.

"Cupcakes, Daddy." She smiles at me, and I close my eyes, my feet walking toward the bakery with her. I'm hoping Everleigh left already, and she's not there. Or they sold out of cupcakes so the display case is empty, and we can just walk out and not have to talk to or see anyone. "Please, Daddy," she pleads.

"Anything for my girl." I walk with her, her hand in mine,

listening to her tell me about her day. But the whole time, I'm thinking about what is going to happen when I pull open that door. We get to it, and I reach out and pull it open. "Here we go," I mumble, not even sure why I'm so nervous. "Cupcakes, and we leave."

Ten

EVERLEIGH

I TAKE A PICTURE of the cupcakes on the stand and upload it on the Instagram page I created for my mother three years ago. A page she hasn't kept up with since the last post, which was exactly three years ago. I've been taking over the social media since I've been in town, and it's grown a ton. I even had one of the reels I created in the morning making the donuts go viral, and a couple of people have reached out and asked if we ship out.

I've even been on Pinterest at night while I'm in bed, coming up with different ideas to spruce up the place and bring the dreary to pop and sunshine. Maybe paint the walls a different color. Put some pictures up from over the years. Put up some little trinkets to make it feel more homey. Maybe put in a couple of tables by the window so they can grab a coffee or even a slice of cake.

I'm posting the picture when I hear the front door open, and then a child's voice calls, "Daddy, they have cupcakes." I smile at her animated voice as I walk out of the back and to the front.

I stop mid-step when I see Brock coming into the door, my eyes going to the little girl standing at the display counter. "Look,

Daddy, they have my favorite." She points at one of them, and all I can do is stare at her. My chest feels like an elephant has just stepped on me, crushing my breathing. I can't help but stare at her, my eyes getting so dry as they burn to stay open, so I blink them furiously. "We can even get some for tomorrow," she suggests happily, and the only thing I can think is she has to be the most beautiful little girl I've ever laid eyes on in my life. She looks exactly like Brock but with feminine features. She looks exactly like the daughter I always thought we would have.

"Hello," I force out, hoping my voice doesn't crack when I get to the counter.

"Hi," she says, "is Ms. Maddie not here?"

I shake my head as the lump forms in my throat. "Not today." I clear my throat in case it stops working. "What can I get you?" I don't look up at Brock, not wanting him to see how this affects me. Even though I think I've put up a brave face, it would take one look into my eyes for him to see how much this is getting to me. And he doesn't get that. He lost that right.

"I'm going to have a chocolate cupcake with the sprinkles," she orders, jumping up and down and clapping her hands, "and Daddy likes the same thing." I stop my head from turning to stare at him because he hates chocolate. He always picked vanilla over chocolate every single time.

"Coming right up." I turn to walk to the back and only when I'm safely there do I let my head hang, and a single lone tear escapes and runs down my face. My hand shakes as I pull the white box off the shelf. Walking back in, I hear her say, "Ask her, Daddy." I have no choice but to look at Brock. His eyes turn soft as he looks up at me, and then I can see the shift in them right before my eyes. "Ask her."

"What can I help you with?" I ask him and then turn to look at his little girl.

"Ms. Maddie usually gives me a cookie while I wait," she announces instead of waiting for Brock to say something, but all he does is put his hands on her shoulders.

I laugh and nod. "That sounds like my mom," I reply, treating her just like I would any other little girl. But she's not just any other little girl. Even my heart knows it. "What cookie do you usually get?"

"She usually has the special ones for me," she shares, her eyes lighting up, "that she keeps in the back."

"Is that so?" I lean my elbows on the counter. "And would you know where she keeps them?" I joke with her and all I want to do is look into her eyes that are very much like her father's. The way they used to be. The ones I longed to look into. "She would only share it with special people."

"I know, I know." She holds up her hand. "Can I show you?" she asks, and I nod as she looks back at Brock. "Can I go, Daddy?"

"Yeah." His voice is gruff and again I ignore looking at him. Instead, I watch the little girl walk behind the counter and come to my side.

"Lead the way." I hold out my hand for her to walk in front of me and I follow her.

"She keeps them in there," she directs, once she gets into the back and points at the fridge in the corner, where she keeps the cookie dough.

"Wow," I say, folding my arms in front of me instead of reaching out and touching her hair and seeing if it's as soft and silky as her father's, "she must really like you."

"She does. She says I'm a very special little girl."

I don't answer her. I just nod as I feel my heart soar in my chest. "She usually warms it up for me," she informs me of how things go. I walk over to the fridge and pull out the cookies I baked just this morning.

"I don't know if these are as good as Ms. Maddie's," I say, putting the tray on the table in the middle of the kitchen, "but here they are." She comes over and stands next to me and I look up to see Brock has followed us into the kitchen. He stands in the doorway, watching us. Does he think I would do something to his daughter?

"Oh, is that one chocolate chip?" she asks, and I nod. "Can I have that one?" She points at what might be the biggest one on the tray.

"You got it," I confirm, grabbing a spatula and then walking over to the oven and putting it in. "It'll be a minute. I'll go and pack your cupcakes and it'll be done by then." She smiles at me, and it's a good thing I'm beside a table so I can hold myself up. The smile is one I've dreamed of for the last nine years. The one where I allow myself to let him out of the box I banished him to.

"I'm getting a cookie." She runs to him and he looks down at her. "And it's a big one."

"Let's go wait in front and get out of Ms. Everleigh's way." He turns and walks to the front.

"She's pretty, Daddy," I hear her say and then I don't hear anything else. I don't know why that bothers me, but it does. Add one more thing on the list of why I hate Brock. I never thought being a good dad would get you a notch on the list, but he was just added there for this.

I walk out and pack the two cupcakes in the box and throw in another one just to piss him off, or at least hope I do when he opens the box and sees. "Do we have a special color for the ribbon?" I ask.

"Green because it's like my name."

"Your name is green?" I ask and she laughs at my question.

"No, it's Saige," she retorts and I nod, looking down at the green ribbon we have.

"That's a pretty name," I say as I put the box on the counter. "I'll get your cookie." I need to get away from this whole situation. I need to get him out of my space, and I need to drink about a whole gallon of wine to erase the fact that not only does his daughter look like him, he won. In all of this, he ends up being the winner. I may have ended up having to bury my dreams, but in the end, he was the one who won at this whole fucking thing. He won because he gets to live a fulfilling life with his daughter, and all I have is the emptiness he left me with.

I put her cookie in a white sleeve bag, bringing it to the front and handing it to her. "Here you go, Saige."

"How much do we owe you?" Brock steps forward and I look up at him.

"It's on the house," I say and then look at Saige. "Enjoy the cupcakes."

"Daddy, can we bake cupcakes this weekend?" she asks him as I turn and walk into the back, not willing to hear the rest of his conversation. My heart can only handle so much.

My phone rings, and I pull it out to see it's Autumn. "Hello," I answer, as if she knew I needed her.

"Hey," she says, "we were wondering, if you weren't busy tonight, if you wanted to come over and just hang out with us?"

"Um." I look at the door and then down at the floor. "That sounds like the perfect night," I admit. "What time is good?"

"You can come over now," she states, "but I know you would probably like to shower."

"I have someone coming in to replace me at four. How about I shower and get there at five?" I tell her. When I hang up the phone, I clean up and prepare my things for the next day. When I walk out of the bakery, I head home. I walk in and spot my mother in her chair. I want to ask her all the questions about Saige and Brock, but instead I tell her everything else about my day except that.

I'm walking out of the door when I hear the sound of the motorcycle coming down the street. My head turns when I see it stop in front of the house, his feet come down as he throws down the stand, and then swings his leg off. "Hey," I greet when Oliver takes off his helmet.

"Hi, Everleigh." He holds his helmet in his hand. "Are you going out?"

"I am," I say to him. "Mom is sitting inside."

"Sounds good," he replies, walking toward the door.

"I'll call before I come home," I joke with him as he shakes his head and walks right in the house.

I get in my car and follow the directions to Autumn and Charlie's house. They are waiting for me outside as she sits in the chair and Charlie is swinging Landon around, making him laugh.

"Hi," I say, getting out of the car and walking over to Charlie, who bends and kisses my cheek. Landon slaps my face before trying to grab my hair in his chubby little hand.

"I'll take that." I rescue my hair from his hand as he throws himself to me. "And you, I guess," I say, cocking him on my hip. "Aren't you the most handsome boy?" He gives me a gummy smile. "And the world's biggest flirt"—he slaps my boobs—"and handsy," I observe, making them laugh. "At least buy me a drink."

"Sorry about that; he thinks all breasts are his," Autumn explains as she comes to stand next to me. Charlie wraps his arm around her shoulders.

"Most action I've gotten in months," I joke and kiss his chubby little cheek as he squeals.

We walk inside and she gives me a tour of the house. We

stop at the table in the hall that has a picture of Jennifer. "Oh my," I gasp at the picture that was taken so long ago it feels like it was in another lifetime. "This is"—I pick it up in my hand and run my hand over the glass—"she looks . . ." I trail off, thinking of the word I want to say.

"She's beautiful," Autumn fills in.

"She really was," I agree, putting the picture down. "Do you find it weird?" I ask. "Sorry, that's a dumb question."

"No." She quickly stops me from talking. "It's not weird. I know how much he loved her. I will never not want him to have that. To have her. That's something that is a part of him. Something I love that he loved."

"You are a saint," I say. "I don't know how I would feel if my husband had a picture of one of his girlfriends in the house we lived in."

"I want to believe she brought us together," she shares, then leans in. "But if the roles were reversed, I would haunt the shit out of Charlie. I would give him erectile dysfunction." I throw my head back and laugh. "And I'm okay with admitting that."

We eat dinner together, the three of us, and then go outside to sit on the same chairs she was sitting on when I got there. "I forgot how peaceful it was at night." I look up and see the sky filled with twinkling stars. My thoughts go to Brock, and I wonder if he's with his daughter. The tightness forms in my stomach as I try to push the feelings away, but it's easier said than done.

"You forget a lot of things until you come back, and then it's all there, and you wonder how you survived without them."

"How long were you gone?" I ask, the guilt of not talking to her rushes through me. I shouldn't have done what I did, but at the time, my own world was falling apart.

"About six years," she answers. "Came back home when I found out my father was dying."

I gasp and reach out to grab her hand in mine. "He's still not one hundred percent but he's hanging in there. He's done chemo and radiation. It could happen at any minute, but for today he is almost the same as he was back then."

"It's all we can ask for," I say. "If I hadn't been on the phone with my mother, I don't know if she would still be here." She wraps her arm around my shoulders. "I'm sorry," I murmur softly, "for blaming you. For not talking to you"—the tear escapes—"and for being a shitty friend."

"I'm sorry," she sniffles, "for not stopping it all before it happened. What I wouldn't do to go back and change that moment." My phone rings in my pocket, and when I pull it out, I see it's my mother calling me.

"Hey, Mom," I answer, putting the phone to my ear. "What's up?"

"Where are you?" she frantically asks me. But her tone cuts me to the bone, before she gasps out, "Fire." I sit up stiff. "There is a fire at the bakery."

Eleven

EVERLEIGH

"MOM." I SPRING OUT OF THE CHAIR, and Charlie is already out of his, and so is Autumn, who grabs a hold of my hand. "What do you mean there is a fire?" The second I say that, Autumn gasps and her hold gets tighter, while Charlie's phone rings from his pocket.

"Everleigh," Oliver says into the phone, no doubt taking it from my mother, "the fire department just called. There is a fire at the bakery." I can hear him rushing on his end as my feet feel like they are cemented to the deck. "We are on our way there now."

"I'm coming." I disconnect with him and then turn to Autumn. "The bakery is on fire."

"Charlie," she calls him over as she moves down the steps, with her hand still in mine.

"Brady just called. Someone called him from the bar," he reports.

"I have to go." I feel like I'm in a daze as she guides me to Charlie's truck.

"I'm going to call my dad to come over," Autumn says to me once she has me buckled into the truck. "I'll meet you there."

"Okay." I look over at Charlie. "We have to go." They share a look and a nod before he pulls out of the driveway and heads toward town. For the first time I think in my life there is traffic getting there. It seems the phone chain is in full effect, and people are rushing over to watch or maybe help.

Charlie honks his horn as he makes his way to the corner of Main Street, where I can see the flames. He pulls over and parks his truck on the side, and I spring into action. I jump down from the truck and head toward the bakery. Two fire trucks are already on the scene, and they have closed down the area, two deputies making sure no one gets close.

"What's going on?" Charlie asks one of them as I look around to see if I can spot my mother.

"We are trying to get the fire under control," the deputy replies. "Fire department just called the fire marshal in. We are also evacuating the rest of the street to make sure it doesn't spread."

"Do we know how it started?" I ask him, and he shakes his head and moves away before I can ask him anything else.

"Oh my goodness." I hear my mother's voice from behind me as she runs to me and takes me in her arms. "I was so scared you went to the bakery to get something and was stuck in there." She holds the back of my head in her hand as I hug her to me.

"No, I'm fine," I assure her as she lets me go. We stand together with our arms around each other and watch the firefighters work to get the fire under control.

"Hey," Brady greets when he makes his way to us, next to Harmony who has tears running down her face. "We came as soon as we heard." They stand with us as they look over and see what we see. Neither of them is able to say anything more.

Harmony walks over to the other side of my mother and slips her hand in hers. "It's going to be okay, Maddie," she comforts, putting her head on her shoulder. No one says anything as the fire slowly dies down.

Some of the onlookers have trickled away and then some new ones have come, but it's mostly just a few of the older folks who are sticking around to see what the damage is. We watch helplessly as the firefighters do what they need to do. I don't think I've ever felt so helpless before in my life. Knowing this is my mother's life and she's watching it literally go up in smoke. My heart breaks for her as she puts her hand to her mouth.

Oliver comes over with a carry out tray of water and coffee. "Here, drink something," he urges my mother, "have some water."

"I'm fine," she replies to him, trying to shoo him away, but he just stands in front of her not moving. "I said I'm fine."

"And I said to drink something." He doesn't back down, which makes my mother glare at him even more.

"Don't you have somewhere else to be," she asks him, "like at the hospital?"

"Or did you want juice instead?" He ignores her question. "I'm not going to move along until you take something to drink, and there are other people here." He leans in. "Some of them are watching us." She bites down on her lip, reaching out and grabbing a glass of water. "There, was that so hard?"

"You better move along, Oliver, before you are wearing this water," she threatens him, and he just chuckles at the threat. Not wanting to deal with him also having to threaten me, I grab a cup of coffee before he moves on.

"He's bossy," I mumble to my mother, who just shakes her head.

I think I only let out a breath when I see the firefighters have stopped using water. I can't even see the damage from here as the fire marshal comes our way. "Maddie," he says, nodding at her.

I feel Oliver come and stand behind my mother, putting his hands on her shoulders and squeezing them. I slip my hand in hers as we both wait for him to start talking.

"How bad is it?" my mother asks.

"There is good news and then bad news," he starts and I close my eyes, not sure I want to hear any bad news. I don't want to hear anything, to be honest. "The good news is we caught it before it burned through the roof and the structure."

"Is that good news?" I finally ask, moving my head to the side. "All the windows are busted out. Where did it start?"

"Started in the kitchen," he reports, and I shake my head.

"I double-checked twice before I left." My heart feels like it's going to soar out of my chest. "I made sure the appliances were all off, and no one had to bake anything or fry anything after I left."

"I don't know how to say this—" He looks down at his feet before looking back up at us. "We think—"

"Don't say it," my mother snaps.

"It's looking like it was arson," he declares, and the air leaves my body.

"There was forced entry at the back door," he explains and I stop him right away.

"There were two guys," I start to say and feel all eyes on me, "there were two guys lurking around. They were acting weird and I didn't think anything of it."

"What else can you tell me about them?" he asks me and I try to wrack my brain.

"Medium height I guess, creepy vibes. They had a black car." I snap my fingers. "Four-door Honda Civic I think." I close my eyes and try to bring up the memory but it's just blank. "I don't know."

"Well, that makes a little bit more sense," he says. "We

found some gasoline canisters that I'm assuming you didn't have in your kitchen."

"What kind of a dumb question is that?" my mother snaps, and Oliver pulls her closer to him and wraps an arm around her waist. "Now what?"

"Now we have to finish the investigation, which will probably be done by tomorrow morning. Then you can get in there and—"

"And what?" my mother barks. "And do what?" He just shrugs.

"I'm sorry. I know how difficult this can be." I just stare at him. "We are going to have the police come over and ask you a couple questions about the two guys you saw." I nod at him, feeling like the rug just got ripped out from under me, looking at what used to be, it actually did. "If you have any questions, feel free to call me."

He walks away and we just stand here staring at him as he makes his way to the bakery.

"Oh my God, this is my fault," Harmony cries. "It's probably because of me."

We all turn to look at her as Brady takes her in his arms, and she cries in his chest. "If you hadn't helped me, this probably wouldn't have happened."

"You don't know that." I rub her back. "It could be anything at this point."

"Well, there is nothing we can do for now," Oliver notes. "Let's get you off your feet." He slips his arm from around her and into her hand, and she doesn't even fight him.

I take one more look at the building before turning and walking with them. "I'm going to get a ride with them," I tell Charlie, who just nods at me, "and come and get the car tomorrow, if that is okay."

"I'll have it brought to you and leave the keys in the mailbox," he states, and I laugh, making everyone look at me.

"I'm sorry, but why does it seem normal to just leave keys in a mailbox and not have to worry that my car is going to be stolen?"

Charlie smirks at me. "This ain't the city, girl." He takes me in a chokehold like he used to do back in the day, making me laugh even more. "Now, I'm going to get home to Autumn, who has been blowing up my phone. I thought she would show up with Landon."

"Sorry about that," I say.

"She'll probably be at your house tomorrow morning, early."

"Good. If she didn't have the whole husband and kid, I would be crashing at her house anyway."

"You can always do that," he invites. "Probably be easier for me to calm her down if you are there."

"I don't want to leave Mom," I admit, looking over to see Oliver open her car door for her, "but I'll call her and make sure she knows I'm okay."

"Sounds good," he says and then smirks. "I'm glad you're home." I nod because all the emotion of the night has come crashing into me. "You make her happy, and that's all I can ask for."

"You love her." I don't know why I say it, but the words come out of my mouth.

"More than my next breath," he confirms. "More than I've ever loved anyone before. Not that I compare it, but . . ."

"I get it," I say, and my mind suddenly goes to Brock. "You have that once-in-a-lifetime love, and sometimes you are lucky enough to have it look you in the eyes every day. It fills your soul and your bones, and you know you'll never be cold a day in your life."

"Everleigh," he says, "you should know."

"I don't want to know." I hold up my hand, knowing he was going to say something about Brock. "It's over; he made his choice."

"Trust me, no one knows more than I do about holding a grudge."

"It's not a grudge," I inform him. "You hold a grudge against someone when you care about them. I don't. It's over. He made it that way." I get up on my tippy-toes. "Thanks for tonight, Charlie." I cut off the conversation before heading over to my mother and getting into the car.

"Are you okay?" I ask while I put my seat belt on. My mother doesn't say anything; instead she shakes her head and looks out the window. "It'll be okay, Mom," I say, my eyes looking at the bakery. "We'll make it okay."

Twelve

BROCK

"DADDY," I HEAR FROM MY SIDE and then feel the bed dip. When I look over, I see Saige putting her knee on the bed as she rubs sleep out of her eyes. "It's morning." She gets under the covers with me and lies down on the other side before grabbing the remote from the bedside table.

"Is it morning?" I ask, turning my head to the side, keeping my eyes closed as I try to wake up. "How do you know?"

"The sun is up." She snorts. "And it's nine thirty."

"Is it that late?" I lift my head and grab my phone from the bedside table and see she is telling the truth. I also see I have a couple of missed texts from the guys at work, and then the last one is from this morning, and it's from Charlie. "We slept in." I toss the covers off me and get up, making my way to the bathroom.

When I return, Saige is still in the middle of the bed with the pillows propped up behind her. "Are we getting out of bed?"

"Maybe," she says. "It depends. Are we going to the park?"

I raise my eyebrows at her. "I don't know. It depends. Are

you going to get out of bed?" I don't wait for her to answer. Instead, I walk out of my bedroom and head to the kitchen to start my coffee before anything else.

"Can I have a cupcake?" she shouts from my bedroom. I look over at the white box on the counter that holds the extra cupcake Everleigh placed in there the day before. Something that made Saige extra happy when she opened it when we got home. It irritates me she did that for my daughter. All night long, I kept thinking of her face when she met Saige. Something I never thought would happen, if I'm being honest.

"You aren't eating a cupcake in my bed," I say as I grab a mug and fill it with coffee. I hear the sound of her feet hitting the floor before seeing her walk into the kitchen. "Good morning, sunshine."

I watch her grab the box and then go to her stool and pull it out as she opens the top of the box. "She gave me a special one," she repeats what she said the day before, and instead of answering her, I just grunt.

Grabbing my phone and going through the messages, I see Tony's message at the top.

Tony: Have you heard about the bakery?

Ryan: It sucks big-time.

My neck tingles as I read through the messages, but no one has said what has happened. And I'm not about to ask about it until I get to Charlie's text.

Over the years, we've drifted apart. We each had our own shit to deal with. To be honest, I wasn't close to anyone and preferred to be by myself.

Charlie: Hey, not sure if you heard, but there was a fire at the bakery last night.

I have to hold on to the counter with one hand as the image

of Everleigh stuck in the fire feels like someone just kicked me in the stomach. I close my eyes, the hiss comes out of my mouth, and I ignore all the feeling in my chest. When I open my eyes, I continue reading the text.

Charlie: Everyone is fine.

I drop my phone on the counter and put my cup down, and I brace on my elbows, my head hanging. Letting out a sigh of relief.

"Are you okay, Daddy?" Saige asks, and I look over at her. Her image is blurry through the tears I fight away.

"Yeah." I nod. "I'm good, baby." I turn around, breathe in through my nose, then exhale through my mouth. "Did you want a breakfast sandwich to go with your cupcake?"

"No, I'm going to do my homework, and then can we go to the park?"

"Yeah," I agree softly, standing back up and looking out the window, forcing my mind blank but failing when I see Everleigh smiling at Saige and ignoring me.

She comes over and washes her hands before drying them and going to her bedroom. I pick the phone back up and continue the message.

Charlie: We should talk when you have a chance. Time is precious, man.

I shake my head and put the phone down, not wanting to read the rest. I don't need him to tell me that time is precious. I don't need him to tell me what I should and shouldn't do.

Instead, I walk over to the back door and slide it open before stepping out and sitting in the chair and just looking out into the distance. The swing set I set up for Saige when she turned four. She was so small it took all of her energy to climb up the ladder on the side. Even on the swing, she could barely touch the ground with her feet, and now she hardly ever looks at it.

Eventually, I should just take it down, but something always tells me not to.

I sit outside, my head a mess, as I try to push away all thoughts of the bakery and the way Everleigh must be feeling. *I don't care,* I remind myself when I hear Saige at the door. "I'm done."

"Okay, I'll go shower quickly," I state, getting up and bending to kiss her head, "and then we can go."

"Okay," she replies, following me inside and going to sit on the couch while I go to my bedroom. I make my bed before taking a shower and getting dressed.

We're walking out of the house when my phone rings, and I look down to see Winston is calling me. I ignore the call and put it into my back pocket, making sure Saige is in her seat before I take off. My phone rings again, showing me Tony is calling. "Hey," I say, answering on the Bluetooth.

"Hey, I'm about to head out."

"Sounds good," I say. "We're on our way to the park."

"Have fun." He disconnects the phone as my truck makes its way over to the shop instead of to the park.

"We're going to walk from here," I say. She jumps down, and I look over at the bakery and so does Saige, who gasps.

"Daddy, look." She points at the bakery, and I see the construction truck in the parking lot, along with a container in the front as workers walk in and out of the door, carrying stuff. "It's all messed up."

"Yeah," I reply, walking down the street and seeing the front windows boarded up. Black soot is around where the windows were and also where the door is. The roof from the front doesn't look like there is much damage, but when you walk to the side, you see half of it is off.

"Daddy, look, it's Everleigh," she declares when we stop by

the side window, the only window that looks like nothing happened to it. I can see the front counter looks like it's still intact, but the glass cases are smashed on the floor. Everleigh has a broom in her hand as men around her are also cleaning up. I don't even notice Saige has left my hand until I see her hold up her hand and she's knocking on the window.

Everleigh looks over, and I see her eyes go soft as Saige waves at her. Eyes that used to go soft like that when I walked into the room and told her I loved her. Eyes I haven't seen for a long time. Eyes I've missed, and sometimes when I dream of her, they look at me like that. Exactly like she is doing right now. She looks like she hasn't slept a wink, and she has black soot on her face. But she smiles at Saige, ignoring that I'm standing right here as she waves at her. "Does this mean that there are no more cupcakes?"

"It looks that way." I reach out for her hand and pull her away from the window. "We'll find another place."

We walk down the street, Saige looking over her shoulder every now and again. I'm forcing myself not to look back over my shoulder.

I sit on the bench and watch her play with a couple of friends from school. The whole time, my stomach feels like I've swallowed glass. My mind sees Everleigh with her hair tied on top of her head. I wonder how the fire started. I wonder if she's going to be okay. I wonder how Ms. Maddie is doing. I wonder all of these things I shouldn't wonder. I wonder all these things I have no business wondering about. I wonder if she even ate anything, knowing she fainted twice when we were together because she didn't eat the whole day. Scared the shit out of me when she walked out of the bathroom and then just fell on her face. That was the first time I ever felt a fear inside me. "Daddy." Saige comes running over to me, panting. "Can we have a mani-pedi night?" She smiles at me, her whole face lighting up.

I smile as I tuck a strand of hair behind her ear. "Whatever you want, baby girl," I agree, the emptiness I felt not a couple of seconds ago being filled by her smile. She's the only one I've let into my heart after Everleigh. She will be the only one who will have a hold on my heart ever again.

"So pizza night and mani-pedi." She sits beside me, taking the water bottle I went to buy at the corner store while she played tag with her friends. Her chest heaves. "When can we go?"

"Whenever you want," I say, and she gets up, putting her hand out. We walk back down Main Street. I see the bar is open, the doors are open with the sign in front that says: "Come in, we are open."

My eyes go to the bakery as we walk past it and see there are just a couple of people left inside. None of them Everleigh, or at least we don't see her, and I'm happy, or else I don't know what Saige would do.

When we get home, I order pizza while she takes a shower and then comes out with her pink mani-pedi case. She puts it on the counter and zips open the top. "What color do you want this week?" she asks as she takes out the bottles of nail polish she keeps accumulating every single time we head over to the pharmacy. "I'm going for a blue," she declares, picking up the baby-blue one she got last week. "What about you, Daddy?" she asks, and I look over at the bottles in front of her, picking out the lightest shade there is and it's a light white. "That's boring." She shakes her head, taking the bottle from me and putting it back in the case. "We are going to do this one," she says of the green one she picked out when it was Halloween. "You said it was a nice color."

"It is," I reply right before the doorbell rings. I get the pizza, and she eats two slices before the two of us settle on the couch. She paints my nails, and then I paint hers.

The cap of the bottle is too small for my fingers. "What happened to the bakery?" she asks softly, as I focus on trying not to get it on her skin.

"I don't know, baby girl," I say the truth. "There was a fire."

"Do you think Ms. Maddie is going to build it back?"

I nod. "Of course she will."

"It's good that she has Everleigh there to help her." She mentions her name again.

"Yeah." That is the only thing I say and hope that she changes the subject.

"Do you think they need more help?" she asks. "If they do, maybe we can help them a bit."

"I think they have all the help they need," I deflect, finishing painting her nails. "Now, do you want your toes the same color?" I make sure I change the subject, and she nods. I finish painting her toes. She sits on the couch not moving and fans her hands to make sure her polish dries, and I do the same. She finally dozes off sometime after ten, long after the paint has dried.

Picking her up, I carry her to her bed and tuck her in before kissing her head and walking out. I turn off the television and the light, and instead of heading to my bedroom to do the same, I head outside and sit in the chair, looking up at the sky. My mind plays tricks on me when I imagine what my life would be like with Everleigh in it. Would we be here in this house? Would we have kids? If we did, would they look like Saige or have Everleigh's eyes?

It happens so fast—it's as if I am having a déjà vu moment when I see myself right here in this chair, with her sitting next to me. Her head is in my lap, her legs stretched out in front of her as she smiles at me. Her hand rests on the small baby bump, with my hand covering hers as I feel our baby kick. I rub my hands over my face to erase the image from my mind. "Maybe in another lifetime." I get up. "And if we were different people." I look up at the sky, seeing a shooting star. "And if I didn't hate her."

Thirteen

EVERLEIGH

I WALK UP THE STEPS to the front door and swear I'm counting down the seconds until I collapse on that couch. My whole body feels like it's been run over by a Mack truck, front and back. Turning the door handle, I really fucking hope it's open so I don't have to fish my keys out of my purse and make me do more work. Closing my eyes and pushing it open, I say a little prayer of relief. "Yesss," I hiss as I step into the house and immediately kick off my sneakers.

"Hey," my mother says from the kitchen when she looks over at the door.

"Hey," I mumble, tossing my purse to the floor, next to my shoes, before dragging my ass to the couch and falling onto my back. "Don't even try to tell me to move because I'm not doing it."

I open one of my closed eyes when I hear my mother laughing from the kitchen. "You are lucky you took your shoes off."

"No." I shake my head. "You're lucky I took my shoes off."

"Are you going to have enough energy to get up and eat?" she asks, and I groan.

"I don't even have enough energy to walk up those stairs"—I point at the stairs—"and take a shower."

"A shower will make you feel better," she advises as she stirs whatever it is in the pot that smells really good.

"This," I say, pointing at the couch, "makes me feel better. Mom, I swear every single bone in my body hurts."

"A nice hot shower will make all the aches and pains go away." I groan when she says that, and I literally roll off the couch.

"You are ruining my peace," I accuse, walking up the stairs with her laughing the whole time. I walk into the bathroom and turn on the shower before getting naked. I close my eyes and put my head back as the hot water runs all over my body. The aches and pains from literally gutting out the whole bakery in the past five days are unreal. From sunup to sundown, I've been in there along with a demolition crew that showed up the day after the fire. As soon as the fire marshal said we could go back in, which was about ten hours after the fire, they showed up. It took five seconds to realize Charlie had called them.

Walking into the bakery was something I don't think I was ready for. Seeing everything my mother worked for in a pile of rubble was a bit too much. I swept the front of the bakery with tears running down my face. *I don't know how I am going to do it, but I am going to make it bigger and better.* I kept repeating that to myself the whole week when all I wanted to do was go home and bury my head under the covers. Finally, the cleanup is done, and we have a meeting with the contractor this coming Monday.

I stay under the water until it turns warm, getting out and wrapping myself in a towel before walking out and heading to my bedroom. I start going through my clothes when I grab my robe and just slide it on before walking downstairs. "Don't you feel better?" My mother looks over at me when she puts a plate on the kitchen table.

"No." I pull out the chair and sit at the table, looking down at the plate of beef stew in front of me. My mouth suddenly waters as I wait for my mother to sit beside me. She puts down a basket of fresh rolls I know she made this morning because she never, ever buys frozen rolls.

Sitting down next to me, she looks at me and smiles. "You can eat," she urges, picking up her fork. "Tell me about today."

I grab my fork and stab a piece of meat and carrot. "Cleanup crew is finally done," I say. "Place is down to the studs, as they said."

"Took me ten years to build that thing up to what it was, and it took a week to gut it." She shakes her head as she takes a bite of her food.

"We have to talk about what is going to happen," I say softly. "I know you said you didn't want to discuss it, but, Mom—"

"I know, I know," she admits, "it's just I don't know what to say."

"Well, why don't we start with all the medical bills," I start at the beginning. "They aren't much since you have insurance, but it's still a debt that has to be paid."

She lifts her hand, waving it. "That bill is covered," she states, and I nod. "I'm more worried about how I'm going to cover building a new bakery."

"What did the insurance company say?" I ask, and she again makes no eye contact with me. She doesn't want to show me how scared she really is. "Mom," I snap. She looks up, and I see big tears in her eyes forming at the bottom. "What is it?"

"They will have to wait for the full investigation to be done in order to tell me if I'm covered or not."

"What?" I gasp, never thinking it would not be covered. That's why you have insurance.

"The fact that it was arson, they have to rule out that I wasn't the one who did it." I slap my hand on the table. "It'll be fine." She tries to hide the fear and her worries. "I'll take another mortgage out on the house, and I do have some savings."

"Mom, that is crazy." I shake my head. "You are going to be working until you're eighty to pay it off. Is it worth it?"

"How can you ask me that?" she questions, as if I broke her heart. "Besides you, that bakery is the best damn thing I ever did. I had a reason to get up in the morning. I love going to work."

I'm about to say something else when there is a soft knock on the door. Before either of us can get up and get it, the door opens, and Oliver comes in. He's been here every single night since Mom has been home. He doesn't spend the night, but he comes over and sits with her. "Hi, guys," he says, his voice chipper as he puts down his helmet on the chair by the door. "What's with the sad faces?"

"Nothing," my mother quickly denies. "What are you doing here?"

"Was in the neighborhood," he answers, and I take a bite of my food trying not to laugh in his face.

"Did you eat?" My mother, even though her voice was annoyed not five seconds ago, has not lost her manners. "Let me get you a plate."

"I got it," he assures her, walking to her and bending to kiss her cheek. "You sit and relax."

I watch him walk over to the stove and grab himself a plate, filling it up before walking over and pulling out his chair. Before he sits down, he goes over to the fridge and opens it, grabbing himself a bottle of beer. I look over at my mother, knowing she hates beer. She has always hated beer, and I've never seen her stock beer in the fridge before. Ever. "This smells good," Oliver praises, sitting beside my mother. "So what's got you all so gloomy?" he asks before he takes a bite of his food.

"We're discussing how we are going to work out rebuilding the bakery if the insurance doesn't cover it."

Oliver's eyes slide to my mother's. "It's fine," she hisses out, "it's not for you to worry about."

"When do they start the rebuild?" Oliver asks, and I know he's definitely not looking at my mother for the answers.

"Monday," I relay. "I'm meeting with them tomorrow morning to go over some drawings."

"Let me know, and I'll get you a check," he states, and we both gasp.

"No." My mother slaps the table.

"It'll be a loan," Oliver explains, leaning back in his chair, "and when you get the money, you can pay me back. Everyone wins." He and my mother go into a staredown, but I see him trying to hide his smirk.

"I was thinking," I say softly, and they end their staredown to look back at me, "while we go through the rebuild"—I move the food around on my plate—"about maybe getting a food truck to tide us over." I look at Oliver first and then my mother. "We can serve coffee and cake out of it. And then make donuts here in the morning. Like we used to do at the beginning before you had a shop."

"I don't know." My mother hesitates.

"That's a great idea," Oliver praises. "People sure are missing the donuts since last week. I heard at least five nurses complaining about it." He takes a pull of his beer.

"That's another added expense," my mother points out.

"All we need is an old van, and we can, I don't know, fix it up for cheap. Put in a couple of coffee makers. I don't know, maybe even serve some sandwiches, or you had a recipe for bagels."

"I don't know," my mother says, not sure.

"I love that idea." Oliver takes my side. "You can park outside the hospital, and you'll be sold out in minutes." I smile at him. "I'll make a few calls and see if I know anyone with a van."

"I know someone who might have a van," my mother admits, and I know exactly who she is talking about.

"I'll wait for Oliver." I push away from the table. "Now, if you don't mind, I'm going to go to bed."

"It's seven," my mother points out.

"And I've been up since like five." I put my plate in the sink. "Leave the dishes. I'll wash them in the morning." I turn and walk over to kiss my mother on the cheek. "Will you leave them?"

"I can't go to bed with a dirty kitchen. It's just gross." She throws her hands up.

"Close your eyes, then you won't see it." I hold up my hand as I walk up the steps, knowing the dishes will not be there in the morning. I'm asleep the minute my head hits the pillow, only waking when I have to go pee at 6:00 a.m.

Stretching as I get out of bed, I go to the bathroom. I brush my teeth before going back and putting on a pair of yoga pants and a white top, then heading downstairs to make my coffee.

The house is quiet, and the kitchen is clean, which isn't a surprise. Until I hear movement to the side and look over to see Oliver trying to tiptoe out of my mother's bedroom. "Busted." I fold my arms over my chest.

"I fell asleep." He holds up his hands. "On top of the covers, fully dressed. Guess I was tired."

"Would you like a coffee before you go?" I ask, and he shakes his head.

"I'm going to get out of here before she wakes up and sees me, and then I'm never allowed back in here." He puts on his boots before grabbing his helmet.

I'm taking my first sip of coffee when my mother comes out of her room in a robe. "Morning, Mom," I greet her, and she glares at me. "I'm going to be going now." I put my coffee in a stainless-steel mug. "Your boyfriend just left."

"I thought you were leaving," she snaps, and I shake my head, laughing as I walk out of the house.

I'm walking down the quiet street, about to cross it, when I hear cursing and a loud cry of pain coming from the mechanic shop. Looking over, I see Brock's truck parked on the side. "Walk away," I tell myself, but my feet move toward the shop. Pushing open the glass door, I hear the bells over the door ring. "Hello," I call as I hear rustling coming from the side where the office is. "Hello."

I stick my head in the office at the same time the bathroom door opens, and I see Brock walk out with a rag wrapped around his finger, oozing with blood. "I was walking by, and I heard you cry out in pain."

"I didn't cry out in pain," he snaps. "I was hissing out."

I roll my eyes, walking over to him. "What did you do?"

"Slipped out of my hands," he says as he applies pressure to his finger. "Landed on my finger, and I think sliced it open." I stand in front of him. "I'm fine."

"Shut the fuck up," I snap, "and let me help, you stubborn mule." He glares at me, but he lets me unwrap the rag, and I see the gash. "I don't think you need stitches. I mean, not like you'd go anyway, but let's get this cleaned up and bandaged." I don't even know why I'm doing this. Well, I know why I'm doing this, because someone is hurt and I've been raised to help. We walk over to the bathroom off his office. It's a lot cleaner than I thought it would be. I turn the water on and feel it with my finger before taking his hand and putting it under the stream. The river of light red blood fills the bottom of the sink. I wait a couple of minutes before grabbing the towel in his hand and wrapping it to apply pressure. "Where is the first-aid kit?"

"At the front, under the desk," he gruffs out, so I walk to the front and find the square white plastic box with the red cross on the front. I go back in and find him near his desk. Opening it up, I grab the antiseptic pads and wipe down the cut before grabbing the big bandage. "You might have to wear gloves today," I advise him as I put the bandage on his finger, wrapping it around, "or not, it's up to you."

He grunts out a thank-you as I lean forward to toss the bandage wrapper, not realizing I'm in his space and my chest is pushed against his arm. I stand as he looks down at me. "Sorry," I say, and it's like the moment is frozen in time. Like we've done this before, and I'm sure after dating for seven years, we may have done this before. I don't even know. "I'll just—" I point over my shoulder. "Go." But my feet stay rooted in the spot as our chests practically touch. His hands come up, and he grips the sides of my neck before his mouth slams down on mine. My mouth opens for him, as if I was waiting for this moment. His tongue comes out to play with mine. My body wakes up as if it's been asleep for so long that this is what it needs to survive. The minute his hands grip my neck, I think I melt into him. I know I shouldn't want this. I know I shouldn't even be here. But what I also know is this kiss is something I might have been waiting for this whole fucking week. A little bit of comfort I didn't know I was missing.

The kiss is almost tender until the bell on top of the door rings again, and I jump back from him. His hands fall to his sides, and I shake my head as the air hits my wet lips. I turn to storm out of the room. "You lost the privilege to do that ever again."

Fourteen

BROCK

"YOU LOST THE PRIVILEGE TO DO THAT ever again," she snaps right before she storms out of my office. The sound of bells ringing as she leaves, my eyes go to the window to watch her walk to the bakery with her head down.

I clench my fist at my side, breathing in deeply, forcing myself not to do something stupid like chase her. Wanting nothing but to chase her, but knowing it would be a big mistake. For the past week, I've watched her walk past the shop with her head down, and even when I left late at night, she was still inside the bakery cleaning.

The number of times I wanted to go over there and see if she was okay was not normal. Especially since I knew I was the last person she wanted to see. "Hey." Ryan pokes his head in the office. "You okay? I saw blood out there."

"Yeah," I confirm, tearing my eyes off the window and turning to look at Ryan. "Part slipped and fell on my finger, sliced it open. I'll be fine."

"Shit, okay." He nods before turning and walking away. My head turns to the side as I watch her shadow move in the bakery. Anger creeps up in me as I hear her voice in my head again. *"You lost the privilege to do that ever again."*

She couldn't be more fucking right as I think back on the day I ruined everything.

"We're going to get you help," the paramedic said, and I shook my head ready to jump off the gurney.

"You need to get your ass back there and make sure Everleigh is okay," I told him. If my arm wasn't broken, I would have gripped the front of his shirt. "Forget about me, I'm fine."

"We have the fire department getting her out," he tried to reassure me, "but we need to get you to the hospital and check out the leg and your arm."

"Fuck my leg," I hissed at him as I heard Charlie yelling from the side of the truck, and I looked back when I saw a police officer coming my way.

"How many of you were in the truck?" he asked, and I looked at him, then over at the truck that was turned upside fucking down. One of the wheels looked like it flew off. The back of the bed of it was slammed against a tree. "Just so we know."

"We were four in the back and two in the front," I answered him as they picked me up and put me in the ambulance. "Get my girl," I pleaded with him as the doors were closed, and I roared out.

"I'm not going fucking anywhere without her," I said, but I was powerless to them. My arm was dangling on the side, and my left pant leg was stuck to me from the blood that was seeping out.

I tried to grab my phone from my back pocket but had to give up halfway through when I about passed out from the pain.

When we got to the hospital, they were pushing me toward the swinging doors. Five people were all over me as I felt scissors move up my leg, cutting off my jeans.

"We have a laceration," the doctor said, "on the left side, right to the bone."

"His shoulder is also dislocated." I looked up and saw the nurse doing something on top of me.

"We're going to get an MRI and a CT scan," the doctor explained. "Make sure everything is good inside," he added before looking at me. "You're one of the lucky ones," he said before they all walked out of the room.

I lay on the bed, looking up at the ceiling when I heard someone walking in. I thought it was a nurse to tell me how Everleigh was doing, but instead it was Winston Cartwright.

"Hey, man," he said as he looked over his shoulder and came to the side of the bed.

"Have you seen Everleigh?" I asked him, and he shook his head.

"No," he whispered, "but listen, we have to talk to you." I lay there, not able to do anything. "Do you know what happened?"

"Not really," I admitted. "You know Waylon, he was on something about going out."

"Yeah." He pretended he was listening. "We are going to need you to help us out," he said, and I should have told him to go fuck himself right then and there. I should have known I was making a deal with the devil. But when they had your whole life in their hands, they were the ones who held the strings, and I was just another puppet to them.

I hang my head, shaking away the memory I've long since wanted to erase from my mind. Before I get back to work, I try to forget about the kiss that made me feel like I was alive again. The way I held the side of her neck like I used to all the time, the way it was just natural for me to do it. Like I was born to do it, but I had to remind myself that it wasn't my place anymore.

I bury myself in my work, forcing myself not to look over at the bakery when I leave. When I get to work the next day, I'm opening the door and walking in when I see her walking down the street. Looking at my phone, I see she's a bit earlier than normal, or maybe I'm here a bit later than normal since I spent the morning making sure everything was ready for Saige tonight.

I'm already working when the guys start coming in, mumbling hello before they start to work.

I'm about to walk into the office when the bells sound, and I turn around to see her walking into the front area. I turn to watch her, wondering if maybe she was mistaken in coming in here. "Can I help you?" I ask as she looks around, and I'm shocked she's here.

"Yes or, I'm not sure," she says before she looks back at me, and like yesterday, she's wearing another pair of black leggings that mold her fucking body. "Do you have any trucks for sale?"

I shake my head. "I'm sorry, what? You want to buy a truck?"

"Or a van," she corrects me. "Basically, I want to make a food truck." I walk back into the area where she is standing but not so close I can smell her perfume. It's enough my cock was hard all day long just thinking about the fucking kiss and smelling her on my hands. So much so I only washed them when I stepped into the shower. "Something that is basically gutted already, so it's easier to add what I need to put in." I look at her with confusion on my face. "The bakery is going to be shut down longer than we thought, so I would like to set up a mobile shop. Something I can serve coffee and cake out of."

"I have a couple of old mail trucks that have been sitting in the back," I mention, telling myself I'm not doing this for her. I'm doing this for Ms. Maddie. "If you want, we can take a walk in the back, and you can take a look at them."

"Oh, yeah." Her eyes light up, and she must forget for one moment that she hates me.

"Let me grab the keys to the gate," I say, walking back to my office and snatching the keys off the hook on the wall. "Follow me." I walk out of the shop and toward the side where the fenced-in area is. We have cars that have been abandoned over the years. We bought a couple of them at an auction for parts, and they just sat here. I unlock the gate and swing it open as she walks side by side with me to the back of the lot, where I have the white vans all lined up one next to each other. I spot a couple of the guys looking out of the open back garage doors, and they earn a glare from me. I'm hoping I'm telling them with my look to get back to fucking work.

Ryan and Tony stand side by side, watching with avid interest. "These are the trucks I have." I point at the five of them. "You can go and check them out if you want."

"Are they unlocked?" she asks, and I nod, turning and walking. More of the boys come out and stand with Tony and Ryan.

She walks up to the first one and slides open the door and steps in, then does the same with the four other ones. "The second one is the cleanest," she mentions and slides her hands against each other to clean them off.

"If you want, Ryan can cut out the side of it and get some hinges on there so you can open her up," I say. I know he has work he is going to have to double up on doing. Worst case, I can come in with Saige and help him. "Are you going to be driving it around like an ice cream truck or just leaving it parked?" I ask, trying to remember if they can actually run. They might have to be boosted to life, but other than that, I think they run.

"Haven't really thought about that," she admits, "but it might be easier to just park it in the parking lot of the bakery. Then I can still keep the customers and then even the construction workers." She talks to me as if we are having a normal discussion as if we're long-lost friends and not like we hate each other.

"When do you need it?" I ask, putting my hands on my hips.

"When do you think it can be ready?" she asks. "Realistically."

"If we take it in today and start the work . . ." I think about maybe even getting a couple of the guys to help work on it tomorrow. "Maybe by Monday."

"That soon?" she asks shocked, and she's not the only one who is in shock. I hear whispering coming from the garage as Ryan glares at me.

"It's for the community," I answer her and Ryan at the same time. "It's what we do."

"Okay," she decides, "let's get the contract going, and if I can speak to your guy who is going to do all the things to it, so we can maybe discuss things."

"Ryan!" I shout over my shoulder for him and see him coming toward me. "Everleigh wants to make a food truck out of that." I point at the truck. "Can you help her out?"

"Yeah, what were you thinking?" he asks, and she starts telling him about what she wants to do with it. There is no reason for me to be out here with them, so I turn to walk away and stop when she calls my name.

"Brock, are you going to do the contract?" she asks, and I just stare at her.

"You'll be doing me a favor by taking that off my lot. Ryan can discuss what he charges." I turn back and walk toward the fence, knowing Ryan is going to ask me questions. I also know the only answer he is going to get is I'm doing it for Ms. Maddie. Who cares if I'm lying to everyone around me? It's not anyone else's business but mine.

Fifteen

EVERLEIGH

I STAND TO THE SIDE talking to Ryan, but my body is on high alert with Brock right there not too far from us. As if it knows, I stop talking to Ryan only when I feel him moving away. "Brock, are you going to do the contract?" His eyes look at me.

"You'll be doing me a favor by taking that off my lot. Ryan can discuss what he charges." He doesn't give me a chance to say anything. Instead, he walks back to the side where the gate is, closes it behind him, and locks the lock. And I stupidly watch him do it as if he has a spell on me.

"Well then," Ryan says, and I turn my head toward him.

"Well then, indeed," I reply. "What do you think it's going to cost to do all of that?" I ask him, and we walk to the side of a truck that is the exact copy of it. "I would love the side to flip up so there is some shade there if it's too sunny," I say, and he nods.

"It'll be easy enough to just cut through it and hinge it on top. I think you should even put windows in," he suggests. "You can maybe open one of them when it gets too hot in there." I nod. "Or close it if it's raining outside."

"What about putting a little counter in front of the

window?" I ask. "We can maybe put napkins and stir sticks and all of that on there."

"That we can do. I can take some metal from inside and weld it." He thinks out loud, and he smiles. "This might be my favorite project."

I smile at him. "Well, that makes me feel better for being thrown on to you."

"Nonsense. Ms. Maddie is the bomb and so are her donuts. I'll do whatever I need to help her."

"Thank you," I say softly, "that means a lot to me."

"Have you any thoughts about what you wanted inside?" He stands with me as I pull up ideas I took down last night while on the couch.

"I'm going to need a counter for sure." He nods. "I want to put in two coffee pots, maybe even three. I'm going to make the donuts at home, so I would need a couple of racks to store them."

"I have a couple of ideas," he offers. "How about I draw them up and run them by Brock, and then we can sit down and see what you think?"

"If it's not too much trouble for you," I state, leaving out Brock's name.

"No trouble at all, Everleigh." He turns, and I follow him into the garage. "I'll probably get all of this done this weekend, and then we can sit down maybe on Monday."

"Are you sure?" I ask, and he nods. "Why don't you take my number down? If you have any questions, you can call me and not bother Brock."

"That sounds good." He takes out his phone, and I give him my phone number. "If I need anything, I'll let you know."

"Sounds good," I reply and walk through the garage, and my

eyes do a sweep to see if Brock is there. I see a station at the corner near the door to get to the waiting area is empty, the stool pushed back. I know it's his station because he has a picture of Saige right in front of the wall, facing the chair. I swallow down the lump and walk out the door, feeling eyes on me but never turning around. I hated that even for a minute, it was as if nothing had ever happened. It felt like it did before everything happened. Before he made decisions for both of us without even talking to me about them. I had him back for those couple of minutes, but then I had to remind myself he really isn't who I think he is.

Instead of heading back to the bakery, I make my way home. Taking my time, I enjoy the sounds of the lawnmowers off in the distance as well as a couple of people outside sitting on their front porches. A few lift their hand and wave at me, and I smile and wave back. It's such a big difference from where I was less than a month ago. In the middle of Chicago, I never even met my neighbors and had no idea what they even looked like.

The company I worked for had lots of subcontractors, so there was no office to go into. Everyone would work in their own space. I knew their faces through Zoom calls we had once a month to discuss contracts coming in. I finished up the last contract I had with them two days after I arrived and gave the next one I would be working on to someone I worked with occasionally. I also took myself out of the rotation for the upcoming contracts. Because I technically work for myself, there was no one to talk to about it.

I walk up the steps toward the house and turn the handle, stepping inside and finding my mother lying on the couch. Her body is to the side, and the smell of something cooking in the kitchen fills the house. I put my stuff down quietly, walk over to the kitchen, and find the crock-pot working its magic. I pull open the fridge before grabbing some sweet tea and then walking upstairs to answer several emails.

One of the graphic designers has gotten back to me with an idea about branding. I go through a couple of the mock-ups she sent me and send them back with a few modifications. I only close my computer when I hear movement from downstairs.

I see my mother in the kitchen, and she looks over at me. "Hey, baby," she says softly, "how was today?"

"Good." I tell her about getting a truck, but I don't tell her I went to Brock's place. I'll tell her if she asks, but I'm not bringing him up. It's like he's the big elephant in the room, right next to Oliver, who we aren't talking about.

We have dinner together, and after dinner, I start making the dough for the donuts I want to try making the next day. I place the bowl in the fridge and go sit outside in the darkness, watching the stars. I get up, and my feet start making their way to the trees that line the back of her yard.

My head is down as I hear the sound of the creek, knowing I'm only hurting myself by going there. The memories and dreams that come after I leave there are torture. It's like I'm trying to hurt myself.

Making my way over to our little spot, I never think in a million years that he is going to be here. I stop when I see him sitting down, looking at the creek. His head turns to the side to see me. "Jesus, fuck," he hisses out, making me angry.

"That's exactly what I was thinking," I snap as he turns and gets up to his feet.

"Great, it's like I can't fucking escape you." He exhales deeply. "You're fucking everywhere."

"Trust me, if I knew you were here"—I shake my head—"I would have stayed far, far away from here. Away from you. The last thing I want to do is be in your presence."

"Good, at least the feeling is fucking mutual." He laughs. "At least we have that in common."

"Trust me, we have nothing in common." I don't even know why I'm answering him. I should just leave.

"What do you want from me?" he asks. I don't know why, but I finally ask him what I wanted to ask him all those years ago.

"Not a damn fucking thing," I snap at him. "Actually, I have a question for you. Why?" I ask the question as my heart beats so hard in my chest I'm sure he can even hear it. "Why did you do it?"

"What?" he asks, his voice in a whisper, and I know the last thing he was expecting was for me to confront him on this. I see his thumb and forefinger rub together, a little thing he does when he's nervous.

"Why?" I ask him again, my voice going higher than it was before. "I want to know why you did it."

"Everleigh," he says, his voice broken when he says my name.

"No, I kept playing things over and over in my head. Wondering and thinking about the whole thing, and for the life of me, I can't find a good enough reason." I shake my head, the tears running down my cheeks, and I don't even try to hide them. "I want to know fucking why."

"I had no choice." The four words he repeated when he broke my heart, four words that he confessed to me a month after the accident. When whispers started that Waylon wasn't to blame. There was no way he could have done what he did. How people who looked at me as if I was doing something wrong when all along Brock had a different story. His story was making us all look like we were crazy. Like we didn't remember that night like he did. "I was out of my mind, worried about you and where you were." His voice sounds just as broken as I feel inside me. "He said all I had to do was tell everyone that Waylon was not reckless. That the accident wasn't his fault and he was struck head-on by another car. That the truck came into our lane and not the other way around." Every single time, it's like a kick to my stomach, feeling like I'm struggling to even breathe. "That he was not drinking, which I thought he wasn't. I handed him a beer that night, and he said no. I thought he was fine." I shake my head. "They had our future in the palm of their hands. They made me a promise they would help me open my own firm, and that all future plans would be with me. They even dangled taking away the contracts my father had with the construction company in my face. They would take away all their business from him. He would have gone belly up if that happened." He shakes his head. "I couldn't let that happen. Not to him. Not ever." He shakes his head as he lays it all out for me like he should have done all those years ago. "All I had to say was he was driving perfectly fine and the other car hit us."

"But he wasn't!" I yell out. "He was reckless, and in the end, he killed four people."

He throws his hands up. "What the fuck would you have done? What the fuck was I supposed to fucking do?" he roars. "I made a fucking deal with the devil, and in the end, I lost. No matter what, the Cartwrights had everyone in their pocket. It wouldn't have changed anything," he says as if he believes it. Like if after all this time he wasn't wrong. Like what he did, didn't fucking destroy us.

"It changed fucking everything," I sob. "You changed everything. You didn't once think about us." My voice goes low. "You never once thought about me." I hit my chest, hoping to stop the pain that is soaring through me.

He takes a step back as if I struck him. "How can you say that to me? You—" he says the words like he's in pain. "You were the only fucking thing I thought about. You were all I ever thought about." His voice trails off, and then softly and slowly, he turns and walks away from me.

Sixteen

BROCK

I SEE HER BREAK DOWN IN FRONT OF ME. "It changed fucking everything," she sobs, a wrecked sob that cuts me off at my knees. It's even a miracle I'm still standing. "You changed everything. You didn't once think about us." Her voice goes down to a whisper, but the night is quiet, and I can hear every word. "You never once thought about me."

I can't help but take a step back when she says the words. With each word, it feels like a blade slicing me open, leaving me to bleed out. "How can you say that to me? You—" The words feel like they are ripped out of me. "You were the only fucking thing I thought about. You were all I ever thought about." I trail off, not sure I can stand here and take much more. So instead of causing her more pain, I do the cowardly thing as I slowly turn and start to walk away from her. There is nothing left to say. Everything that should have been said should have been said all those years ago. Not now. Not when everything is done and buried.

"I wouldn't have done it," she snaps to my retreating back, her voice so tight I know her hands are balled by her sides.

"I would have given up being set for life. I would have done everything to make sure that would have not been taken away from you." I close my eyes, stopping in my tracks. "I would have done nothing that would have jeopardized us. That would have taken your love away from me."

"You can't say that." I turn to the side, seeing her exactly the way I thought she would be, but also looking more beautiful than I remember. More beautiful than my dreams. More beautiful than my memories. "What would you do if they told you they would take away everything from you? If they showed you how set up your mother would be and she would never have to work again?" I know she would go to hell and back for her mother. She would lay her life on the line to take her place. I'm sure she would have done what I did. Or at least in the moment, that is what I tell myself. "Would you not do it for her after everything she's done for you? You stand there and are able to tell me you wouldn't do it for her?"

"You're right," she finally says. "I don't know what I would have done. But I do know one thing, Brock. I especially wouldn't have hidden it from you." The hits just keep coming, but she's right on that. "I would have never hidden it from you. I would have told you the first chance I got. I would not live with you month after month and not say a fucking word."

"I will forever regret not having the courage to tell you what I did," I confess, my heart soaring with pain. "It killed me." If only she knew, if only she fucking knew how much I hated myself. If only she knew the destruction I did to myself. If only she knew I was dead inside and the only piece alive was what Saige had.

"I guess two more people died that night," she states what I've been thinking all along. That night I may not have flatlined, but that was the day I died. I swallow down the lump in my throat before finally turning around and leaving. Nothing else needs to be said. Nothing I can say will make anything I did right.

I walk through the darkened woods, feeling as if someone is kicking me in the back with each step. I left home after dinner, not knowing what to do since Saige was supposed to be with me this weekend. But she came running out of school, asking me if she could go with her best friend's family to their cottage for the weekend. They would be back Sunday afternoon. Even though I didn't want to lose any time with her, I knew she would have a good time, so I let her. Never knowing what the night would hold in store for me.

My head spins, and I feel like I'm in a daze when I finally walk up the steps to my house. I open the door and head straight to the cabinet on top of the fridge. The cabinet where I put the bottle of whiskey I rarely touch, but after what just happened, I need to be numb. I unscrew the gold cap and bring the bottle to my lips, taking three gulps before putting it down and letting my head hang. Her words come at me so fast and so hard. The vision of her sobbing in front of me makes me lift the bottle again to my lips. Hoping not to see it anymore. Hoping I can erase it from my mind. Hoping I can drink until I'm numb enough that it doesn't hurt.

Sitting on the couch, slouched down, I finish the bottle. My vision goes blurry as the memories come back when I close my eyes, remembering one of the last times I was at that creek. Before I ruined everything.

I leaned down to kiss her naked shoulder as she lay on the blanket on her stomach. I was lying on my side, with my arm draped across her naked back. Another blanket covered her from the waist down. She just finished riding me as we listened to the sounds of crickets filling the night, as we listened to the sound of the creek trickling down. "I love you," I said as she tucked her arms under her. She turned her head toward me to smile.

"Yeah?" she returned softly as she turned to face me. She wrapped one arm around me as she placed the other arm on my naked chest, cocking her leg up over my jean-covered hip. "How much do you love me?"

"Baby." I sighed big and pulled her to me until she was flush with my chest. "Don't ask me stupid-ass questions." She laughed softly. "You know exactly how much I love you."

"But it's always good to hear." She kissed the underside of my jaw. "Like I can name some of the reasons I love you." She leaned back to make sure she was looking into my eyes. "I love that you make me laugh. I love you can come into the room, and with just one look, I feel better. I love that I know with you nothing can hurt me. Nothing will happen to me because I know you'll take care of me. I love how hot you are." I laughed at that. "I love how you fight with me just to be able to have make-up sex."

"Baby," I said, laughing, "you are the one who starts the fight so we can make up."

"Not always." She tried to push away from me, but I tightened my hold on her. "Most of the time, you start it."

"Why else do you love me?" I asked her.

"I love your heart." She leaned in to kiss the middle of my chest. "The way you love with everything you are. I love how you support me. I love how you know when I've had a bad day, so you make sure to make me smile."

"I'm going to do that for the rest of my life," I told her. "Soon, I'm going to get down on one knee, and I'm going to ask you to marry me."

"Is that so?" She smirked.

"Yeah." I kissed her lips softly. "I'm going to marry you." I

was so fucking sure of myself. "I'm going to marry you, and we are going to have all the babies you want to give me. We are going to grow old together."

"That sounds like fun." She kissed me again. "And just so you know, I can't wait to marry you. I can't wait to take your name. I can't wait to build an even better life together. I can't wait to have your babies grow inside me. I can't wait to grow old with you." She kissed me with her whole heart, and I thought we would forever be happy.

If only I had known that what we had was a ticking time bomb, slowly counting down until it exploded. My eyes shut, and I fade into the blackness, into the abyss.

The phone ringing the next day makes me sit up on the couch, as I look around for the phone. My hands move everything on the table in front of me, knocking down the bottle of whiskey to the floor. Luckily, it just bounces instead of shatters as I find my phone and see it's Winston Cartwright. "Fuck that." I toss the phone back on the middle of the table before getting up and walking to the kitchen. I see it's just a little bit after noon. Grabbing a bottle of water and then the ibuprofen, I drag my ass to my bedroom and in the shower.

My head is pounding, but it should be gone soon. I get out and dress in jeans and a T-shirt before I head back to get my phone and call Saige, who answers after two rings. "Hey, Daddy."

"Hey, baby girl, you didn't call me," I scold, and she groans and then laughs.

"Sorry, I forgot."

I let it go. "How was last night?" I ask, and she tells me how much fun she is having. She promises to call me tonight before bed.

As soon as I hang up with her, I decide to go to the shop

to get some things done. When I get there, I find Ryan closing up the shop. "Hey, what are you doing here?" he asks, tucking his phone in his back pocket.

"Saige is at a friend's house." I shrug. "Thought I would come in and work."

"You look like shit, man." He laughs at me.

"I feel like shit," I admit. Finishing a bottle of whiskey was not my best idea. "What about you? Did you get your things done?"

"More than I thought," he replies. "Got the door cut out, and my contact for the window said he'll bring it by on Monday. I even stripped the inside of it." I nod when I look over at the truck in the corner.

"Did you discuss payment?" I ask, and he shakes his head.

"I'll do the work for free." As soon as he says the words, my eyebrows pinch together. "For Ms. Maddie. You can charge her for the parts and all that."

"You don't have to do that," I say.

"I know I don't have to, but I am going to. Plus, you gave her the truck, figured I could do this," he reasons. "It's the least I could do."

"Whatever you want to do." I don't want to continue this conversation because I don't want him to ask me questions as to why I gave away a perfectly good truck when I could have sold it.

The bells ring from the waiting area. "I'll handle it. You get out of here." I motion with my head, and he walks to the side door. I don't have to go to the waiting room because the person comes into the garage.

"You're a hard man to get ahold of," Winston states, coming to stand in front of me.

"Thought maybe you would take that as a hint that I don't want to talk to you." I stand taller, showing him I'm not a fucking kid anymore.

"We need your help." He finally ends the staredown. "It's the least you could do."

"I thought I made it clear to you and your father, I know nothing about the drawings. Just like I told you a month ago, just like I told you two months ago. I didn't work on them, so I can't help you." He doesn't say anything. "Now, if you don't mind."

"You owe us," he finally snaps with a sneer.

"I owe you fucking shit." I take a step into him. "All fucking debts were paid."

"I would watch yourself if I were you." He puffs out his chest. "I would hate for another building to go down on this street."

"You threatening me?" I ask, and he holds up his hands. "You wouldn't be stupid enough to do that." I take a step closer to him, and he goes back a step. "Especially not in the middle of my shop. A shop that has surveillance cameras all around it." His eyes show the surprise right before he laughs.

"Just two friends having a chat," he backpedals. "Take care, buddy." He slaps my shoulder with his hand. "Let me know if you remember anything."

He turns and walks out of the garage. "I'm not going to tell you guys again," I inform him before he walks out. "You show up again, I'll have to go to the sheriff. He might not believe me, but with all the phone calls you've been making, plus this visit, it might pique someone's interest." His eyes go to slits. "Take care, Winston."

Seventeen

EVERLEIGH

I'M TAKING THE DONUTS out of the oil when my phone rings from the kitchen table. Wiping my hands on the dishrag, I walk over and look down, seeing it's Ryan calling me. "Hello." I put the phone on speaker before going back over to the donuts.

"Hey, Everleigh," he says, "truck is ready."

I gasp. "It's been a week, and it's already ready?"

"It was a group effort." He chuckles. "Everyone was jealous I was working on something for Ms. Maddie, so they wanted to help out."

I stop and blink. "What?" I ask again, not sure I heard what I heard.

"Yeah, I gutted the inside and then I did the paint outside. Tony did the inside with the cabinets and everything. Eddie made sure there was ventilation going on from the top. It was really a group effort."

"That is—" I shake my head, almost in disbelief. "I don't know what to say."

"The keys are ready for you to pick her up," he adds, "or

if you don't know how to drive it, I can move it to wherever you want."

"I'll swing by later and pay Brock," I say, not looking forward to seeing him. Especially after what went down by the creek. Or better yet, what didn't go down by the creek. I asked him the loaded question, and even though he gave me the answer, it didn't make me feel any different than I did all those years ago. Instead, I was more angry.

"Not sure what he is going to charge you, if anything. You can take that up with him." Ryan laughs.

"Thank you so, so much. I don't know how to thank you."

"You can buy me a coffee." His voice is smooth, and I wait to see if I get anything from talking to him. For the past week, we've talked every single day, and I've waited to see if maybe it would pique my interest, but nothing. It was like I was talking to Oliver or Charlie. There was nothing there. It's official, I'm broken.

"Coffee for life and maybe donuts," I joke with him, making him laugh.

"Let me know what you decide," he says.

"Will do." I disconnect the phone and walk over to the stove, turning it on and then adding the glass bowl on top of the pot of boiling water to melt down my chocolate chips. I'm stirring it gently when the front door opens.

"It smells good in here," Oliver declares, coming in dressed in jeans and a white T-shirt. Both his arms are tatted, and one of his hands holds a bike helmet. I smile at him as he comes into the kitchen and looks around. "Where is your mom?"

"Sulking in her room." I motion with my head toward her bedroom. "She got snippy with me this morning when I told her she wasn't helping me. It led to a long glare and a hiss before she stormed back into her room."

"Oh, dear. I'm going to take her out today on the bike. Maybe she'll be in a better mood." I nod at him as he walks toward my mother's bedroom.

Once the chocolate is melted, I walk over and grab the donuts that have been cooling on a rack before lifting one up, swirling the top in the chocolate, and placing it back down. I'm almost done when Oliver and my mother come out from her bedroom. I can see my mother's cheeks are pink and Oliver has a smile on his face. "We are going to go out for a drive."

"Sounds good." I look at her. "Want to try one of the new donuts I made?" I ask. "It's this new concept I was trying."

"What do you mean?" my mother comes over and asks me.

"It was something I thought about. I rolled out the dough super thin, then added twenty of them to one, seeing how they would fry up. It looks like it's stacked." I show her the donut. "I'm wondering if they are lighter."

"I'll try one." Oliver picks up one and bites into it. "Holy smokes," he says, chewing, "it's light and flaky."

"Yes." I nod. "That is what I'm going for."

My mother also tries one, and she smirks at me. "She's got the touch, I tell you." They both finish their donuts and head out.

When I look over, I see it's almost two o'clock in the afternoon. With nothing to do, I decide to maybe head into town and see if they have started work on the bakery. From the phone call I got last week, it would be any day now. They were going to start right away, but I thought that we could expand a little now that we are starting over. So I'm waiting on him to tell me how much extra it will be. But I think adding a seating area will bring in more business, and my mother reluctantly agreed with me.

Washing the smell of donuts off me, I slip on a white T-shirt and then grab my ruffled yellow skirt. It wraps over in the front and is longer in the back. The T-shirt falls just on top of the waist, showing off a hint of my stomach. I slip on my brown sandals before grabbing my phone and walking out. Leaving my hair down and flowing, I head to the bar, wondering if Autumn is in town with Landon.

I stop at the corner and am about to cross the street when I see Brock's truck parked at the garage. It angers me to no avail. Especially after the way he just walked away from our conversation. Again, leaving me feeling battered and bruised, and he didn't even have to lift a finger. My feet are moving before I even can stop them; with each step I take I get angrier and angrier. I pull open the door and the bells ring. I look around, seeing the waiting area empty and then sticking my head into his office and seeing it empty also. My heart jackhammers in my chest and I turn and storm to the garage, finding him in front of the workbench with a rag in his hand, and it looks like he's just finished cleaning the stainless-steel top.

The look on his face is of utter shock at seeing me here. "Everleigh," he says my name, and my knees turn to jelly. Just from the way he says my fucking name. And I hate it. I also hate when my eyes do a sweep of him from head to toe, and I see him wearing black Dickies with a black T-shirt that I wish made him look dreary and sloppy. But it doesn't, it fucking doesn't, he looks fit as can be.

"Fuck off," I say, walking into his space and stopping in front of his workbench as he rounds it. "I want to know how much I owe you for the truck."

"I told you," he says, and I shake my head furiously side to side to stop him from talking.

"I don't give a shit what you said," I snap at him. "I don't want anything from you. Not one fucking thing." My head moves into his space, my teeth clenched together.

"I don't give a shit what you want," he hisses back at me. "I'm not doing it for you. I'm doing it for your mother. So take your snit and fuck off." He motions with his head.

"That isn't how it's going to work!" I yell at him. "You aren't going to get to have a say in this."

He laughs in my face, and if I wasn't seething before, that pushes me over the edge. "I can see you are in full form today."

"Fuck you." I'm about to push him away from me, but the minute my hand touches his chest, he grabs my wrist. "Don't touch me." I'm about to rip my wrist from him when he pulls me to him.

"You came in here full of your attitude." He turns and backs me toward his workbench. "For what I don't know, nor do I fucking care." My breathing is coming in pants as I look into his eyes, eyes that are hooded over with a look I've seen far too often before. "Don't bring your shit to my door."

"I want nothing to do with your door," I retort, almost whispering. "I want nothing to do with you. Not now"—the lump starts in my throat, and I regret coming in here—"not fucking ever."

"Good," he replies. His head advances, and his mouth is open on mine. His tongue slides into my mouth as the kiss is primal. I move my hands to his shoulders to shove him away at the same time his hands grip my hips so tight, I'm going to have his mark on me. I move my head to the side, planning on stopping the kiss, when he picks me up and places my ass on the shiny stainless-steel top. My legs open when he steps into them, he pulls my hips forward so I can feel his hardness.

This is crazy, my head tells me while my body arches into him, his hips thrusting forward. I want to push him away from me. My fingers squeeze his shoulder to do just that, but instead, one hand moves to the back of his head. Sliding it into his hair,

I fist it in my hand, ready to pull his head away from me. But the more he kisses me, the more I forget even my own name.

"Fuck," he hisses when he lets go of my lips for a second before his tongue again invades me. His hands move down to my legs as he bunches the skirt into his fists. My hands are frantic to touch him now. The urge is more powerful than the need to walk away from him. One touch from him is all it's ever taken. The two of us are in sync as my body aches for his touch, so much I might cry. It's this overwhelmingness that I can't explain.

My hands go to the hem of his T-shirt as I pull it off, and he lets go of my mouth long enough to rip it over his head. My hand touches his chest, trailing down, feeling his heartbeat mimicking mine. His hands move to my own shirt as he rips it off and tosses it to the side. His mouth goes to my neck as I close my eyes and feel his heat invading me. His hands cup my tits as he rolls one nipple before pushing down the cup to the other one, and his mouth doesn't go to kiss it. No, he attacks my nipple, first biting down on it, making it shoot straight to my core. I moan before he sucks it into his mouth. My hands go to the button of his jeans; at the same time, his hands move from my outer leg to my inner thigh, moving up until his fingertips touch the lace of my panties. The touch sends shock waves through me. "Shit," he swears, and he makes sure my eyes are looking into his when he slides the fabric to the side and slips two fingers into me. "Wet."

My eyes instead go to my hands at his button, getting it open and then sliding down the zipper. I'm about to push his pants down and free his cock when he slides out of my reach and down. His hands pull me so my ass is on the edge so I have to put my own hands by my sides. The coolness of the stainless-steel top should make me stop whatever it is that is about to happen, but I'm mesmerized by his tongue sliding out of his mouth and licking me. I have to close my eyes; it feels like I'm about to fly off the table. His mouth devours my pussy, sucking in my clit at the same time that two fingers slide into me. I lift my hips off the counter, wanting to fuck his fingers. "Oh my God," I can't help but cry out when he bites down on my clit and doesn't let it go. Instead, he rubs his teeth together and savagely finger-fucks me. "Yes," I hiss, moving one of my hands to his hair and pulling it in my fist, hoping he feels the pain also. His fingers slide in and out of me as he manipulates my clit. I need more, and he knows it. If anyone knows my body, it's Brock. He has played with it like he's the conductor and I'm the instrument.

"No." He pulls his fingers from me. "You come on my cock." He licks his fingers, and I'm about to cry, but he moves one of my legs so my foot is on the top, leaving me open for him. He pushes his pants over his hips, his cock springing free, making my mouth water. My hand comes out to rub the precum into the tip of him before palming his shaft. "Put me inside you," he orders, and I do exactly what he tells me to do. I rub his cock head through my slit three times, dragging it out, hearing him growl before placing him exactly where he needs to be. He doesn't hesitate for a moment, and in one swift move, he's inside me. My mouth opens in a gasp before his mouth finds mine. His tongue sweeps into my mouth once before letting it go and then he looks down at us joined. His cock is buried to the root, filling me as if he was made for me. He puts his forehead on mine and I look up to see his eyes looking at me.

I quickly close my eyes, not wanting to watch him watch me. The feeling is too intimate. "The eyes are the key to the soul," he used to tell me. Even if I can't say no to this, he doesn't get to look into my soul. He can have my body, but that is all I will give him. "Fuck," he hisses, "open your fucking eyes."

"No," I deny, and I feel him bending down to suck my nipple into his mouth as he slams into me over and over. I can feel his anger toward me, his hatred radiating from his body.

I squeeze his cock with my pussy, wanting him to know I hate him as much as he hates me. "Fucking look at me." I put my other foot on the counter, hoping he can get deeper in me. "Baby," he says my nickname, and it's all I need for me to come all over his cock. One fucking word that makes me forget everything but the goodness he could always give me.

Eighteen

BROCK

"FUCKING LOOK AT ME," I hiss at her as I pull my cock out of her to the tip and then slide it back home. Fucking heaven, every single time. She puts her other foot on the counter as I try to get deeper into her. "Baby." The nickname slips out of me softly. My guard's coming down when I look at her. When I feel her clench around my cock, when I kiss her. It's my own personal hell. Her body arches as she comes on my cock, and I bend down to bite her where my mark always is. Where I always left my mark. Where I would touch her, knowing my mark was under my fingertip. I suck in deep as her pussy clenches over and over around my cock. It's so tight I have trouble pulling halfway out before slamming back into her. "Open your fucking eyes," I demand of her, my teeth clenched together, "and fucking"—I slam back into her—"look"—I pull out, slamming back into her—"at"—watching her face—"me."

She takes a deep inhale, and the only sound I can hear is the sound of our skin slapping against each other. All of the anger I've felt just makes me fuck her harder and harder. "Fuck," I finally hiss out when I feel my balls getting tight, and I know

I'm going to come, but I want her to come again. I need her to come again, and this time, she's going to open her fucking eyes and see who is making her come. I pick up my hand, pinching her nipple, and she hisses at the same time she arches her back.

"Open your fucking eyes." I lean down to bite the same nipple, and she hisses this time before her hand slides into the back of my hair, and she pulls it. I suck her nipple into my mouth until she stops pulling my hair. The whole time, I feel her pussy getting tighter and tighter. I move my head up, putting my forehead on hers, and I see her eyes flutter open. She looks into my eyes for a second. For one split second, I have my Everleigh back. For one split second, I feel whole. Until she looks to the side and she closes her eyes, but it's too late. We are both jumping off that ledge. She gasps out her moan, and I swallow it with my mouth. My tongue slides into her mouth gently as I plant myself as far as I can get into her, and I let go.

Her hand slowly slips from the back of my head to my neck and then to my shoulder. Our lips separate as our chests rise and fall. Her feet fall from my workstation to the side of her, hanging down. It's like we both remember we hate each other, and we want to get away from each other as fast as we can. But the minute I slip out of her, I want to pull her to me. I want to bury my face in her neck and smell her as she hugs me. But I just step away from her as she closes her legs. "That's the second time we've done that," she chides. "It better be just me you're fucking."

I bend to grab my T-shirt. "You lost the privilege to tell me where to put my dick the minute you left me." I see the hurt in her face as I walk away from her and head to my office and the bathroom. Closing the door behind me, I put my head back on it and close my eyes, taking a deep breath.

I look to the side, not the side with the mirror on the wall.

I'm not sure I can look myself in the eyes right now. The hurt in her eyes flashes back, making me hate the words I said to her. I walk over to the sink, turning the water on, holding on to the sink, and hanging my head. I cup water in my hands and wash my face before cleaning up and tossing the towel to the side.

I zip up my zipper and button my pants before turning and walking out of the bathroom. I make my way back to the garage, and I don't know why I'm expecting to still see her there. There is no way I would stick around; I don't know why I was hoping she would. I walk over to the workstation and see her handprint there. The scent of her perfume still lingers, making my cock hard. I close my eyes, tucking my stool under the bench I fucked her on without a care in the world. The front fucking door wasn't even locked. Ryan had just left, and he could have returned and seen me plowing into her. I let that thought burn in my stomach for a bit before I remind myself it's not my job to take care of her.

I lock up and head to the bar before going home. Something I don't do often, but occasionally. Walking in, I see it's almost packed, so I make my way over to the bar. Usually, it's Brady, but ever since he's hooked up with Harmony and her son, he's off on the weekends. He's a family man, and I'm happy for him. I slip out a stool and sit down as the new bartender approaches. "Can I have the house blend, one shot?" I tell him, and he nods at me as he moves to prepare my order. I tap the bar, looking around, spotting a couple of people I know. But usually Sundays are spent with families. He places the drink in front of me, and I take the shot before getting up and leaving a twenty on the bar.

I walk back to my truck and head home. The black clouds look like they are rolling in fast, and it feels like a downpour is about to come. My mind wanders to Everleigh, even if I know it shouldn't. This whole fucking week I've thought about her every fucking night. Waking up thinking about her, going to bed after having to jerk off because I couldn't get her image out of my head. Today, she walked into the garage, looking for a fight, and it felt like we were right back where we were all those years ago. The fight would always be intense, but then the make-up sex would be even more intense. I swear, we fought just to fuck some days.

Pulling up to my house, I get out, and a gust of wind makes the leaves in the trees rustle along with the wind chimes I put up for Saige a couple of years ago. She loves the sound of them, always has. At first, I didn't want to put them up because they would make me think of Everleigh. She hung one right outside our window in the apartment we shared. Growing up, she had one outside of her bedroom and said it made her feel at home listening to the sound.

I'm about to go over to the tree and rip them down and see if Saige will notice when a car pulls up on the street. I look over and see a Mercedes stop right in front of my house. The car door opens and I turn around to see my old boss get out of the car. He looks around, taking off his sunglasses before he turns and faces me. I take a moment to look around also, to see if anyone is outside to watch this if anything happens. Like I throat punch him for fucking me over.

He smiles when he sees me here on the steps. "Brock," he says, walking up the path to the front door, "I was hoping you would be home."

"You got car trouble?" I ask, and he looks at me confused.

His eyebrows pinch together. "No."

"Then why the fuck are you here?" I ask, folding my arms over my chest.

"I was in the neighborhood and thought I would stop by

and see an old friend," he says, and I take a step down to make sure he can see my eyes.

"A friend, is that what you call yourself?" I ask. "You stole my fucking designs and called them your own. The only problem with that was you didn't copy them right and now the whole fucking place looks like it's sinking." I shake my head. "What the fuck do you want from me?"

"I'm sorry about that," he says and runs his hand through his thinning black hair. "I didn't want to do it. They made me do it." I nod.

"Yeah, they made you steal my designs?" I ask, not surprised in the least, but I was hoping he would have stolen them to get ahead. You see, he was my boss when I was working for the Cartwrights, and when they handed him the development to create, they also put me on there. I spent hours upon hours drawing and recreating the perfect housing plans. The perfect development would make the Cartwrights a lot more money than they had.

However, they didn't consider that I set it at eight stories and not twelve because the soil wouldn't hold up the weight. This idiot just added floors to make it look different as if I wouldn't know it was my design.

"Well, good for you, then"—I laugh—"and good luck with fixing it."

"You need to help me, all right?" he pleads, his voice in a panic. "They are threatening to—"

"Get," I say, with my teeth clenched, "the. Fuck. Off. My. Property." I grab him by the collar of his shirt. "And don't fucking come back. You can also deliver that message to the Cartwrights. I want nothing to do with them." I push off him before I jog up my steps and get into my house.

Shaking my head, I slam the door and head over to the

fridge, grabbing a beer out of it as the thunder rolls in. I look out the window to see the Mercedes gone from in front of my house. The sky lights up at the same time the booming rolls in, sounding like two boulders hitting each other. My phone rings, and I look down and see it's Saige.

"Hey, baby girl," I greet her and hear rustling from her side.

"Daddy," she says in a whisper, "I'm scared."

"Oh, baby girl, where are you?" I ask and look outside to see the rain has started.

"In my bed and Mommy is in the shower."

"It's okay," I soothe, walking over to the couch. "You'll be fine. Are your shades closed?" I ask.

"Yeah," she confirms, and I can tell she's crying.

"It's okay. Why don't we talk until Mommy gets out of the shower?" I suggest. "What did you do today?" From the minute she was born, she hated the thunder and lightning. One night, it was so bad she was trembling, but it got a bit better as she got older. But the minute the thunder starts, she hides.

"Nothing, we did cookies, and then we had pizza," she reports, and for twenty-five minutes, we talk about the little things. Her voice gets higher and higher, and I wish I was with her so I could hug her.

"Okay, Mommy is here," she relays, and I smile.

"Love you, baby girl," I say.

"Love you too, Daddy," she replies before she hangs up. I place the phone on the table in front of me, the silence of the house almost deafening. I sit here in the family room and stare out the window at the storm that is brewing, wondering how much longer I can go on like this. How much longer before one of us finally snaps? How much longer can I pretend to hate her, when I know deep inside, I have never stopped loving her?

Nineteen

EVERLEIGH

"WE'RE GOING TO BE LATE!" my mother yells up the stairs for me as I'm exiting my room.

"We are not going to be late," I huff as I walk down the steps and find her wearing almost the same outfit I'm wearing: black jeans and a white T-shirt, our hair also piled on top of our heads in a messy bun. "Look, we're twinsies," I joke, and she smiles at me.

"Okay, can we go now?" She claps her hands together. "I don't want to keep them waiting."

"Mom, they are contractors," I say. "Their number one job is to always be late." Again, the joke ends with me getting a smile before a glare.

We're about to head out the door when I hear the sound of a motorcycle coming, and there is only one person I know who comes on this street with a motorcycle, and that's Dr. Oliver. "Oh look, Mom," I say, pointing at the street to see him getting off his bike and taking off his helmet. He runs his hands through his salt-and-pepper hair. "Your boyfriend is here." That earns me a smack on my arm. "Ouch." I rub the spot where she hit me.

"He's not my boyfriend."

"Then what is he?" I ask finally.

"He's a friend."

"With benefits." Her glare should make me stop talking, but for once, I don't. "Mom, why are you hiding this? He obviously cares about you, and you care about him."

"Why do you say that?" She folds her arms over her chest.

"Well, for one, you haven't killed him yet, and he's been here every single night since you got out of the hospital."

"He's an old friend," she reiterates, her eyes going to the door when it opens. "No more talk," she says before she sets her eyes on Oliver. "What are you doing here?"

He shuts the door and puts his helmet down where he always does. "Good morning," he greets as if my mother didn't just ask him a question. "How are you feeling today?"

"Irritated," she answers him. "You have to go; we are just leaving."

"I know," he says, walking over to the table by the door and picking up the keys to my mother's car. "I'm coming with you."

"For what?" I watch the exchange going back and forth, really wishing I was taping this showdown.

"Well, for one, I want to make sure you follow my instruction on not overexerting yourself. And for two, I want to make sure everything is what the two of you want."

"I don't even know what that means," my mother retorts, "but I don't have time to argue with you, so let's go." She grabs her purse before walking out of the house.

"That went well." Oliver looks at me.

"She didn't stab you in the foot with a fork," I joke. "It's the best you are going to get."

"Why a fork?" he asks, and the memory of Brock assaults me.

"So it's more painful, obviously. Four entry wounds."

"You are your mother's daughter." He shakes his head, walking out of the house. I follow them out and into the car.

Putting my phone in my back pocket, I get into the back seat as Oliver gets in the front seat, and we take off for the bakery. My eyes look out the window as my mind goes back to yesterday when I showed up at the garage.

After he said what he did and left me there sitting on his fucking workstation, I jumped off and ran out, not looking back. I also decided that I was done. He probably did this to get another rise out of me, except I'm all out of fight. I have nothing left to give him. There was nothing that needed to be said. There was nothing that needed to be done. We are both adults, and we can coexist in the same town.

We pull up to the bakery, and I gasp when I see the coffee truck parked in the middle of the lot at an angle so everyone can see it from the street. "Oh my God," I say of the truck that is painted all white with the writing that says *The Best Coffee and Sweets in Town*. "Momma." I reach out to touch her shoulder as she looks out her own window, and I see tears running down her face.

"It's so pretty," she states, getting out of the car when Oliver puts it in park and shuts it down.

We walk, holding hands, up to the truck, and I see Ryan running over from the garage. "Hey," he pants, "Brock just drove the truck over and forgot to leave the keys." He holds up the keys for me. I fight the pull to look over at the garage and look for him. Ignore the way my heart speeds up just thinking about him. How my body aches for his touch and my heart yearns for him. Even though my head tells me I hate him.

"Thank you so much," my mother says. "I can't wait to see inside."

"I'll see you around," Ryan replies, nodding to us before running back to the shop.

"He's nice, isn't he?" My mother pushes my shoulder with hers. "He's good-looking, has a good job, and he's a sweet man."

I look over at her. "Then you should date him," I retort, knowing what she was getting at.

She glares at me as Oliver chuckles but grabs her hand as we walk into the shop. It's the first time my mother has been back since the night of the fire. She gasps, and I can hear her sob a little. Her hand goes to her mouth as she looks at the gutted space. Literally gutted with nothing there but the four walls that were salvaged. "It's finished."

"It's not finished." Oliver takes her in his arms. "It's a clean slate is all."

"Stop doing that." She pushes away from him. "You always do the glass half full. It's fucking half empty." Instead of arguing with her, all he does is nod his head. She turns in a circle. "Is it even worth it?"

"You tell me," I urge her. "Do you want to throw in the towel and close shop?" I raise my eyebrows. "Or do you want to rebuild and make it better than ever? Put your stamp on things the way you want them and not how you inherited it."

She shrugs when the door opens, and I see the contractor enter. "Hey," he says. "Jensen." He extends his hand to mine. "We spoke on the phone."

"Yes," I reply, extending my hand to him. "I'm Everleigh and this is my mother, Madeline, and her friend, Oliver," I introduce, earning me a chuckle from Oliver. "What? I don't know what to label you."

I look at Jensen, who just rolls his lips to stop from laughing. "Shall we get started?" I ask, and he nods, walking over to the middle of the room and squatting down before unrolling the plans.

My mother squats down next to him and looks at the plans.

"This looks like scribble writing to me," she admits. "I'm going to need you to just explain this."

"Will do," Jensen assures her and walks over with my mother as he explains where walls will go and how the kitchen is going to be set up. Then he walks over to the front. "And from here we are going to knock down this wall," he says of the front wall, "and push it out twelve feet so we can add some tables. We were also thinking of maybe even extending this side wall about ten feet, so we can make an even bigger kitchen."

"A bigger kitchen," my mother ponders, "I don't even know what to say."

"Mom, you were always complaining that it was too small and you were bumping into things and there wasn't enough storage," I remind her. "Now is the time."

"How much would all of that cost?" she asks nervously.

"That isn't an issue," Oliver speaks up, "we'll do it." My mother whirls toward him. "She'll do it." He smirks at her. "Better?"

"No, not better."

"Okay, lovebirds, no fighting in front of company," I tease, looking back at Jensen. "What are we looking at in terms of how long it will take?"

"Well, believe it or not, we have some folks here who will volunteer to do some of the work. Plus, my crew and another crew coming down from another section, we should be able to be working around the clock."

"What?" my mother whispers as Oliver goes to her and puts his arm around her shoulders.

"The community has banded together to help rebuild this," Jensen explains and even I am shocked.

She turns in his arms and cries into his shoulder as he rubs her arm. "So we can start tomorrow?" Oliver asks, and he nods.

"Our supplier had everything in stock. I already got approval from the county to expand, so let's say, we start tomorrow at six a.m."

We finish talking to Jensen, and when he walks out, I look over at my mother. "This is going to be good," I assure her, and she nods. "It's going to be everything you've ever dreamed of."

"Not everything," she mumbles, "but it'll be close." I look at her, trying to catch her eye to see what she meant by that, but she turns her head toward Oliver. "We're going to have a nice chat, you and I."

"Oh," he responds, "I can't wait. Shall we get going so we can get this chat over with?" He slips his hand in hers and brings it to his lips. "Or how about I treat you guys to breakfast at the diner?" He pulls her out of the shop, and we head over to the diner.

We have a late breakfast and head home. When my phone rings, I look down to see it's Autumn. "Hey," I answer, smiling when I hear Landon in the background.

"Hey," she says, "are you free tonight?"

"That depends. Does he have chubby hands and a gummy smile?"

"Sadly, no." She laughs. "Our bartender called out sick. Brady has a baseball game with Wyatt, so I'm up to work."

"Oh, fun," I say. "Do you need help?"

"Yes, I need someone to help me not fall asleep."

"Done, I'll be there after dinner."

"Actually, come early, and we can grab a burger."

"Fine, twist my arm." I laugh. "I'll see you at five."

"Perfect," she says, disconnecting.

I take a shower before putting on a touch of makeup and sliding on the pair of tight white jeans I think I wore in high school. Putting on a white lace bra, I see the mark he left me yesterday on display, so I change it to one that is more of a bralette. I slide on the light peach, button-down, short-sleeved shirt, leaving the top four buttons open before tucking the front in and letting the back hang down past my ass. I grab my beige wedges before heading downstairs and finding Mom in the kitchen cooking. "Where are you going all dressed up?"

"I'm going to have dinner with Autumn," I inform her. "By the way"—I kiss her cheek—"I started the dough for the donuts, so I'll be up at around three to start frying them."

"I'll come and help you." I shake my head as she says the words and I start to make my way to the door.

"I can nap when you leave," she says.

"Don't make me call Oliver," I throw over my shoulder. "I'll be back early."

I opt again to walk to the bar instead of driving, missing the walks I've been doing these past couple of weeks. I get to the bar and see it's not full at all, just a couple of tables lingering. I catch Autumn behind the bar. "Hey, what happened to everyone?"

"No tours today," she explains, and I look at her confused. "We offer tours of the distillery," she fills me in, "and usually, they always stay to drink and eat. But Monday is our off day, which means we have to depend on the locals. And, well"—she points at the tables—"that is what you get."

"Well then, better for me." I sit on the stool. "All to myself."

"All to yourself," she confirms and then stops talking when she looks up and sees ten people walking in with Charlie as the leader of the pack. "What are you doing here?"

"You didn't think I'd let you work at the bar by yourself." He pffts out, stopping in front of me and kissing my cheek. "Everleigh, these are my boys." He points at the men following him.

"I'm Emmett," the tall one beside him tells me. His blue eyes are striking, and his blondish-brown hair sticks out from the back of his baseball hat. They are all wearing Mustang Creek Ranch shirts. "I don't believe we've met." He smirks at me, holding out his hand.

"I'm Everleigh." I extend my hand to shake his. "But we've met before," I remind him. He started working for Charlie when he opened the ranch. Even though we only met a couple of times when I went out there to ride with them.

"Oh, I know," he says, "I was just wondering if you remembered me." He winks at me. "How are you doing, darlin'?" He pulls out the stool beside me as Charlie groans, and I laugh.

"How are you doing?" I ask, and he folds his arms on the bar.

"I would be better with a beer," he tosses out, and Autumn just looks at him. "Please?"

She walks over and grabs two beers, handing one to me and then another one to Emmett. "So what have you been up to?"

"Not much," I reply, taking a pull. "What about you?"

"Same old, darlin'." He brings his bottle to his lips. "Same old thing."

Charlie comes over and leans by my side on the bar as the rest of his crew grabs tables, giving the server something else to do. "So when are you going to come and let me take you for a ride?" Emmett asks after we finish eating. He's standing beside me, leaning on the bar, while Charlie sits on my other side. The music is a bit louder than it is normally, and a couple of the guys have gotten up to show a couple of the other guys how to line dance. I'm about to answer him when a shadow fills the doorway. I would know that shadow anywhere, even in the dark.

He walks in and looks at the guys dancing on one side before shaking his head, laughing, and then coming up to the bar. His eyes look around and stop when he sees me, but he quickly looks away to where Charlie is sitting, which is right beside me. He walks toward where Charlie is and nods at Autumn.

"I'm sorry, what?" I turn back to Emmett, giving him my attention and not showing that Brock has any effect on me. We can be in the same room without anything happening.

"When are you going to let me take you on a ride?" He grins at me, and then his grin turns into a smile. He said it so loud you would think the whole bar would stop to wait for an answer.

"What kind of ride are we talking about?" I flirt back with him, but I feel like I shouldn't because I'm only doing it to take my mind off the one person I should stop thinking about.

"Whatever ride you want me to take you on." He winks at me, and then we both laugh.

"I don't know." I push out the stool. "Can you dance?" I ask him as my head screams at me *this isn't going to end well,* but my heart. My heart is beating for someone else entirely. Someone who I vowed I would never love again. "Let's see you move those two left feet." I hold out my hand to him, not knowing what he's going to do. I feel all eyes on us, but the ones I want on me are looking straight ahead.

Twenty

BROCK

I STAND AT THE BAR, facing ahead, trying not to let anything show on my face when I hear her voice. "What kind of ride are we talking about?" The minute she says the words, the tightness happens again. I don't know what I was thinking by coming here today. I should have just walked away when I heard the loud music. But my feet had a mind of their own, and my heart felt as if it was beating for the first time today.

"Whatever ride you want me to take you on," Emmett replies to her. I've never had a problem with him, but I suddenly want to throat punch him.

"I don't know." I don't turn my head as she pushes her stool away. I can see from my side view. "Can you dance? Let's see you move those two left feet."

"Autumn," I say, holding up my hand, "can I get a double of the house blend?" I ignore the need to turn around and watch her. I can hear the hooting and laughing coming, and I can imagine what is going on. She always could turn heads when she would dance.

"You good?" Charlie asks from beside me.

"Yup," I reply, keeping my eyes looking straight ahead. Autumn places a coaster in front of me and puts down the glass. "Thanks." I take the glass up and hold it tighter than I should. It's a miracle that it doesn't shatter in my hand. I bring the glass to my lips and take a gulp instead of downing the whole thing so I can get the fuck out of here.

"Sent you a text," Charlie states, and if I look at him, I'll see her, but if I don't, she'll know it gets to me. Either decision means I lose, and she wins. But it's no surprise. She's always won when it came to me.

"Yeah, I got it," I confirm, turning and staring at him but wanting to go over to Emmett and rip his fucking arms off him.

"You never got back to me."

"Didn't know there was a need to reply." I look forward, feeling the ache fill my chest, finishing the drink and then placing the empty glass on the bar. "Thanks, Autumn." I reach in my back pocket and toss two twenties on the bar. "See you guys around." Charlie nods at me. He looks like he has other things to say, but I need to get out of here. Even my breathing is becoming labored.

I turn and walk straight past the dancing, seeing the sight of peach turning around and hearing her laugh as I make my way out into the darkness. I think the tightness will get better, but instead, it's so tight I have to stop beside my truck and put one hand on the side of it, or else I think I'm going to fall on my ass. I close my eyes, and instead of getting into my truck, I make my way to the forest and toward the creek.

I don't even know why I keep coming back here at this point. It's like I'm a glutton for this punishment. It's like I want to feel this pain, but in the end, I know it's the only place I can go to where I can feel close to her without admitting it to anyone, least of all to myself.

I get to the creek to our spot and sit down, putting my knees up and leaning my forearms on them as I look out at the water trickling by. Closing my eyes, I think of all the fucking times we came here. All the moments we've shared here.

Fuck, so many that it's all coming back to me, from the first time I kissed her to the last time I made love to her here.

I hear the sound of the branches snap and close my eyes, wiping away the tears that have escaped from the corners of my eyes.

I hear her before I see her. Getting up to my feet, I watch her walk down here with her head down. She looks up when she must feel me looking at her. "Brock," she says my name in a whisper.

"Why do you always keep coming back here?" I ask the loaded question, hoping her answer is like mine.

She folds her arms over her chest. "Why do you?"

I think about fighting with her, but I'm just tired of this. I'm so fucking tired. "I was thinking about that same question when I got here," I admit, putting my hands in my back pockets. "It's probably because it holds so many memories for me." Her mouth opens as she silently sighs. "Now, why do you keep coming here?"

"I don't know." She shrugs. "I just do. It's peaceful."

"It is," I agree with her. "It's why we picked it in the first place." She walks to me. "All of our moments were here." She looks up at me. "So again, why do you keep coming here?" I ask, almost begging her to answer me with what I want to hear. She just stares at me, not giving me anything. "I'm tired, Everleigh," I confess, my voice broken and even I hear it. "I'm so fucking tired of this."

"What are you saying right now?" she asks, her chest rising and falling as if she's running a marathon and not standing in front of me still.

"I'm saying I'm fucking tired of pretending I hate you. I'm tired of fighting with you. I'm just fucking tired of this." I close my eyes and look to the side. "Don't get me wrong, you leaving me broke me, and I hated you. I hated you so much for giving up on me so easily. Hated you for not being by my side during the biggest hurdle of my life. Hated you for not knowing I would have never done anything to hurt you." The tears finally escape the corners of my eyes, and I hope in the darkness she doesn't see them. "I've never, ever loved anyone the way I love you. Not ever. Not before, not now, and I now know I never will."

"You're a liar," she hisses, right before she softly sniffles back, then advances on me. "I don't believe you."

"How can you even say that?" I ask in disbelief. "There was never any question about how much I loved you."

"You moved on," she retorts, her own tears running down her face, "and pretty quickly too—"

"I never moved on," I cut her off, "never."

"You moved on," she repeats in almost a whisper. "I may have left town, but I never moved on," she sobs. My hand comes out of my pocket to grab her neck, but she moves away from my touch, and my hand falls to my side. "She was carrying your baby two months after I left!" she shouts at me. "Two fucking months." She shakes her head. "Sixty fucking days and you moved on."

"You left me, and I was destroyed. I was either drunk or in a daze, taking whatever pills I could have taken, drinking whatever I could to make sure if the pills didn't work, the booze would," I explain, and her eyes go big at that. "Anything to numb the pain. I don't even know why I did it. But I did, and then she was standing there telling me she was having my child. I fucked up in the most momentous way, but I had to do what was right. It wasn't the child's fault I was a fuckup." I take a step toward her, closing the distance, hating that I'm hurting her again. Hating I've caused her this pain. Hating she thought I would ever move on from her. "Baby."

"Don't say that." She closes her eyes. "Don't call me that." Her head hangs down, and I move to her, taking her in my arms, and she finally lets me touch her. I hold her in my arms, closing my own eyes as her tears seep into my shirt and into my skin.

"I can't do this anymore," she says, moving away. "I can't. I don't have anything left in me."

"I don't want to hurt you." I sigh heavily. "I don't want to fucking hurt you. I never wanted to hurt you." My heart seizes in my chest.

"But you did." Her voice is broken. "You broke me to the point where I didn't even think I would be able to live another day. To the point where breathing hurt. To the point where every single limb on my body felt dead." I listen to her break in front of me. "Then knowing someone else was carrying your child. Carrying what was supposed to be ours. What was supposed to be mine."

"I can't regret Saige," I say. "I won't. She was the only reason I got up in the morning. The only reason I didn't just end everything. I won't regret her."

"Of course you wouldn't," she gasps. "You wouldn't be the man I thought you were if you did. She's yours, fuck, Brock, she's so beautiful." She smiles through the tears. "So fucking beautiful, she took my breath away."

"Another reason I love you. You are the strongest person I know." I close my eyes. "I know if I would have come face-to-face with a child you had with someone else, I would not have survived it."

"Stop saying that," she whispers. "Stop saying that."

"I can't," I admit. "You think because I had a child with someone else, that I never loved you. That I could stop loving you. You left me, and you broke me. Ruined me."

"You married her," she states softly. "You made vows to her. Vowed to love her forever. Made her promises." I shake my head.

"I married her in a courthouse. I didn't say any vows to her. They asked me if I took her to be my wife, and I said yes, but I never made her any promises. I couldn't make her any promises. I couldn't even vow for it to be forever. I thought it was the right thing to do, but she knew. She knew it was never going to be like that. She knew she would never have that. She thought she could live with it, and even if she could have, I couldn't. I couldn't do it. Couldn't live with it anymore, and I left her." I run my hands through my hair.

"It's never been anyone but you. It will never be anyone but you. I can't fight it anymore. I won't fight it anymore. I'm a shell of a man. I'm existing and living for my daughter. I thought I would be okay with that, and then you came back to town, and all of a sudden, everything feels so empty. My life is colorless. You come back to town, and all of the hurt of you leaving me is gone. All of the hatred I thought I had toward it is gone, and all I want to do is come to you and tell you how sorry I am. How much I love you. How much I want to make it up to you. How much I've missed you. How just looking at you and seeing you smile makes it all better." I take a deep inhale.

"I love you, Everleigh. My heart is yours. It was always yours; it will always be yours." I bend my head and kiss her lips softly. "It will always be yours. If anything, I wanted you to know that. I need you to know that. I won't bother you anymore," I say. "I won't cause you any more pain than what I've already caused you. But you had to know." My hand comes up to cup her cheek, my thumb sweeping side to side. "I'll love you forever." I take one more look at her before walking away from her, not willing to be the cause of any more pain that comes to her. Also, not willing to hear her say it doesn't matter. Not willing for her to tell me she doesn't care. Knowing my body and soul wouldn't be able to survive that for sure.

Twenty-One

EVERLEIGH

"I LOVE YOU, EVERLEIGH. My heart is yours. It was always yours; it will always be yours." He bends his head and kisses my lips softly, the tears just rolling down my cheeks. I thought my tears had dried up. I was wrong. All I want is for him to wrap his arms around me. "It will always be yours. If anything, I wanted you to know that. I need you to know that. I won't bother you anymore," he says, and the way he says it sounds like closure. It sounds like it's over. It's been over since I walked out on him, but a part of me never shut that door. "I won't cause you any more pain than what I've already caused you. But you had to know." His palm that has held my face countless times before comes up to cup my cheek. I push my face into his hand while his thumb sweeps side to side, brushing away the tears. "I'll love you forever." I stare into his eyes, the lump in my throat making it hard for me to breathe, before his hand drops from my face, and he walks away from me. I close my eyes, not willing to open them to see him walking away from me. Not willing to see the back of him. Not willing to watch the heartbreak yet again.

I don't even know if he's gone before I drop to my knees.

I sit back on my feet, looking up at the sky, not able to see it. "I love you," I whisper back to him and think back to the day everything changed.

I knew the minute I walked into the apartment that something was wrong. Fuck, I knew something was wrong for the last six months. I found him on the couch with a bottle of whiskey in front of him and his elbows on his knees, with his head hanging down. My eyes went from him to the empty bottle. "Hey," I said, putting my purse down. I took one step into the living room, and his head came up. His eyes were bloodshot, from the whiskey or crying, I didn't know. "Are you okay?" I asked even though nothing had been right since the night of the accident. Instead of us being closer than ever, we were miles and miles apart. At first, I made excuses for him: he lost his best friend in the accident and his other best friend, Charlie, was off the rails.

"The court case starts tomorrow," he said, his voice husky, and I took steps toward him. "I'm being called as a character witness for Waylon." Some of the survivors were suing Waylon's estate for wrongful death.

"What?" I asked, shocked. "What do you mean?"

"It means, I'm going to go on that stand and tell them what kind of guy Waylon was." I waited for him to tell me he was joking. "And the accident wasn't his fault. He wasn't being reckless."

"But he was," I snapped, my heart pounding. "He was not in his right mind, and we both knew it."

"We knew fucking nothing." He stood, and I guess he was more drunk than I thought he was because he fell back on his ass. "He was fine."

"He was all over the fucking place on that road, and you know it!" I shrieked. "Why are you saying this?"

"Because they asked me to," he admitted, his voice soft, "and I'm doing it."

"Why?" The loaded question. "Why would you do that?"

"Because it's the right thing to do." He avoided my eyes.

"You are not." I shook my head. "You are not going to fucking do that. Are you crazy? You will be lying under oath." He shook his hand away, and I was livid, so livid I had tears running down my face. I stood. "Brock, you do this and it'll be the end of us." I finally had enough, and I knew he would choose me. He had to choose me.

Instead of looking at me with the love he'd shown me over the years, it was a glare. He was mad at me. "Don't you fucking threaten me."

"I'm not threatening you," I said calmly. "I'm telling you if you go into the courthouse tomorrow and you lie, it will be over between us." I turned, not willing to stand there any longer. I picked up my purse by the door and looked back over at him.

The following morning, I waited outside the courthouse for him, and when he saw me there, he stopped in front of me. "I'm begging you not to do this."

"I'm doing it, Everleigh," he said. "Get over it." He walked past me, and I grabbed his hand, not knowing it would be the last time.

"Brock," I said his name so soft. "I love you, please don't do this. Don't do this to us."

"It'll be fine." That was all he said before he walked away from me and went to the courtroom.

"Brock," I called him, and he looked over his shoulder one last time, and all I could do was shake my head. He gave me a chin up and walked away from me. I didn't even attend the hearing. Instead, I went to the apartment and packed up all of my stuff. It was the last time I spoke to him. It was the last time I touched him. It was the last time my heart beat normally in my chest.

I wipe the tears from my face before I get up from the ground and make my way home. I open the front door and see the house dark, except for the light on top of the stove. When I walk up the steps, it feels as if my heart is broken like it was all those years ago. I don't sleep a wink that night, not one fucking wink. I keep hearing his voice in my head over and over again. *"I can't do this anymore. I can't hate you."* Seeing his face so broken and defeated, I hate that. Hate that he felt that way. Hate that, after all these years, the pain is still so fresh and the wounds haven't healed. Not one fucking bit.

The alarm doesn't wake me up because my eyes never shut. Getting out of bed, I head downstairs, tying my hair up on my head as I walk over to the fridge before starting my day. Three hours later, I'm rushing out of the house with bins and bins of donuts. My mother helps pack them all in the car, and when I get to the truck, my stomach flips with nerves, wondering if people are actually going to come.

I open the back door, grabbing a couple of bins and carrying them over from the truck. Putting them down, I then open the door. I'm putting them on the counter and I'm about to go back to my car when the bakery door opens and a man comes out, a tool belt around his waist and his white shirt looks like he's got dirt on it. "Hey," he says, "I'm Caleb." He wipes his hand on his shirt, where more dirt is added. "My father is Jensen."

"Hi." I smile at him and extend my hand. "How are you?"

"I'm good." He nods. "I'm going to help you unload your car," he announces, walking with me to my car and the back door that is still open.

"You don't have to do that." I look over my shoulder.

"Yeah, I do." He chuckles. "You can go and set up, and I'll get these over to you." I look at the man with his light hair and green eyes.

I think about arguing with him, but a truck arriving has me looking over, and I see Harmony getting out of it and walking over to me with a smile. "You didn't think you could have a grand opening without a couple of my cakes, did you?" She laughs, and then I shake my head. "And Autumn is coming with balloons." I gawk at her as Autumn arrives with not just a couple of balloons but two bouquets of ten.

"There," she says, putting one at each end of the truck. "Now, that is much better." They give me both a hug before rushing back home to take care of their families.

I shake my head, grabbing my phone out of my pocket and snapping a picture. Opening social media, I post it on all the platforms we are on with the caption "Open for Business" before walking up to the food truck and starting the coffee. It's almost done when my first customer arrives. "Hi," I greet, looking at Ryan and the boys from the shop. "My first customers. What can I get you?"

"A coffee for each of us," Ryan orders, "and can I try the new donut I saw on Instagram?"

"Will do," I reply, grabbing the paper cups and pouring in the coffee, and then placing them all on the stainless-steel ledge that is welded on there. "Here you go," I say, turning and walking over to one of the bins and taking the donut out. I place it in a small white bag before walking over and handing it to him. He's about to hand me money when I shake my head. "On the house. Thank you for all the help, boys," I state, and even though I tell them it is free, they still each leave a couple of dollars on the ledge.

By the time noon rolls around, we are sold out of all the donuts, and a couple of the construction workers come out and ask if I make lunch. I have to sadly tell them I don't. So I make a list of things I would need if I made wraps and sandwiches. I could prepare them in the morning and maybe my mother would be able to bring them to me. I'm cleaning up and closing up the truck when I look down and see my social media has lots of comments. I smile while I take a second to answer a couple of questions before I look over at the garage.

My feet move before my head tells me to get in my car and go. Pulling open the door, I hear the sound of machinery, and I stand here in the waiting area for someone to come and help me. Ryan is the one who comes out, and he smiles at me. "Everleigh," he says, "what can I help you with?"

"Is Brock here?" I ask, the tightness in my stomach forming as he nods and yells over his shoulder for him before walking back into the garage.

It's a couple of minutes later when Brock walks into the waiting area, a grease rag in his hand as he wipes them clean or at least tries to. His eyes widen in surprise to see me, and I can't help but see he looks tired and wonder if he had a hard time sleeping like I did. "Hi," I say, lifting my hand, suddenly nervous around him.

"Hey," he returns, his tone softer than it has been the last couple of times when I've seen him. There is no harshness to his voice. "Everything okay?"

"Yeah," I confirm, nodding my head and looking behind him to make sure we are both alone. "I was hoping you could talk."

"Everleigh," he says my name on a whisper and a sigh.

"You said what you had to say, but you didn't give me a chance to say anything," I point out to him. I have no idea if I have anything more to actually say, but I know we are not finished with the conversation.

"I don't think there is anything left to be said." He reads my thoughts.

"I think there is." I stand firm. "There are things I want to know, and forgive me, but you owe it to me to explain."

He takes a deep inhale. "Fine," he agrees, "but I'm not doing this here." He looks over his shoulder, also making sure no one is there. "Come by my house tonight after six. I'll make dinner for us."

I try not to smile, but I fail. "Okay, I'll bring dessert," I offer. Then I realize what that sounded like so I backpedal, "I mean donuts, I'll bring donuts." He chuckles, and it brings a warmth to my body I didn't know I needed at that moment. "I'll see you then." I quickly turn and walk out of the garage before he changes his mind.

Twenty-Two

BROCK

INSTEAD OF GOING AFTER HER and telling her there is nothing else to talk about—fuck, how much more can there be to talk about—I watch her walk away. My heart hammers in my chest so fast that it feels like it's going to come out of it. My eyes fixate on her as she walks over to her car and gets in. Her hair blows a bit in the wind, and I can admit that my heart aches watching her. I knew it would, knew it would fucking hurt. But again, instead of turning away and saving myself the pain, I'm adding more to it by inviting her into my home. A space that is reserved for Saige and me. A space I longed to have her in, so she could see what I created even though she hated me.

I close my eyes, breathing in deeply. "You okay?" I hear Ryan ask when he walks in with a work order in his hand.

"Yeah." I nod, tucking the rag in my back pocket. "I'm going to head out," I say, and he just looks at me with his eyebrows pinched together as he sits on the chair, fixing all of the papers on the front desk and putting them in a pile.

"You have Saige this week?" he asks, knowing that unless I have Saige, I'm always the last one to leave.

"No," I reply, "but I have something to do." I don't give him a chance to ask me anything before I walk back to my office and grab my keys. When I walk back out, he's still there figuring out all the paperwork and where to put everything. "Leave that. I'm going to see if I can figure it out tomorrow night."

"Nah," he says, "I just finished my work order, and it's too late to start another car, so I'm going to fix this." He holds up the papers in his hand. "And then head out early unless you need me for anything."

"I'm good. Take off early," I say, pushing open the glass door and heading out to my truck. I stop by the grocery store before heading home. Marinating the steaks I bought, I wash the potatoes and then place them in the oven with some carrots before heading back to my bedroom, undressing, and taking a shower.

I don't think I've ever been this nervous before in my life. I don't even know why I'm that nervous. At almost six o'clock, I open the fridge door to grab myself a beer when I hear a car door slam. My head turns and my eyes immediately go to the front window, where I see her standing there by the driver's side of the car, parked on the street, looking at the house. I'm sure she's looking at the changes I've done to the front. Like the big glass window that gives the whole house light. Especially with the extension of the two-car garage on one side. The house is painted a bright white with wooden shutters, which is different from the brown it was painted back in the day. I open the beer, watching her from the kitchen as she just looks at the house. I'm wondering if she's thinking about running away, getting back into the car and taking off. I wouldn't blame her. Fuck, I might do the same if I was in her shoes. But I watch her take a huge inhale, close her eyes, and then walk back to the back passenger door. She grabs a plate out of the back before making her way up the walkway. I take a pull of the beer and walk toward the door, making it at the same time that she rings the bell.

I pull open the door, and she looks up at me. She is the most beautiful woman I've ever set my eyes on. She always has been. Her beauty used to take my breath away, but now it's so much more. My breath is taken away, but my heart soars in my chest. I know right then and there that I will never love anyone like I love her. She was it for me, and I let her go. I ruined it all. "Hi," she says with a smile and tears welling in her eyes as she blinks them away.

"Hi," I say, moving out of the way for her to come in. She steps in, and I smell her perfume, and my dick stirs just by the scent of her. My hands itch to come up and touch her, but I can't do it to myself. I don't think I would just stop at touching her. "Welcome," I add nervously, closing the door behind her. "Come in."

"Wow," she declares as she follows me inside and sees the open concept I made the house. "You've changed it quite a bit," she observes. I nod at her, watching her turn, her long, flowered skirt floating around her. The tank top shows off just a touch of her smooth stomach, and I want to get on my knees to kiss her right in the middle and see if she still gets goose bumps from my touch. If she will still shiver. "It's beautiful," she finally says, standing looking at the big family room that faces the kitchen. "I made my new donuts." She holds up the plate, and I lean forward to grab it from her, hoping I can touch her fingers, even if it's just grazing them. Nothing happens when I take it from her as I look down and see the sugary goodness.

"Do you want something to drink?" I ask as I take the plate to the island, and she looks at me.

"Are you having something?" Her voice is soft as she fidgets with her hands nervously.

"I'm having a beer," I say, putting the plate down next to the open bottle of beer.

"I'll have one too, I guess." I walk over to the fridge, grabbing her one and tossing the cap in the trash before turning to her.

"Cup or bottle?" I know she would always drink out of the bottle back in the day, but she is older. It's suddenly dawned on me that she had a whole life without me, and I know nothing about it.

"Bottle is fine," she states, and I walk around and hand it to her.

"Would you like to sit?" I ask, and you could cut the tension with a knife. The air between us is electric, yet there is a huge elephant in the room.

"I think I need to sit," she admits, walking around and sitting at the edge of the couch. Her hands are on her knees, with the bottle in both hands, as she looks at all the pictures I have of Saige and me, as well as a couple of pictures of my parents. "You've made a beautiful home," she compliments. I can hear the heaviness of her voice at the end, the pain it must have taken to say it.

"Thank you," I say, bringing the bottle to my lips, "it means a lot." She takes a pull of her beer, and I'm jealous of a fucking beer bottle.

"So," I say, sitting in front of her and not beside her, "you said you had questions."

"I do," she confirms, and I see her finger peeling off the label. "I want to know it all. What happened? When did it happen? Why didn't you tell me? I want to know everything, really. I think I need that for me to move on, so we can both move on."

I swallow down the lump that went from the pit of my

stomach to my throat when the words sink in. What if I don't want to move on, then what? Where will I . . . "I think we'll start with the first question," I say, and I don't know why, but it's going to be good to finally get it all out there. "They came to see me in the hospital. I had just gotten there and was yelling for you when Winston came in." She listens to me. "Pretended to care, see if I was okay. He told me Waylon didn't make it. He was crushed but then said he had to do what he needed to do to protect his brother and their family. I didn't understand it at first. Until two weeks later when I went into work. Winston and his father came to see me, said they would like to take me out to lunch." I shake my head. "I should have known something was happening, but I was still shaken up over what just happened. I was worried about you and how you would be healing. I was worried about Charlie, who was a ticking time bomb, and I was afraid I would wake up and he would be gone too. It was just too much. I think they knew my head wasn't there. So they took me out to the golf course for lunch. Sat me down, said that I was like a brother to Waylon. Then said there was rumbling that people were going to try to say Waylon was drunk even though his tox report came back clean. They wanted to make sure I would be able to stand behind Waylon, since he would have done it for me. I was on the fence, not sure. They must have sensed it because then the promises came. They wanted me to take over the big project. Knew I was going to kill it. They told me all the right things. I would have my own team; it would be huge. But the biggest thing is that they would help me create my firm. Everleigh, you had to know the only thing I thought about was how it was going to help us," I say, and she lifts a hand to wipe away the tears, breaking my heart.

"Like, you have to know that the only thing I thought about was you. Was us. Was the future for us, making sure you were taken care of." I swallow down the lump. "They knew they had me on the hook, but it wasn't good enough for them because then came the blackmail." I laugh bitterly. "They would take away the contract they had with my father. The only contract he had. The only one that was keeping him afloat. They were already six months behind in payments, something I didn't know, but if they took it away, chances are they were not going to fucking pay him, and he would have to close the doors." The anger grips me exactly how it did that day. "I couldn't do it. I couldn't let him suffer because of me. So I told them I would do whatever they wanted. I would do it for Waylon because I want to believe he would do it for me."

"He wouldn't do shit for you," she hisses. "He was the most self-centered asshole."

"I know that now," I admit, "but I did what I did, and I have to live with that. Coming home to you every single day, knowing I was hiding it from you, killed me inside. You have to know this. I wanted to tell you everything, but then again, I didn't want it to touch you. I didn't think it would blow up the way it did. I thought I was protecting you."

"But what about you?" she asks and leans forward to put her beer bottle on the coffee table. "Who was going to protect you?"

"I didn't care about me," I admit. "After I lost you, I wanted to die. I begged to die." She gasps and puts her hands in front of her mouth. "I couldn't even look at myself in the mirror. I knew you would be pissed at me, but I never thought you would leave me. I guess I had hoped it would all work out. I took the risk, and it was bigger than I thought it would be." I look down, afraid to look into her eyes, but knowing I have to. I have to see them when I say it. "It will forever be the biggest regret of my life."

Twenty-Three

EVERLEIGH

"I DIDN'T CARE ABOUT ME." His words feel like they are tormented. "After I lost you, I wanted to die. I begged to die." I gasp at this information. Never, and I mean never, would I have thought that my big, strong, protector of a man would go down to that. "I couldn't even look myself in the mirror. I knew you would be pissed at me, but I never thought you would leave me. I guess I had hoped that it would all work out. I took the risk, and it was bigger than I thought it would be." I watch him go through the emotions that he should have gone through all those years ago, but now, sitting in front of him, I can see I wasn't the only one who suffered from this. He did too; he suffered along with me. I may have blocked it out because it was easier for me to hate him, thinking he did it because he didn't care about me. "It will forever be the biggest regret of my life." His words feel like they are ripped from his soul.

"Thank you"—I feel my body shaking—"for finally being honest with me." I can see the hurt on his face, and I hold up my hand. "I don't mean it like that. I mean it . . ." I look up at the ceiling and use the back of my hand to wipe away the tears from my cheeks. "I thought it was easy for you." It's my turn to give him my side of it. "I thought you did all that, and you didn't care that you were doing it." He shakes his head furiously back and forth. His elbows go on his knees as he looks down at his shoes and then looks back up at me, and I can see his own tears in his eyes.

"Fuck, Everleigh." He uses my name instead of baby, and it hurts. "It ate me up inside."

"You should have told me, Brock," I whisper. "You should have been honest with me."

"I didn't want it to touch you." He runs one hand through his hair. "I didn't want their hands on you. I wanted you as far away from them as I could get you."

"But don't you see," I say, "they had you, and in return, they had me, and I had no idea." I wait for it to sink in, wait for him to see it. "I needed to know what I was up against, and you took it away from me."

"I'm sorry." His voice is so soft. "I'm so fucking sorry. I wish things were fucking different."

"I do too," I admit. "I do too." He looks like he wants to say something else, but the oven beeps. He gets up and walks over to the kitchen, and I take a look around, seeing the home he created for him and his daughter. Little picture frames are scattered around the house. There are pieces of Saige everywhere. One of her sweaters is folded on the end of the couch, a couple of her notepads are in the middle of the coffee table. I suddenly wonder what kind of father he is. I suddenly want to know more, but I'm not sure my heart can take it.

"Did you still want to stay for dinner?" he asks, and my head turns from the notepads on the table to him standing in the middle of the kitchen, taking off an oven mitt.

"I do," I confirm, getting up. "If that is okay with you, that is." I walk over to the island and stand with it between us. "I could also leave if you don't want me here."

I wait with almost bated breath for him to answer me. "I would like nothing more than to have dinner with you." He stares into my eyes as he says the words.

"Good." I try not to smile, but it fills my face anyway. "What can I do to help?"

"Sit down"—he motions with his head to one of the stools—"and relax."

"That I think I can do." I turn back and walk to the table to grab our beers before heading over to the kitchen. I walk around the island to hand him his beer. He reaches up for it and gives me a soft smile.

"Thank you," he says, and I can feel the electricity in the room between us. It's always been there. My question is, will it always be there? He stares at me longer than he should, yet not long enough for my liking.

I pull out the stool and sit on it. "Tell me what you've been up to."

He walks over to the fridge, grabbing the meat. "Not much. You left." The words sting. "Dad died soon after. I was stupid and drunk and got Karla pregnant after one night with her." He takes a deep inhale, and the words hurt. "Had Saige, and she's been the second-best thing that ever happened to me." He tosses down the package of meat before grabbing his beer, extending one hand to the side of the counter. "You being the first thing."

I pick up my own bottle of beer, bringing it to my lips. "She's pretty amazing." I take a pull. "Your daughter, not Karla."

He chuckles. "I would agree with you on that one." He puts his beer down and grabs a bowl. "So tell me," he says as he walks around his kitchen, grabbing things, "what have you been up to since you left?"

"Well, I live in Chicago," I say, and he nods. "Which you probably know anyway."

"I don't," he admits. "I know nothing about you. I know you left, but I refused to hear anything that had to do with you."

"Well, same," I confess to him with a chuckle. "I knew you had a daughter." I bring the beer to my lips to keep my hands busy. "But I stopped Mom from telling me anything else."

"What do you do in Chicago?" He veers away from the conversation about him having a child with someone else, someone who was always all over him.

"I work for a company that does marketing for all different companies," I say. "If you need marketing for whatever, you come to the company and they outsource it."

"Do you like what you do?" he asks as he prepares the steak, and I shrug.

"It's work, so sometimes I love it, sometimes I don't." He nods. "What about you? Why didn't you ever go back to architecture?"

"I wanted nothing to do with it. I didn't want to look at another drawing. I wanted none of that," he explains. "I'm happy running the shop. I make my own hours. I'm there to take Saige to school and pick her up. I provide a decent house for her."

"It's beautiful." The words slip out of my mouth before I can stop them. "You created a beautiful home."

He doesn't say anything, but instead, he nods at me. "I'm going to go and do the grill." He motions with his head toward the door. "Can you set the table?"

"Yeah, I can do that." I push away. "Do you want to eat at the island or—"

"You decide, baby," he says softly, walking out of the room, making me watch his back. Trying not to let the way he said my nickname get to me, I walk behind the island and open a couple of cabinets before I find the plates. I grab two plates and then walk over to the dining table off the kitchen, and I'm wondering if we should eat at the island. I'm in the middle of looking from one to the other when the back door opens, and he comes in and looks at me. "What's wrong?"

"I'm thinking I don't know if you eat at the table or the island."

"Breakfast is at the island," he says. "Dinner, we sit at the table."

I nod at him, the tears stinging my eyes.

"Are you okay?"

"I don't know," I say because I may not have seen him in nine years, but I am not that different of a person that he doesn't know me.

"Well, what did I say that you got that look on your face?"

"The fact you eat breakfast at the island and then dinner at the table," I say, putting down the one plate. "That you have this routine you never had with me."

"We had a routine." He doesn't move from his spot by the back door. "We would always have coffee sitting out on the deck," he reminds me, "no matter what time it was, and dinner was always with us sitting next to each other. Whether it was on the couch, side by side, or standing, you were always beside me." I nod. "I wanted Saige to have a routine."

I smile at him, and I don't plan to have the sob rip out from me, but it does, and it takes him five steps to take me in his arms. "I'm sorry." I close my eyes. "It's . . ." I shake my head. "I have to get over it." I step out of his arms. "You should check on the steaks," I say. "Is there a bathroom where I could freshen up?" I ask, and he looks at me.

"There is one in my bedroom." He points at one side of the house. "The guest bathroom is right there." He points at the other side of the house. "You can use either."

"Thank you," I reply, and even though my feet want to go to his bedroom, I walk to the other side of the room, into the guest bathroom. Once the door is closed behind me, I see that it's really Saige's bathroom. Her towels are hanging on the hooks, and her hairbrush is by the sink with a couple of hair ties. A laundry basket on the side is halfway full, and her toothbrush is in the holder with a tube beside it.

"He had a life after you," I remind myself. "You need to move on." I wet my hands and dab my cheeks before wiping my hands on a towel hanging on the rack and stepping out.

Brock is in the kitchen. The steak is on the table, along with a plate of potatoes next to a bowl of salad. "Are you okay?" he asks, and I shrug.

"I'll get used to it." I smile at him. "Now, where do you sit?"

He pulls out the chair he sits at, and I look at him. "Where does Saige sit?" I ask, not wanting to sit in her seat, and he motions to where I put the empty plate down before. I smile and walk over to the opposite side of the table next to him.

"You didn't have to do that," he says, and I sit down and smile up at him.

"It's her spot, and no one should take it." He nods as he sits down in the chair beside me. "It smells good."

I grab the salad bowl and put some on my plate before offering it to him. "Stop making this weird."

He chuckles as he grabs the bowl from me. "This is fucking weird," he finally admits as he puts some on his own plate. "Never thought I'd be sitting at a table with you."

I grab the plate of potatoes. "Well, to be honest, I never thought I'd be sitting at a table with you either." The two of us just laugh as he takes his bottle of beer and brings it to his lips. "So now that all the heavy stuff is sort of behind us"—I cut into the steak he put on my plate—"Charlie and Autumn?" I question, and he nods.

"Did you hear about Brady and Winston's wife?" he asks, cutting his own steak. "Well, ex-wife now, but it was so—"

"I know, Autumn told me a little bit about it." I shake my head. "Crazy, right? Like holy shit."

"It's good for Wyatt," he says, of Harmony's little boy, who Brady has taken under his wing and treats him exactly like he's his. "He had a sorry excuse for a father, and now he has a real father."

"I mean, Waylon wasn't much of a prize, and I don't want to talk ill of the dead." I cut another piece of steak. "Actually, fuck that, I don't care. I hope he's rotting in fucking hell where he belongs. He ruined all of our lives. And like the coward he was, he's not even here to face it."

Brock leans back in his chair. "Even if he was, you think he would have answered for any of it?" I look at him, thinking, *I was hoping with the time that went by, looking at him wouldn't make my heart speed up.* Hoping with the time that went by, that looking at him I would forget how much I loved him. Hoping with the time that went by, I would be able to sit at this very table, or any table, and not long for him. To be in his arms. To be kissed by his lips. To be loved by him.

"You're right," I agree with him, blinking away the tears. "As always," I joke, and he puts his head back and laughs so loud I can't help but join him in the laughing.

We finish eating the meal not really saying much, not sure what to say. When I push away from the table, I start to help him clean up. "Where do you want to have dessert?" I ask when I wipe the water from my hands. I can see the twinkle in his eye, and then he looks away as he smirks. "For my donuts," I stress, and his eyebrows just shoot up at me. "That didn't sound better either." I toss the dishrag at him, and he catches it with one hand as I stand in front of him.

"We can have it outside, sitting on the porch," he suggests. "Do you want coffee?"

"No, I have to be up at three," I explain to him. "I'm making the donuts in Mom's kitchen."

"How much is she itching to get back to work?" he asks, taking the plate from the island and unwrapping them.

"She's fit to be tied," I share as he picks up one and takes a bite and then looks at me.

"These aren't your mom's," he says to me right away as he looks down at the donuts. I shake my head.

"No." I smile, putting one foot on the other. "Those are my creation. I roll them until they are paper thin and then stack them on top of each other so they are flaky." He takes another bite. "Are they good?"

"No." He shakes his head, making my heart stop in my chest. "They are better than good." I roll my eyes and breathe a sigh of relief.

"You're a jerk," I kid with him, and he puts the donut down on the plate.

"I should go," I say, and he looks up at me.

"I don't want you to," he says softly and slides his hand in mine. "Come and sit with me outside." He moves quietly outside to his back deck, where there is a long L-shaped patio couch. He goes to sit in the corner, stretching out his legs. "Sit with me," he urges, pulling down my hand.

I sit beside him, looking out into the darkness and curling my feet under me. He wraps his arm that was holding my hand around my shoulders, pulling me into his side. I shouldn't be here with him, but there is nowhere else in the world I would rather be than right here. I put my head on his shoulder, looking out into the darkness. The next thing I know, my eyes are so heavy I can't open them.

"Baby." I hear his voice softly, and when my eyes flutter open, I'm lying with my head in his lap, right on top of his hard cock. I push up, looking at him. "It's almost three."

I sit up. "What?" I ask him, and he rubs his eyes.

"We fell asleep," he explains, and I sit up, blinking away the sleep from my eyes.

"Shit," I swear, getting up. "I closed my eyes for a minute."

"Well, it was a little bit more than six hours," he corrects, getting up with me.

"I have to go," I say and walk to the door with him on my heels. "Thank you so much."

"For what?" he asks, standing there looking at me with sleep in his eyes.

"For dinner," I reply, and I want to lean up and kiss him. So I do, but instead of kissing his lips like I want to, I kiss his cheek. I'm about to walk out the door, but he spins me to face him. His hands go into my hair. Fisting it, he tilts my head to the side, and he kisses me. It's wet, it's wild, and it's fucking everything. My tongue mixes with his, and he kisses me until I don't even know my own name anymore.

He finally lets my lips go, and I open my eyes. "Have a good day, baby," he says as I turn and walk out of the house, my lips still wet from his kiss and tingling. I'm in a daze, and when I get home, the last thing I'm expecting is for my mother to be sitting up waiting for me.

"Hey," I say, walking in and kicking off my shoes, "did you just get up?"

"What are you doing?" she asks, getting up from her spot in her chair.

"I don't know what you mean," I reply to her, confused, as she stands in front of me with her hands on her hips.

"That man has been a shell of a man since you left," she says, her voice tight but soft at the same time. "And now you are doing the same thing to him that you did back then." Her words shock me, but she's not done. "You are going to leave here and go back to your life, and he is going to stay here. But now he's older and he has a daughter he has to worry about and not just you."

"Mom," I say as my chest tightens, her voice and words penetrating so much that my breathing is coming in pants.

"And what about you?" She raises her hand, pointing at me. "What are you going to do? How are you going to feel when you leave here?" I swallow down the lump in my throat. "You haven't had anyone in your life since him." I softly gasp. "No, I want you to be happy. You have a life, and you haven't done a thing since you left here. Sure, you're successful, but what else do you have?" She shakes her head, and she wipes the tears away that are rolling down her face. "You don't think I know what it's like to love someone from afar?" she says. "I know more than you think I know. You get one chance at love in your life. I'm not talking about loving someone. I'm talking about falling in love with someone so much that your heart hurts when you aren't with them. That you literally don't think you'll be able to live if they are not there. It's a love that is so consuming you know you will never love someone like you love that person." The way she is talking, it's like she's reliving something. I watch the pain on her face, and I know this isn't only about me.

"Are you talking about me"—I point at myself—"or are you talking about you?"

"I'm talking about walking away from someone and sacrificing what you want for them." Her voice rises. "You are going to leave here and then what? You are going to have to walk away from him again. This time without the hatred in your heart. Without thinking that you never want to see him again. This time, you are going to have to walk away from him knowing in your heart you will never love anyone like you love him, and where will that leave you?" She shakes her head. "You live there; he lives here. He has a child he has to think about. He's living for his child. I've watched him for the past nine years. Watched him live his life just existing, and the only time I've seen him smile is with his daughter. The only time I see a little light in his eyes is when he's with her." She inhales. "I hope you know what you're doing," she finally says before walking away from me and toward her bedroom. She leaves me in the middle of the living room, asking myself the same thing. How the hell am I going to leave him again?

Twenty-Four

BROCK

I WATCH HER WALK TO HER CAR, or better yet, jog to her car. She doesn't look back when she gets into it and all I can do is watch her drive away. I hate she is leaving, but I'm happy she was here for as long as she was, especially since it wasn't supposed to be like that.

I felt her head get heavy on my shoulder as we watched the darkness, neither of us saying anything. I was too scared to say a word and then have her leave, so I just stared into the darkness, and for the first time in a long fucking time, I wasn't angry. There was no anger left inside me, and it felt like a fifty-pound weight was lifted off me. Her head slipped from my shoulder and I softly laid it down in my lap.

My arm then came down and rested on her arm, she curled up in a ball and slept with her head in my lap. I put my head back, looking at the stars, and thanking whatever forces of nature for bringing her back to me. I didn't think I would be able to fall asleep, but I did and woke when my neck was sore. As I looked down at her, still with her head in my lap, seeing her, feeling her, my cock was awake even before I had a chance to talk it down. Looking at my watch and seeing it was two thirty, I knew she had to get up. I had no choice.

I wasn't going to kiss her. That was never my intent. Did I want to kiss her? You bet your ass I wanted to kiss her. I wanted to spend the night kissing her on my couch. Wanted to spend the night lying with her in my arms. Just that, lying with her, nothing else, and I would have died a happy man. She got on her tippy-toes and kissed my cheek. It was one of the sweetest kisses I've ever gotten. My arm moved before I knew what was happening, and I buried my hands in her hair. Hair that felt like silk on my fingers. I wanted to just peck her lips. My head, however, wanted so much more, and it took it. Fuck, the kiss was everything I remembered it would be and more.

I watch the car until the lights disappear from view and walk back into the house. Picking up my phone from the counter, I text her, pulling up the group chat that Ryan has me in when he was discussing things for the truck.

I save her number to my phone, wondering if it's the same number she had all those years ago. After she left, I deleted everything about her, almost everything. There was a locked part of my phone where I stored all the pictures I had of her. Someplace I never opened. I pull up her name and text her.

Me: Let me know when you get home.

I walk toward my bedroom, not wanting to take off my shirt that still smells like her, so I just fall on the bed. The phone beeps ten minutes later with her text.

Everleigh: Home.

I put the phone down on the side table and close my eyes, dreaming of her. Always fucking dreaming of her. This time, the dreams are with her smiling and laughing. I don't even hear the alarm when it goes off, so when the phone rings, I open my eyes, snatching it up and seeing it's Saige.

"Morning," I answer, putting the phone to my ear.

"Hey, Daddy," she says cheerfully, "you didn't call me."

I sit up in bed and look over to see it's almost seven thirty. "Sorry, baby, I overslept," I say something that I've never done. "Did you check your spelling words?" I ask, getting up and walking back into my closet and peeling my shirt off, putting the phone on speaker.

"Yeah, Mommy and I did them yesterday and I got them all right," she says, "and I am on chapter twelve of my book. Mommy said I had to put it away until all my homework was done."

"Well, Mommy is right," I agree with Karla even though we both know Saige is reading at a seventh-grade level, even if she's only eight. She started reading before kindergarten and was always with her nose in a book. She still is that way. Sure, she has playdates and plays outside, but if she's inside and the television isn't on, she's got her nose in a book.

"She said we can't see you this week," she whispers softly, and I close my eyes. "We are having dinner with someone else."

"That's okay," I assure her, trying not to show her I'm pissed about it. "We get to see each other in four days."

"I know," she mumbles sadly, "but I miss you."

"I know, baby girl. How about we have movie night on Friday?" I try to change her mood. "We can order pizza and camp out in front of the television, and we can watch whatever movie you want to watch."

"Ohh!" she squeals with glee. "Okay, let's do that." I hear Karla yelling at her in the background that she needs to get dressed.

"Call me tonight when you get home and let me know how the test went. I love you, Saige."

"Love you too, Daddy," she replies and then hangs up before Karla starts in on her again.

I know I shouldn't text her, but I do anyway.

Me: Hey, can you call me when you have a minute?

I get dressed in my Dickies pants and black T-shirt before rushing out of the house. I get to the garage at the same time as Ryan gets there, and he looks over at me like he's confused.

"Are you getting here just now?" he asks.

"I'll let you know when you become my boss," I snap, and he rolls his lips to stop from laughing at me and my guilt of coming in later. My eyes move up to the bakery, and I see about ten construction men standing by the truck, some of them waiting on their order, a couple of them already with their coffee but eating a donut beside the truck. "Did you get coffee?" I ask Ryan as my feet start to walk toward the bakery.

Ryan rushes over to walk beside me. "I did, but something tells me I need to come with you."

I turn in the parking lot and spot her right away, leaning out of the side of the truck with a smile as she hands the man in front of her a coffee. My jaw gets tight. "She's fucking gorgeous, and she can make a mean donut."

I don't even feel my jaw getting tighter. "Maybe we should come back." Ryan tries to pull me away from the construction men who should be fucking working.

I stand in line behind two men, who are also standing behind a man, as they talk about some game that was on last night. But my eyes are on her as she pours two more cups of coffee. The man in front of them tells Everleigh, "You are going to have to let me take you out, or better yet, let me cook for you." He winks and smirks at her, and she just smiles, not saying anything as she turns and prepares his coffee. "I'll see you later, Everleigh," he says, and she nods.

"I'll be here until three thirty." I don't think she's flirting back with him as much as she's just telling him what her hours are.

The two men in front of us walk up to the window to

order their stuff. She goes to prepare their items. Her eyes meet mine when she sticks her head out again and the smile that is on her face goes even bigger. "Hi," she says over the two guys in front of her, taking one more look at me before turning to the guys and telling them how much it is. They each give her a five, which is double their bill. She puts it in the tip jar in the front, which I see is almost full, and she's only been open for about an hour.

"Hey." She leans on her elbows on the counter inside the truck. "What can I get you guys?"

"I'll have a coffee," Ryan orders, "and one of the donuts." She nods and then turns to me.

"I'll have the same." I motion with my head toward Ryan, and she pushes back as she makes the two cups of coffee, placing them on the stainless-steel ledge I know Ryan and Eddie soldered on there. I look behind me and see a couple more guys coming out to get some coffee.

"Are you okay?" Ryan asks, looking around.

"Yeah, why?" I answer.

"You look like you are about to go all Hulk." He snickers as she comes back with two donuts wrapped in a white bag.

"There you guys go." She hands me mine.

"Thanks, baby," I say, and as soon as I say it, it feels like everyone around us stops talking and looks over to us. "I'll pay you tonight, yeah?" I tell her, and she smirks, looking down at her hands. "Have a good day." I wink at her, turning and walking away from her, knowing everyone, and I mean everyone, saw, including the douchebag who flirted with her.

"Oh my God," Ryan finally blurts when we are on the sidewalk as he huffs out a deep breath. "I thought we were going to get pummeled to death with stones and hammers." He looks over his shoulder. "What the fuck, dude?"

"I have no idea what you're talking about." I take a sip of the coffee.

"You are one crazy son of a bitch." He shakes his head. "I thought you didn't like her."

"We dated," I finally tell him and he stops walking, literally stops in the middle of the sidewalk.

"What?" he shrieks, his voice high and pitchy.

"A long time ago," I explain to him. "Didn't end well."

"Wait a second." He holds up his hand.

"Before or after Saige?" he asks, trying to piece everything together.

"Before." I don't wait for him, so he has to jog to me. "Way before. Was going to marry her."

"Shit," he swears. "I'm so sorry, man."

"Yeah, you aren't the only one," I reply, pulling open the door. "Now get your ass to work. You're five minutes late."

He laughs, shaking his head, walking into the garage while I walk to my office. I toss my keys on the top of it and look out the window to see the construction workers have also left to go to work.

I pull out my phone and text her.

Me: Have a great day!

It takes her a couple of seconds to send me back a text.

Everleigh: What was that all about?

I shake my head and smile.

Me: I don't know what you mean! Dinner tonight, my house? Five?

I'm waiting for her to answer me, looking down at the phone, when a call comes in from Winston, and my hand grips the phone even tighter. I press the red decline button, sending him to voicemail, knowing the mailbox is full and he won't be able to leave me a message.

My phone beeps in my hand, and I see I have a text from Winston.

Winston: You need to call me back, and we need to settle this.

But my eyes are on the next text that comes in, and I'm smiling even bigger than I did when I saw her.

Everleigh: We shouldn't . . . but I'll be there.

Twenty-Five

EVERLEIGH

I INHALE AND OPEN MY BEDROOM DOOR, walking out and down the steps. I find my mother in the kitchen walking to the stove wearing cutoff jeans and a loose tank top. "Hey," she says, looking over her shoulder as she bastes the chicken she has been roasting. "Dinner is almost done."

"I'm not eating at home." I stand here in the middle of the kitchen. "I'm going out."

"Where are you going?" She tosses the dish towel on the counter beside her.

"This morning I couldn't get into it," I say, pulling out a chair and sitting down, "but now I can." She eyes me. "What did you mean that you knew what it was like to let go of the one thing that you've loved?"

She shakes her head. "This isn't about me."

"What did you mean, Momma?" I ask softly. She's about to say something when the door opens, and Oliver stops dead in his tracks, taking in the scene. My mother has tears running down her face, and she quickly wipes them away.

"What's going on?" Oliver questions, coming into the room and looking at both of us.

I turn to him. "Oliver, how long have you known my mother?"

"Everleigh," my mother snaps, and I shake my head.

Oliver walks over to my mother and smiles at her. "She's old enough to know."

"I would hope so. I'm in my thirties." I about slap the table, losing patience with both of them.

"We've known each other since high school," Oliver answers, wrapping one arm around her neck. "We dated back then." My eyes open as I look at him and then my mother. "I got into medical school at the same time I asked her to marry me."

"Oliver," she hisses at him at the same time I gasp out in shock, my hand going to my mouth.

"Maddie," he says, dropping his hands, "it's enough time, don't you think?" He shakes his head, looks up at the ceiling, and lets out a huge sigh. "Call me later," he says, walking out the door and slamming it behind him. My eyes followed him across the room and toward the door, and I just stare at it before turning and looking over at my mother, who is now in front of the sink, looking out the window.

"Mom." She turns back to me, and I think she's going to blow me off, but instead, she looks straight at me. "Is it true?"

"Yes," she whispers. "We met in eighth grade. His family just relocated, and we struck up a friendship in science class." She smiles. "God, he was the cutest boy I had ever seen. We became inseparable. I loved him with everything I had. Then he got into medical school. And it was so big, but he was on the fence about leaving me. I knew there was no way I could keep him back. There was no way I could tell him not to go, so I broke up with him." My hand goes to my mouth. "Worst day of my life." She shakes her head. "Started dating someone right after to show him that I was over him, and even though we used protection and I hated every single second of it, it was too late." She smiles at me, but her smile is sad. "I would never, ever wish that you weren't here."

"I know that, Mom." I get up, and she holds up her hand to stop me from going to her.

"The best thing that ever happened to me." She pushes through the tears.

"But Oliver," I say, my heart breaking for both of them.

"He found out I was pregnant and left town shortly after that," she explains, her voice sounding as broken as I thought it would be. I know exactly how they both feel. "When you were ten, he came back to town. Just to visit, I think. Was here with his wife." I gasp. "The way that hurt me to this day, I cannot explain it." She puts her hand to her stomach. "This is what I wanted for him. This is why I did it. Heck, I had a child with someone else. But seeing him and his wife together, holding hands and laughing, it was a bit too much for me. I avoided him like the plague until he walked into the coffee shop one day. Both of us were shocked that we were in front of each other. It took one look at him, face-to-face, for me to admit I would never love anyone like I love him, so after that, I didn't even bother. I was happy just being with you. Two years later, he came back, but this time he was divorced. Came to the coffee shop and we spent an hour talking to each other. But his life wasn't here, it was in New York, where he was working as a cardiologist in one of the biggest medical hospitals in the country. He was working his way up the ladder, but every single week he would call. Then he would visit occasionally, and when you turned sixteen, he told me he was moving here. That he was tired of loving me from afar. Tired of living his life half empty. I couldn't give him what he wanted. I had to think about you."

"Mom, I would have wanted you to have that."

"Oh, I know, but I was just fixated on pretending it was nothing and thinking that any day he was going to leave."

"Mom, you almost died," I remind her. "It's time for you to live your life and be happy."

"I am happy," she finally says, shouting.

"Then go after him and be happier," I say, and she looks up.

"What if we did all this, and he doesn't feel the same way about me?" She finally gives in to her fear. "What if it's working so well because we aren't together?"

"What if it's even better than you thought it would be?" I ask. "Mom, that man loves you so, so much." She rolls her eyes. "With the attitude you give him, he is still here day in and day out. Do you love him?" I get up and face her. "Like, do you really, really love him?"

"Do you really, really love Brock?" She turns it around.

"Yes," I say without a question in my mind.

"You love him?" she asks again.

"Yes. I don't think I ever stopped loving him, to be honest."

"What are you going to do about it?" she asks the loaded question, and I shrug.

"What are you going to do about it?" I ask, and she laughs, wiping her nose.

"Look at us," she says, laughing. "Aren't we a pair?"

I walk to her and give her a hug. We hear the door open, and both look over at Oliver. "I've had it," he huffs out, "we're done."

I open my eyes wide. "Oliver," my mother yelps, her face showing she's worried.

"No, Maddie." He shakes his head. "Enough is enough. We

are going to stop this fucking shit right now. I love your mother." He looks at me. "More now than I did back then. Never stopped loving her, and she knows it. She knows how I feel for her. I'm tired of living like we aren't together," he snaps. "So from now on, we aren't. You are going to move in with me, or I'll move in here. I don't care. But we are moving in with each other, and we are also getting married."

I gasp but not as loud as my mother. "Yeah, you heard me."

I look at my mother and expect her to tell him to go fly a kite, but instead, she just shrugs. "Okay, fine," she concedes, as if he's forcing her to go out with him, "but we are not going to leave my daughter by herself."

"Your daughter is thirty. She's fine." He looks at me. "And you will be more than welcome to live wherever we are."

"Your daughter is also leaving," I interject. "You guys can hash out the details on when you are getting married." I smile at him. "I'm not calling you Dad."

"I wouldn't expect you to, but I'd be honored." I smile at him and secretly thank him.

"You guys celebrate," I tell them. "I'm going to go have dinner with a friend."

"Is that what you are calling him?" my mother asks, and I hold my hand up and wiggle my fingers before walking out of the house.

I look at the car and then look up at the sky, opting to walk to his house. I pull up the text thread on my phone.

Me: Hey

I press send as I walk down the street. The phone rings in my hand, and I look down to see he's calling me.

"Hello." I put the phone to my ear.

"Are you calling me to cancel?" I hear him moving around on his end.

"No." I laugh. "I'm just letting you know I may get there earlier than five, but not sure since I'm walking there."

"You're walking to my house?" he asks, and I hear the door shut.

"Yeah. It's a nice day, and I figured I'd walk there."

"Okay." I hear a car door slam. "See you soon, then."

"See you soon," I repeat, disconnecting and wondering if he's just leaving the shop and heading home. I'm about to cross the street when his truck pulls up right beside me. I look into the open passenger door window, seeing his hair wet from his shower. "What are you doing here?"

"Get in." He reaches over and pushes open the door. I shake my head and climb into the truck. "Hi," he says, and I see he's wearing gym shorts and a white T-shirt that has drops of wetness on his chest from his hair.

"Were you in the shower?" I ask, and he shakes his head.

"No, I was just getting dressed," he states as he makes his way to his house. We pull into the driveway at the same time as a car pulls up to the sidewalk. I step out of the truck and round the front of it, standing by Brock, who goes tight.

"Fuck," he hisses and then looks at me. I raise my eyebrows when I see Winston get out of his car, taking off his sunglasses.

"Well, well, well," he says, and his voice makes my skin crawl, "isn't this a nice surprise?"

"Thought I made it clear the last time, I don't want you here or on my property," Brock declares and turns to look at me. "Let's go inside."

"We need to talk," Winston insists. I walk up the steps with Brock and watch him slam the door behind us.

"What is going on?" I ask him, looking out the window at Winston walking back to his car.

"That," he spits, putting his hands on his hips, "is the aftermath of them trying to fuck me over."

I stare at him, confused. "I don't understand."

"Before you left, they brought me in to help the lead architect," he explains as I watch him. "Well, after you left and the truth came out and they were done with me, they stole my designs and then fired me." I gasp. "Except they fucking put more apartments than the foundation was built for. Now it's not only cracking, it's sinking."

"So what do they want from you?"

"To tell them how to fix it," he states, and my eyes go big.

"Can you fix it?" I ask, and he shakes his head.

"The only way to fix it is to demolish it and start over, and they don't want to do that."

"What are you going to do?" I ask, and he looks at me.

"There is nothing for me to do. I lost everything because of them. I would never have been behind that. He stole it and passed it off as his own design, doubling it. I don't think he gave much thought about the foundation, thinking it would be fine."

"Wouldn't he know?" I ask the loaded question.

"Yes, but he probably didn't give a shit, thinking that nothing would happen." He shakes his head.

"Were you going to tell me?" I ask the loaded question, and he stares me in the eye.

"Tonight at dinner," he states. "No word of a lie. I was going to tell you tonight at dinner."

"Is there anything else I need to know?" I ask, waiting.

"There are a couple of things," he admits, and my mouth gets dry.

"Saige wants to see me once a week when she isn't with me."

"Okay." I'm not sure why that is something I need to know.

"Karla isn't keen on it."

"What?" I ask, shocked. "Why not?"

"No fucking idea. Besides the fact that she fucking hates me. I'm going to talk to her one more time, and if that doesn't help, I'm going back to my lawyer."

"Don't you think that would just upset her more?"

"I don't know. I also don't care. I'm a good dad, a great fucking dad, and I love my kid. She can hate me all she wants. She needs to put her feelings for me aside and focus on Saige." I watch him run his hands through his hair. "That's it. That's all of it." I nod at him as he inhales deeply. "Do you have any questions?"

I try to hide my smile but I can't. "Are we going to make out before or after dinner?"

Twenty-Six

BROCK

I STAND IN FRONT OF HER, giving her all of it. Not keeping one thing from her because I did that once, and I'm never, ever doing that again. Knowing it might be too much, knowing she already left me once without looking back. Knowing this time it might actually kill me. Each second feels like a lifetime. She looks down at her hands, and she tries to hide her smile, but she can't. "Are we going to make out before or after dinner?"

The minute she says the words, I'm halfway to her. "The question is, couch or bed?" I don't wait for her to answer. Instead, one hand wraps around her waist, pulling her to me, the other hand goes to the side of her head, tilting it before my mouth slams down on hers. We both let go of a moan, both moans swallowed by each other's mouth. Our tongues go around and around. "Decide?" I urge her, walking her back toward the couch or the bedroom.

"Bedroom," she finally replies. I pick her up, and her legs wrap around my waist, her mouth going back to mine as I make my way to my bedroom.

She kisses me as soon as I walk into the bedroom. "Not to

be a total Debbie Downer," she says, "but"—she looks at me and then the bed—"just so we're safe."

"I haven't had sex with anyone but you for the last six months," I begin to tell her and I see the relief wash over her face, "and I never brought them here. You're the only woman I have had in that bed." I motion to the bed, leaving out she's the only one I want in the bed. One thing at a time.

She slides her legs off my hips, planting them right on the floor. "Same," she says, and I don't want to think of her with someone else. Her hands go to my shirt, lifting it up over my head, before she gets on her tippy-toes and kisses me again. My hand goes to the hem of her shirt and lifts it up over her head. My hands come up to cup her tits in the lace bra that leaves nothing to the imagination. Her nipples pebble and tighten, waiting to be sucked. My hands push down the cups viciously, before I take one in my mouth. I roll the other nipple with my forefinger and thumb before pinching it. "Brock," she moans my name, her hand running into my hair as my head moves from one nipple to the next. "You know what this does to me," she says, and I do know. I know every single thing about her. I know when I suck her nipples, she needs me to rub her clit at the same time, but I've made her come a handful of times just by sucking her nipples. "I want you naked," she states, pushing down my shorts and gasping when my cock springs free. "Hmm." She licks her lips and I shake my head.

"I need you on my lips first," I say and her eyes gloss over; she knows exactly what I need. I slip her jeans over her hips, down to her ankles, and then wait for her to step out of them. When she does, I kiss her pussy through her panties. "Fuck, I can't wait to taste you." She turns to walk toward my bed, her hand coming up to the back where her bra is and unclipping it, so it falls to the floor. She puts one knee on the bed and crawls to the middle of it, turning around and looking at me.

"Before you get my pussy on your tongue"—she sits back on her feet, before kicking her feet out and lying down—"I want your cock down my throat." I close my eyes as my hand goes to my cock, fisting it. It is throbbing to get into her. Her mouth, her pussy, her ass, fucking anywhere. "You going to join me?" she asks. I open my eyes and the five seconds I had to calm down did nothing when I see her with her feet on the bed and her knees up, as she moves them side to side.

I walk over to the bed and lie down beside her. "It's not fair that you still have your panties on," I declare as she puts one knee between my own and holds herself up by my side before she bends to kiss me. Her tongue slides into mine as my hands go to her bare ass, thanks to the thong she's wearing. She moves her hips back and kneels in the middle of one leg, making me sit up and twirl my tongue around her nipple before she pushes my chest so I can lie back down. She wastes no time moving down and gripping my cock in her hand. I can't help but hiss out when she swallows the head into her mouth. My eyes watch her suck it in and then let it go. She gets on her hands and knees as she swallows the head of my cock into her mouth again, her hand working with her mouth. "Fuck, baby," I mutter when she looks into my eyes as she bends to take one of my balls into her mouth, sucking it softly. Her eyes never leave mine as she licks up the shaft, all the way to the tip—licking my cock like it's a lollipop—before taking half of it in her mouth. She closes her eyes, trying to take me all the way to the back of her throat. "That's it, baby." I lift my hips to go deeper into her throat. "Open up for me." She moans as I push to the back of her throat, fucking her mouth like I would her pussy. "If you don't stop, I'm going to come down your throat," I warn her and she opens, her eyes looking up at me. "You want that?" I ask, knowing that look.

Her mouth lets go of my cock, but her hand doesn't let up, gripping me even tighter. "I want you to show me how much you missed me." She sucks the head in. "Show me how much you missed my mouth." She takes me all the way down to the root, gagging a bit. "Paint every single part of me that you missed with your cum." She sucks me back into her mouth. "My mouth." She lets me go, repeating the movements. "My tits." I groan, my cock getting bigger in her hand. "My pussy." I have to close my eyes, but I'm fixated on watching her. "My back," she moans, and I can see her hand playing with herself. "My ass." That's all it takes, the visual of fucking her ass, and I groan again.

"I'm—" I start to say, but her mouth has already covered my cock, and I'm shooting in the back of her throat. Her hand works with her mouth to drain every last drop from me.

"That was—" I say when my cock plops from her mouth, and she looks at me with a sly smile on her lips. She crawls to me, and I bend to leave my mark on her. A mark that I had left all the time. Right next to her nipple, close to her heart. "I want you to lie down in the middle of the bed and spread your legs for me."

"You don't have to tell me twice." She moves around me, my hands catching the lace of her panties, and they rip off, and she gasps. "I see we're starting this again," she retorts, trying to sound annoyed, but there is a twinkle in her eyes. I used to rip at least one pair of panties a week off her, so many that when we were starting to make out, and it was about to get even hotter and heavier, she would take off her panties in the middle of it to save them.

"I can't talk," I inform her as she lies down and opens her

legs, "my mouth is full." I suck her pussy into my mouth, and her taste is like euphoria. She is my drug; a drug I didn't know I was addicted to until now. A drug I know now I will never get over. "Fuck." I slide my tongue into her, tasting her sweetness before licking to her clit.

"Brock." She runs her hands through my hair, pulling it in her fisted hand.

"You like that?" I ask, knowing full well she likes when I play with her clit, sucking it into my mouth. Her back comes off the bed. "Baby." I kiss the inside of her thigh at the same time I rub two fingers up her slit, getting them wet before I slide one into her. Her pussy immediately tightens on my finger. "Baby"—I look up at her as I slide another finger into her—"you like that?"

"Yes," she pants out as I move my fingers in and out of her. "Right there."

"Oh, I know," I assure her, feeling her G-spot and curling my fingers up. "I know this pussy better than you do." I bite her clit, pulling my fingers out of her, and she cries out, grabbing my wrist to put my fingers back. "Such a greedy girl," I tease her. She opens her eyes as I lick my pinky and then move back down, her eyes on my fingers as I slide it into her ass. She hisses out and opens her legs more. "Your pussy is greedy." I slide two fingers into her pussy at the same time my pinky fingers her ass. "Your ass is even greedier."

"Make me come," she begs. "I need to come."

"Your wish," I say, finger-fucking her hard, "is my command." I move my fingers in and out of her. "You are getting so close." I suck her clit in as I watch her move her hands to her tits, where she rolls her nipples.

"Need you to fuck me," she pants. "I need your cock." She lifts her hips. "Need to feel full." She rotates her hips. "Make me feel full," she begs. "Only your cock is going to do."

"You are going to have to lose my fingers," I say, and she groans out in frustration, knowing she'll lose my fingers.

"Need your cock more," she pleads but holds my hand, "but I need you to fuck me hard."

"Is that so?" I smirk, my fingers still playing with her pussy. "I think I can do that."

She nods at me as I pull my fingers out of her, crawling up between her legs with my cock in my hand. I look at her and see she's moved one hand down and she has her two middle fingers in her, fucking herself. Her eyes are on my cock and not on me. "You want my cock, you are going to have to get your fingers out of there," I state, leaning down and taking her nipple into my mouth. I let go of her nipple, taking my cock and slapping her clit with it, and she knows I'm ready to slide into her. It was code when we were together all those years ago. She moves her legs back, slides her fingers out, and in one thrust I'm buried balls deep. Her pussy comes as soon as I enter her. She comes on my cock, almost choking it to death. "Fuck, baby, I can't even move."

"You better fuck me hard," she hisses as she moves her fingers to her clit and moves it side to side. "None of this soft bullshit."

I laugh as I pull out until the tip of my cock, and then slam into her. "Yes, like that," she cheers, "but you can do it harder."

"I can." I slam into her, her wetness leaking out of her and down my balls. "But I want to get deeper." I take her leg and place it over my shoulder and then pound into her. She screams when I do that. "You like that?"

"Yes," she confirms. "More." I fuck her with everything I have. "I'm there again."

"I know." That is the only thing I say, my eyes watching her pussy swallow my cock. "All you have to do is watch." I look down and see her doing the same. "Greedy pussy," I say, and she moves her hips up to meet me. "I'm going to come."

"Yes, I'm coming!" she shouts, closing her eyes as I fuck her through her orgasm. "You going to come in my pussy or my mouth?"

"Pussy now, mouth later." I plant myself all the way inside her, shooting into her, pulling out, and shooting again. My head goes back as I roar out her name, "Everleigh!"

Twenty-Seven

EVERLEIGH

I WATCH HIM fuck me, and I can feel when he is about to come. His cock gets even bigger in me, filling me so full I never want not to have him in me. My pussy knows his cock, and it's like he's finally back home. He roars my name, his head going back as he pours into me. My hand rubs my clit, wanting to go with him. It takes nothing for me to come with him. He knows my body like it's his favorite toy. "Yes!" I shout, coming again at the same time he stops moving in me. "Just like that," I praise as he stays planted inside me. "Fuck, just like that." His fingers help mine move against my clit. "That was," I start, moving my fingers but watching him still play with me, "something."

"It was," he agrees, pulling out of me. "So fucking greedy," he teases, looking down at my pussy. His hands go to my pussy as he rubs his cum into me. "Make sure you don't lose any of this," he says, shoving his cum into me. "Don't want you leaking out."

"You know I'm going to leak out," I say, watching his fingers in me. When he pulls them out, he looks at me. "Let me clean that for you." I grab his wrist and bring his fingers to my mouth and lick them clean.

The taste of us together makes me want him again. "My baby needs to come again?" he questions, and I nod. "We are going to have to get your toys in here," he states, and I'm about to fly off the bed. "Fuck you with your vibrator while you suck my cock."

"Yes." He looks at me, bending to kiss me. His tongue slides into my mouth as he sucks my tongue to also taste us. Sex with us was always, and I mean always, open and free. We grew up learning together. Neither of us was shy about what got us off. He would tell me what I needed to do, what he liked. Just like I did, he knew how to eat my pussy like no one else. He knew every single part of me. There were times when we would spend the day naked, with our hands all over each other.

"I'm going to sit with my back against the headboard." He gets into position. "And you are going to get on all fours above my legs, and I'm going to play with you until you are ready for my cock again."

He doesn't have to tell me twice, I crawl over to him, getting in position. "Look at this ass." He slaps it softly. "Perfect." He rubs where he just slapped. "But it would be better with my mark on it," he mentions, slapping the spot again before going to the other ass cheek.

I open my legs more. "Did I forget to slap that pussy?" he asks, and I am shaking for his touch. He slaps my right ass cheek again, going to the left, and then rubbing softly. I close my eyes while he moves his hands between my legs. "Hmm." He moves from my slit to my clit, rubbing it side to side before slapping it.

"That's nice," I say, my head hanging down, waiting for his next touch. I wiggle my ass side to side.

"You have no idea." He slides a finger into me. "Your pussy is begging for me."

"Yes." I close my eyes as his other hand goes to my tits that are hanging, as he pulls the nipple and twists it.

"Brock," I hiss, and I really wish we had our box of toys here, "we are going to have to get some toys."

"Oh, I know, baby." He slides another finger in me. "You want one in your ass or your pussy?"

"My ass," I choose unabashedly.

He slides his finger out of my pussy, slapping my ass. The hand that was playing with my nipples moves down my back and into the crack of my ass before he slides a finger into my ass and two in my pussy. "Yes," I cry out.

"You like this, baby?" he asks as he fucks both of my holes. "So fucking wet, it's running down my wrist."

"Only you." I close my eyes, feeling like I'm going to self-combust. "Fuck, only you can make me feel like I'm going to crawl out of my skin."

He pulls out of my pussy, slapping my ass. "Don't you ever fucking forget who owns this." He leans down and bites my shoulder, and I look over at him. His mouth covers mine as he ravenously kisses me while finger-fucking my ass. I move into his finger as he slides two into my pussy. "You are a dirty, dirty girl." He puts his forehead to mine. "After I make you come, you going to ride my cock?"

"Yes." I would agree to anything right now. "I'll do whatever you want."

"Watch what you agree to," he warns, the sound of the wetness from my pussy filling the room.

"I'll do anything you want," I repeat, closing my eyes and coming all over his fingers.

"Gushing down my fingers." He fingers me faster. "That's it, gush, baby." I close my eyes, the orgasm ripping through me so hard and so strong I cry out.

By the time he's done with me, I literally can't walk. My pussy and my ass are both sore. "I think I'm addicted to your cock," I finally confess after riding him.

I wake up at 2:00 a.m., and I know I have to leave soon, so I wake him up, sucking his cock. One thing leads to another, and I'm climbing onto him. Even knowing how sore I am, I can't say no to it.

"I'm addicted to you," he says, grabbing me around my waist and pulling my pussy to his mouth, sucking my clit. "Tonight, I want you to sit on my face, and then I'll fuck your face."

"Don't tease me with a good time." I get off the bed and walk toward the bathroom. "I need to hit the road and then shower."

"I'll drive you," he offers, getting out of bed and following me, but I stop him.

"I can walk." I slide my pants up my legs before grabbing my bra.

"Yeah, and you can get that sweet ass into my truck and I'll take you home," he instructs, getting dressed and covering his favorite part that I love.

He drives me home and makes out with me in the truck before I walk into the house. Tiptoeing in, it's all for nothing when my mother is in the kitchen with a cup of coffee to her lips. "Someone had a good night," she jokes with me, and I look over and see that Oliver's shoes are by the couch.

"I wasn't the only one." I motion with my shoes.

"It's different," she deflects. "We live in the same town."

"Mom." I hold up my hand, not sure I want to hear it. "I know. I'm trying to live in the moment."

"Don't waste time like I did," she urges softly. "I should have done this a long time ago."

I nod, walking over to the kitchen, pinning my hair on top of my head, and then washing my hands. I make the donuts, and when I get to the bakery, Caleb is just getting there while the night shift is walking out.

"Want to see something cool?" he asks, and I nod at him. He motions with his head to follow him, and I walk with him into the bakery. "The walls are up and ready to paint," he points out, and I look at him in shock. "Flooring goes in tomorrow."

"Holy cow," I reply, looking around at the bigger space. "This happened so fast."

"I think by next weekend it should be done and you can start using the kitchen here," he explains and a pang hits my chest. "So you can start painting by Friday."

"That sounds amazing. I'll call the painter."

He nods at me. "The kitchen will be arriving sometime on Monday, and they should have it installed before Wednesday."

"That's just"—I turn around in the space—"so fast."

"You have the town to thank," he shares with me, and I nod as he walks back to his truck to get his stuff.

Taking my phone out of my pocket, I snap a picture to post it to social media later. I put

the phone back in my pocket before getting my stuff out to start the day. I start the coffee before walking back and unloading the car.

I open the front of the food truck when I feel arms at my hips. "Hey, baby," he whispers in my ear, and I look over my shoulder at him.

"Hey yourself." I smile as my chest feels like it's getting even fuller than it was when I left him, which was pretty much so full I felt like my chest would explode. My hand comes up and holds his cheek. I smile as he leans to kiss my lips.

"Can I help?" he asks, and I nod.

"You can get the rest of the donuts from the car," I say, and he walks away at the same time Harmony gets here.

She comes over with her own box of cakes. "I know you were selling only donuts, but I thought I would bring this by. Maybe cut one up in pieces and serve the boys and then sell them," she suggests.

"Oh, that's a good idea," I say, grabbing the box from her. "I can pay you tomorrow."

"Nope." She shakes her head. "That one is on the house," she says, looking at Brock with her eyes wide in surprise when he stops by her with the plastic containers in his arms.

"Hey, Harmony," he greets cheerfully before walking away.

"Hi, Brock," she replies, unsure what else to say. She waits for him to walk away before she leans in. "Is that Brock, Brock?"

I try not to laugh. "Um, yes, I think." I look at him putting the containers down inside. "He's helping unload my car."

"Yeah, I saw. I thought I was in some parallel universe."

"Nope." I can't help but laugh. "Not unless I am also." I look at him walking down the steps of the food truck. He's wearing his black Dickies with a matching shirt, when the phone rings from his pocket.

"Oh, I get it now," Harmony murmurs. "I did not see that coming." I turn to look at her. "Although Brady called it before you got here." She smirks at me. "Text me later."

"I will," I assure her and walk over to the truck, up the steps, and hear him on the phone.

"Okay, baby girl," he says softly. "You have a good day and call me when you get home from school," he finishes and then hangs up. "Sorry about that."

"You don't have to apologize for ever taking her call," I say. "She takes priority."

He looks like he wants to say something, but he doesn't. "You have to get to work," I remind him softly, walking to him, "and I have to start the day."

"Yeah," he says, gripping me by my hips and pulling me to him. "You going to have dinner with me again?"

"You going to play with me after?" I ask him with a smirk.

"Before and after," he confirms, and I laugh at him. "Now I'm fucking hard, and all I can think about is bending you over and fucking you."

"Well, considering people might see, how about we table that?" I step away from him. "I'll make you a coffee and send you on your way." I grab a cup and make him a coffee. "And don't you go and take care of yourself." I look at him and make sure no one is around. "The next load is going down my throat." I wink at him. "It would be a shame if it wasn't a mouthful."

Twenty-Eight

BROCK

SHE SLIDES DOWN my cock, and my hands come up to hold her tits in my hands. I bend forward and take one nipple in my mouth as she rides me. "I'm almost there," she moans, her head going back and her hair swaying on my legs.

"Take what you need, baby," I encourage her, letting her ride me the way she wants to ride me. My own release simmers, waiting for her. "You need my help?"

"Play with my clit," she instructs me, not even shy about it. It's what I love about her. She's unapologetic about what she wants in the bedroom. I move one of my hands from her tits, down her stomach, and my thumb plays with her. "Yes."

"Get there," I urge between clenched teeth. Her pussy's so wet and squeezing me, it's making my balls get tight, and I know I'm almost there. "Now." I pinch and twist her nipple, and she gasps but also comes on my cock. I empty into her, my eyes watching her face as she moans out. "Milk me, baby," I say, and she even speeds up. "Take all my cum."

"All of it," she assures me finally when she collapses on my chest. "I want all of it."

I wrap my arms around her. "Good morning." I kiss the top of her head, and she just mumbles.

We've been waking up with each other for the past four nights. Coming home after we finish work and then fucking, eating, and then lying together. Last night we both crashed at eight, maybe it was even seven thirty. The alarm softly wakes us up at two thirty, which gives me thirty minutes to get her to her house.

"I can't wait until the bakery is done, and I can start at five instead of three," she mumbles, and I kiss her shoulder.

"Soon, baby," I say, and she nods as she pulls herself off my dick.

"I'm going to go and get cleaned up." She gets off my bed and I watch her walk to the bathroom. Getting out of bed myself, I follow her. She pins her hair up on her head as she turns on the shower and steps in.

I watch her as I grab a facecloth to clean off my dick and then grab my boxers. "I'm getting Saige tonight," I remind her, and she looks over at me as she lathers herself in my body wash.

"Oh, you must be excited," she replies, rinsing herself off.

"Yeah, I miss her when she isn't here."

She shuts off the water and then walks out, grabbing the white towel she hung up last night, making me feel off about her not using it until next week. "What are your plans?"

"Pizza and a movie tonight," I say. She smiles at me, but I feel like the smile is just to get me to think she's okay.

"That sounds like a perfect night." She wraps the towel around her before she walks out of the room. I walk out, and she's already dressed.

I am feeling bittersweet about getting Saige and then not sliding into bed with Everleigh. "I'll be ready in two," I say as I grab the shorts from the floor that I tossed after getting into bed with her. I slide them on and the T-shirt that she slipped into after taking a shower.

We walk out, more quiet than usual. When I pull up to her house, she leans over. "Have a good day," she says softly, kissing me lightly on the lips before reaching for the door handle and getting out of the truck.

I watch her walk inside the house and head back to mine, sliding into bed and smelling her all around me. I drift off to sleep with the alarm set for six thirty so I can be at the shop by seven and help her unload. It's something I've been doing also, just to make sure everyone knows she's with me.

I pull up to the shop at the same time as Harmony gets there with her box of cakes. Everleigh steps out of the truck wearing acid-washed jean shorts with a loose white tank top that is tucked in. Her hair is piled on top of her head in a messy bun. She smiles and shares a laugh with Harmony as I walk over to them.

"Morning, ladies," I greet them, and Harmony smiles at me.

"Morning, Brock," she replies. After the first morning, she's not that shocked to see me. "I'll see you later," she tells Everleigh before walking away.

"Did you unload the car?" I ask, and she shakes her head. "I'll go get them."

I help unload the car and watch her place the plastic bins to the side before she hands me a cup of coffee. "There you go, good sir," she jokes, and I smile.

"Have a good day," I say, leaning and kissing her. "I'll call you later."

She nods and someone comes to the truck, so I don't have a chance to ask her if she is okay before I walk away. All day long, I feel a heaviness on me, and when I leave at three thirty to go get Saige, the truck is closed.

I pull up her number.

Me: Was going to drop by and say hello.

Getting into the truck, my phone buzzes.

Everleigh: They wiped me out. I had nothing left to sell. I think I might make fifty more donuts for Monday and see if they sell out.

Me: I have no doubt.

Everleigh: Good answer.

I put the phone down and make my way to the school. Waiting by the fence, I watch the door and see Saige run out. "Daddy!" She runs to me, waving her arms all around.

I catch her in my arms and lift her, kissing her neck. "Hey, baby girl." I turn and walk to the truck with my arms wrapped around her and her laughing since my beard tickles her neck.

"Daddy." She tries to push me off, and I finally let her go when we get to the truck.

"How was your day?" I ask as she climbs into the back seat.

"Good," she answers at the same time my phone beeps from my back pocket.

Pulling it out at the same time I shut the door, I see it's from Everleigh.

Everleigh: Dropped off a couple of cupcakes for Saige. Left them at the front door.

I get into the front seat and feel a fullness I don't think I've ever felt before. She went out of her way, knowing that I used to always get cupcakes with her on Fridays, and dropped them off at my house. I then get really pissed she didn't go inside and drop them off. But I'm not sure how she was going to do that with no key.

Me: Thank you, baby. I'll let her know you dropped them off. Also have to get you a key for my place.

She doesn't answer me, and when I pull up to my house, I immediately see the box. "Everleigh dropped off some cupcakes for you," I tell Saige, and her eyes get big as she gets out. She runs straight to the door and picks up the box.

"Daddy, it's heavy." She picks it up and then looks at me. "There is a note on top." She looks down and reads it. "Here are some sweet treats to go with your pizza night. E."

"That was nice of her," I say, trying to gauge how she feels.

"She's the best, and she's really pretty."

"She is," I agree, letting her into the house. "You know, we were friends a long time ago."

"Really?" she asks. "You knew her?"

"Yeah," I reply, not ready to give her the full story just yet. I will eventually, but for now, let's just go with we were friends.

"Was she pretty back then too?"

"Oh, yeah." I smile at her. "She was the prettiest of all the girls."

"Did you like her?" she asks as she pulls out a cupcake that has a mountain of icing on it.

"I liked her a lot," I admit, not sure we should get into the whole I love her yet.

We spend the night camped out on the couch watching movies, and I have my phone next to me in case Everleigh texts, but she never does. I don't even know what she's doing.

When I slide into bed after nine, I take my phone and text her.

Me: Going to bed.

I think about adding that I miss her, but I don't and instead just press send. I put my phone on the side table before crashing. When I get up in the morning, it's just after eight, and I reach over expecting her to be there. Getting out of bed, I walk out and see Saige is sitting on the stool in the kitchen eating a cupcake.

"How long have you been up?" I ask, starting the coffee, and she shrugs.

"I was reading my book in bed," she states, taking another bite, frosting on the tip of her nose.

"What do you want to do today?" I ask as I take a sip of my coffee and walk back to my bedroom to grab my phone and check the weather.

I see Everleigh texted me at seven.

Everleigh: Crashed on the couch at six. Moved to my bed at eleven. I'll be at the shop today trying to paint. Have fun today!

"Want to go to the park?" I ask Saige when I walk back into the kitchen, making a plan to pass by the bakery and see if Everleigh will come with us.

"Yeah," she agrees, and I make her breakfast. We walk out of the house close to eleven, after I start the laundry and tidy up the house. I remove a couple of steaks from the freezer for dinner.

I drive toward the shop, pulling up not too far from the bakery and seeing a couple of construction workers walking into the shop. "Want to go and check on the bakery?" I ask, taking her hand in mine and walking over. I spot Everleigh right away talking to one of the contractors, and Saige walks up and knocks on the window.

Everleigh looks up and spots us and has a huge smile on her face. She walks over to the door and opens it. "Hey, you two," she chirps, "what are you doing here?" She's wearing a pair of jean short overalls with a white tank top with black stripes.

"We're going to the park," Saige tells her.

"Oh fun, would you like a little tour of the bakery?" She holds open the door. Saige doesn't even wait for me; instead, she walks in. I follow her and squeeze her hip as I walk in, and I'm in shock at the progress that the shop has had in two weeks.

"It's so big," Saige says, turning around in a circle.

"It is, isn't it?" Everleigh agrees. "This is going to be a little seating area." She motions to the front where they made it bigger. "And then this is where the cases are going to be for the donuts." Her eyes light up as she discusses it all.

She looks around. "What do you think, Saige?" She walks over to the wall at the end. "Should we do the walls a cotton-candy pink or a baby blue?"

"I like the pink," she declares, and Everleigh smiles as she nods.

"Me too," she says, folding her arms over her chest.

"Want to come to the park with us?" I finally get the courage to ask. "And then after, ice cream?" I don't even know I'm holding my breath.

"I don't want to intrude on your time," she says softly.

"It's fine," Saige says. "Dad usually sits by himself, so you can sit with him."

I raise my eyebrows. "And then we have ice cream from Wild Billy's."

"Well, I can't say no to Wild Billy's," she says to her. "Only if you promise to try out all the new donuts that I'm going to make this week."

"I can do that," Saige assures her, making me laugh.

We walk out and over to the park. Saige runs to play while I sit on the bench with Everleigh beside me. I want to lean in to kiss her, but I'm not sure it's the right time. So instead, I put my arm on the back of the bench and rub my thumb up and down her bare arm. We sit quietly as we watch Saige run around with friends of hers, before she comes over and asks Everleigh if she ever did the monkey bars. Everleigh laughs at her as the two of them go off, and then back and forth on the monkey bars.

"My whole body is going to hate me later," Everleigh complains when she finally walks back over to me. Watching the two of them spend time together is something I didn't know I needed in my life.

We don't stay at the park long enough for my liking, and after ice cream, she gives Saige a hug goodbye before walking back to the bakery.

I ache to kiss her. I ache to hold her. I ache to be with her, with the both of them at the same time. I make dinner with Saige on the couch reading her book. A shower is next and then she goes to sleep at around nine thirty.

I pull out my phone, and instead of texting her, I call her, and she answers after two rings. "Hey," she says, and I close my eyes and lean my head back on the headboard.

"Want to come and make out with me?" I whisper and hear her laugh. "We have to be quiet. We can make out on the couch or my bed."

"You are incorrigible." She laughs. "Be there in five." She disconnects the phone.

I walk out of the house to sit down to wait for her. She gets out of her car wearing a pair of loose shorts and a matching top. "Are those your pj's?"

"Well, yeah," she admits, walking toward me, "I was in bed."

"Really?" I say when she is close enough, and I don't wait a minute more before my mouth is on hers. "Fuck," I hiss when I slide my tongue into her mouth. "Bed or couch?"

"Bed. That way, I can sort of hide if she comes to your room," she decides. I slide my hand into hers as I make my way into the darkened house, feeling like my house just became a home.

Twenty-Nine

EVERLEIGH

"I HAVE TO GO," I whisper to him as he bends his head to give me another mouthwatering kiss. My hands come up to grip the front of his shirt as I listen to the birds chirping in the background. He finally lets go of my lips for just a second before coming back and softly pecking them. "You need to stop doing that." My eyes finally flutter open as I stare at him, taking him all in. His hair is all over the place from my hands running through it.

"I don't want you to go," he admits, and my heart surges in my chest because I don't want to go either.

"You have to go and be a dad." I smile. I kiss under his jaw, the bristles from his beard pricking me. "Call me later if you can."

I slowly slip out of his arms and jog slightly to my car, not slamming the door, afraid I'm going to wake Saige up. I start the car, hoping that it doesn't make noise, before I drive away with a last wave. I look in the rearview mirror until I get to the stop sign at the corner of his street. I see him standing there in shorts that are hanging on his hips. Shorts he slipped on about five minutes before he walked me to the door. Opting to lie on his bed next to me in his boxers, even though I made it one thousand percent clear to him that we were not going to do anything that would require either of us getting naked. So instead, we made out like we did when we first started dating, dry humping each other, and it was magnificent.

My phone beeps as soon as I get home with a message from him.

Brock: Text me when you get home. I'm waiting for you before I go into the shower.

Me: I'm home, but why don't you go back to sleep?

Brock: I've been rock hard since you lay down next to me. I need to go and jerk off.

I can't help but laugh.

Me: Um, same.

I laugh as I get out of the car, the phone beeping in my hand.

Brock: You are going to jerk off in the shower?

I smirk as I walk up the two steps and then stop.

Me: No, I'm going to get naked in my bed and get my vibrator out.

I'm hoping that it drives him as crazy as it's driving me. Opening the door quietly and stepping in, the phone buzzes as I kick off my flip-flops.

Brock: That isn't helping.

I see the light on top of the stove is on, as always, as I walk over to the steps and slowly creep upstairs, my eyes on the hallway where my mother's room is. I really do feel like I'm in high school again, and I'm sneaking in.

I tiptoe until I close the door behind me and then slip into bed. I don't get naked like I told him I was going to. Instead, I turn on my side and fall asleep with the smell of him on me. When I wake up, I grab the phone and see that it's a little past 10:00 a.m.

I blink the sleep out of my eyes, about to text Brock, when the phone rings in my hand, and I see it's Autumn. "Hello," I mumble, turning back to my side and closing my eyes.

"Ugh," she groans, "please tell me that you did not just get up."

I smile at her tone. "Okay, fine, I didn't just get up."

"I was up at four thirty when Mr. Man over here thought it was a good time to start the day."

"I really hope the Mr. Man you are talking about is your son and not Charlie." I turn on my back and look out the blinds, seeing the sun shining high in the sky.

She laughs. "Yes, Landon William. What are you doing today?"

I wish I was hanging with Brock and Saige, I almost say. "I am actually going to the bakery, and

I'm going to paint."

"Oh, that sounds like fun," she replies. "Want some company?"

"Are you sure you want to spend your Saturday painting?" I ask, and she laughs.

"That sounds like a perfect day. I'll be there in about an hour."

"Why don't we head out to the diner for some lunch for you and some breakfast for me, and then we can start?"

"See you then," she confirms, and I hear her yelling Charlie's name as she hangs up.

Getting out of bed, I head to the bathroom and wash my face before I head downstairs to make myself coffee. The sound of emptiness lets me know my mother is not home. She's no doubt out and about with Oliver. He's been holding her at bay, telling her she can start working part-time in two weeks, but in the meantime, she's been going to all these estate sales trying to find decorations to tie into the new place. So far she's found a lamp that is now in our living room since she loves it so much.

I get dressed in a pair of old jeans and a tank top before

heading out. Autumn is sitting at a table when I get there. We both order breakfast, and forty minutes later, we are spreading the plastic tarp to cover the floor before she starts on the baseboards. "I can't believe how quickly this was done."

"I know," I answer her from across the room, the paint roller in my hand as I roll it up and down on the wall. "The whole town came through for Mom."

"Gotta love the small town." She laughs. "What are you going to do when it's done and your mother is back at work?"

The question in itself makes my stomach turn. "I don't know," I answer honestly. "I thought I would come back and just leave after."

Autumn laughs. "Girl, same." She moves on her knees as she dips her paintbrush in the paint. "Now here I am with a thriving business, a husband, and a child." She smiles when she says it. "How are you and Brock?"

I look over at her. "Is there talk about us?" I ask, and she side-eyes me. "Shit . . . really?"

"He threw down with you in the middle of the parking lot with about twenty people there listening. It's not like he was keeping it to himself."

I exhale. "I don't know," I finally admit to her. "I mean, I do know. I never stopped loving him even though I convinced myself all these years that I hated him. I think it was easy since I didn't have to see him every single day. But the minute I finally laid eyes on him in the flesh, I knew I didn't really hate him. I also knew that I never really hated him to begin with."

"How are you going to handle that?" she asks, and I shrug. Even if I did, I wouldn't be able to answer her. "You still have a ways to go anyway."

"Do I?" I ask, not really sure. "And what is that going to do? More time spending it here. More time spending it with

Brock. More time for me to see my life is empty without this." I open my arms. "I know two of my neighbors," I admit to her, "and one because we sometimes bang." She snort-laughs. "The other one because she complains my wind chimes that I keep outside wake her up at all hours of the night, so I had to bring it inside my bedroom near my window." I roll the paint roller in the paint. "I haven't been to my apartment since I came here, and I don't think anyone noticed. Not one person even texted to check on me or ask me how I am doing."

"I'm so sorry," she says softly. "I had a friend when I left here. She sort of saved me, and I will be forever grateful for her."

"I'm sorry," I reply quietly, "for turning my back on you when you needed me. For how everything went down."

"I'm sorry too, for not being brave enough to tell you guys what was going on with Waylon. For not—"

"Hey," I snap, "you don't have to apologize for anything. You were not driving that truck. Don't let him continue to have a hold on you. That was his decision. I knew he wasn't all there. I mean, I didn't know he was drinking that night, but he was always so pissed off and reckless. We all knew deep down inside, and none of us said a word."

She shakes her head. "Now I have to know"—she raises her eyebrows—"have you been with Brock since you've been home?"

I think about lying and keeping it more to myself, but it's been so long since I've had a girlfriend to talk about these things with, all I can do is smile shyly. "Yes, and before you ask, even better than before."

Her mouth opens. "I know, shocking since it was like out of this world before, but now it's like kablam." I shake my hands and some of the paint drops on my pants. "Like he just got better with age, which is not fair, by the way. He was supposed to get older and have saggy balls."

She throws her head back and laughs. "I never want to picture Brock and his balls again in my life. Thank you for the visual." It's my turn to laugh. "Word on the street is that he's smiling now and not all grouchy and shit. Grunting instead of using words. It's a phenomenon, really." I can't help but laugh a bit. "We are all saying that it looks good on him."

I look down at the wall and then back at Autumn. "Anything looks good on him," I admit. "He was always too handsome for his own damn good."

"We'll agree to disagree on that." She makes me laugh as we switch topics, and she asks me how I'm going to decorate the shop.

We paint for a good couple of hours before there is a knock on the window. We look over to see Landon with his balled-up baby fists in his mouth as his face goes into a gummy smile, looking at his mom before he finally shrieks out in a high-pitched squeal.

"There is my man," she says, putting down her paintbrush and wiping her hands on her pants before reaching out and grabbing him. She pulls him to her and kisses his neck. "Did you miss me?"

"We did," Charlie confirms, leaning down and kissing her lips, "so, so much." I smile at the three of them having their moment.

"This is perfect timing," I say, putting the paintbrush down, "because I am done for the day." I clap my hands together.

"I'm going to clean up and then head out."

"Oh no," Charlie says, "why don't I clean up for you two, and you guys can go to the bar and take a load off?"

"Isn't he the best?" Autumn asks, looking at me and then looking up at Charlie.

"He's something," I reply, trying not to laugh at them.

"Are you sure?" I ask, and he nods. "Fine."

I walk out with Autumn. "Are you sure he's okay?" I ask, turning my head. I don't even look where I'm going and almost run into something.

"Oh my, I'm so sorry," I finally say, looking forward and coming face-to-face with Karla. My stomach literally sinks down to my feet. It was bound to happen; the town isn't that big.

"Well, well, well," she snips with a sickening smile on her face, "I heard you were back." She folds her arms over her chest. "Didn't really believe it until my daughter said she hung out with her dad's friend." She chuckles. "It was no big secret who that could be, considering he doesn't really have any friends."

It's my turn to smirk at her. "I guess you don't know him like you think you know him." Her grin turns into a glare.

"I knew him enough to have his child and marry him."

I put my hand to my stomach to hold in my laughter as Autumn gasps beside me. "Oh, yeah, you would have to know him enough to spread your legs for him." I put my finger to my chin and look to the side. "And how was the marriage? From what I heard, it was so good it lasted a whole what . . . six months at that."

"Fuck you, Everleigh," she snaps.

"Now, now." I shake my head. "Must have touched a nerve."

"I don't want you around my daughter," she finally hisses.

"Well, it's a good thing Brock is a good father, and he also gets to decide who is in his daughter's life." I wait for her to tear him down as a father, and I know if she does, I'm throwing hands. "Now, if you'll excuse me, I'm going to go and have a drink. You have a blessed day, Karla."

"Enjoy my sloppy seconds." She thinks she's taking a parting shot at me.

"Oh, trust me, I will." I smile big. "Considering he was

mine before he was yours, and well, I think we all know that he never really did move on, even if he fucked you." I look over at Autumn, who is trying to hide her smile behind Landon's head. "Shall we?"

"We shall," Autumn agrees. "Also . . ." She looks at Karla. "How fucking sad is it that you used your daughter for any of this?" I don't even wait for her to answer. I just pull Autumn away from her.

When we are in the bar, she looks over at me. "Walk all the way to the end and go to my office, now."

"I'm fine," I say even though deep down I'm not fine. She puts her hand in mine and drags me to the back to her office.

"Now, you can let it out," she urges me, and I actually put my hands on my knees.

"I shouldn't let it get to me," I tell the floor. "It's not like I didn't sleep with anyone after him." Autumn doesn't say a word. She knows I have to talk this out with myself. "I have a neighbor who I fuck monthly. I've had a couple of guys who I've hooked up with. It shouldn't fucking bother me." I get up and feel the tears. "Why does it fucking bother me?"

"Because you love him, and the thought of him with someone else is just too much," she says. "Just like I'm pretty sure if you told him that you have a neighbor you fuck monthly, he would probably burn down your building." I can't help but laugh at that. "I know how you feel," she finally shares softly. "Charlie pretty much fucked the entire town." I gasp. "Yeah, so you have only one woman; I have them on every single corner."

"What is going on?" Charlie walks into the office and sees us.

"Nothing. I was telling her what a womanizer you were." She glares at him, and I have to roll my lips. "And I'm constantly face-to-face with all the women you banged." His face goes white. “Yeah, exactly. Don’t think I don’t see them batting their eyes at you.”

“What happened from the time you left the bakery until now?” He puts his hands on his hips. “And how did it become my fault?” He looks at me, and I fill him in. “He never loved her,” Charlie reveals quietly, “not for a second, and everyone knew it, including Karla. She just didn’t want to see it.”

“We all have our pasts.” I look at him. “The question is, can we get past them?”

Thirty

BROCK

"I LOVE YOU, BABY GIRL," I say, giving her a hug and kissing the top of her head. "I'll see you next week, and I'll talk to you tonight when you get home from school."

"Okay, Daddy." Her voice is lower than it was five minutes ago in the car as she sang out at the top of her lungs about Vermont and seasons of sticks. She hugs me tighter for a second before letting me go and walking into the fenced-in yard. Looking back over her shoulder, she waves to me before walking into the school. My hands up, I clench the chain-link fence with one hand, and I hold up the other to my heart as I give her a chin up.

Only when the door closes behind her do I drop my head for a second before looking up at the sky and exhaling. Every single fucking time, it feels like half my heart stops beating when she leaves me. I push off from the fence and walk back over to the truck, pulling out my phone. Knowing this conversation would be happening today, I've played it over and over in my head the whole week.

I pull up her number and dial, my heart beating faster in my chest, waiting for her to answer. "Hello," she answers on the third ring, no doubt doing it on purpose. I know she works with her phone beside her computer keyboard, so there is no excuse.

"Hey," I say, "just dropped off Saige."

"How is she?" she asks, clicking away on her side on the phone.

"She's okay," I answer and then take a deep inhale. "Listen, Karla, I wanted to talk to you before I go to my lawyer." The clicking immediately stops, and the tension on the phone is so thick you could hear a leaf fall off the tree outside from inside the cab of my truck.

"Your lawyer?" she questions, her voice tight.

"I would like to have dinner with her once a week when it's not my turn, and also, you should have a chance to see her too when it's not your week." My index finger taps the steering wheel nervously. "It would still be the same time that we spend with her, just it won't be that long between when we switch."

"Listen, Brock," she says, her voice going low, "there is no reason to do this."

"What do you mean there is no reason to do this?" I repeat. "I miss her, and she misses me. If you think there is no reason to do this, then why can't we do it?"

"It's been working all this time." She trails off. "The schedule is fine the way it is."

"No, it hasn't," I bite back. "I've been asking you to spend time with her during the week when you have her, and you always have an excuse. I'm tired of it, to be honest, so I'm asking you one more time if we can do it. If not, you are going to leave me no choice but to go and speak to my lawyer and see what we can do."

"This is because of her, isn't it?" she hisses out, the venom in her voice filled with anger and rage, and everything in my body tightens when she says the next part. "Like I told your little girlfriend . . ." I think I stop breathing when she mentions

Everleigh. "I'll tell you, I don't want her around my daughter. Not now, not really fucking ever." My whole body feels like ice has filled my veins, and if she was in front of me, I'm not sure I would be able not to say something I shouldn't say, especially not to the mother of my daughter.

"I guess we'll have to go through our lawyers, then." I don't show her how pissed off I am. "I had hoped it wouldn't come to that."

"Whatever," she snaps and hangs up on me.

I shake my head, turning the truck on and then heading to work. I get in a little after eight and there is a line at the food truck, but it doesn't stop me from going over there.

She spots me right away and smiles my way before handing the man in front his order. It takes five minutes for everyone to finally leave, and I walk into the back of the truck. "Hi, you, how was drop-off?" she says with a smile on her face, coming over to me and putting her hands on my hips. Her touch calms me down just a little.

"Sucked," I admit to her. For the past week, I've seen her every single morning, kissing her hello and then coming to see her before I pick up Saige. Even though I've thought of begging her to come over and see me at night. It fucking sucks going to bed without her, even more than not waking up with her. I haven't had sex with her in over a week, and I'm so ready to slide into her tonight.

"Did you want a coffee?" she asks softly.

"Yeah," I mumble before she leans up and kisses the side of my ear, and I watch her walk to make my coffee. "Is there something that you might have forgotten to tell me?" I ask, and she looks over at me. She's wearing another pair of shorts that show off her legs, making my mouth water, with a regular T-shirt. Now she pairs her outfit with a pink apron that has three cupcakes on the top with Maddie's written underneath them.

She chuckles. "I don't know, is there?" She puts the lid on the coffee, turning to face me. "From the look on your face, there has to be something I didn't tell you. But for the life of me—"

"Called Karla to discuss me seeing Saige during the week," I say, and her face pales when I mention her name. "She said she spoke to you."

"Spoke to me is pushing it a little there." She folds her arms over her chest.

"What did she say to you?" I ask, trying not to go over to Karla's work and cause a scene.

"Nothing, really." She tries to play it off, but the look in her eyes tells me everything I need to know. "She heard I was in town." All I do is raise my eyebrows. "She heard that I met Saige, would like me not to be near her daughter."

I stand straight, my body tight. "I need you to tell me exactly, and I mean word for word, what she said."

"Why?" she asks, confused. "It's nothing."

"She's had five live-in boyfriends since we got divorced," I inform her. "All of them moving in after a month or so. All of them lasting maybe six months. One of them lasted a whole year."

"Okay," she replies, not sure why I'm telling her this.

"I called her today after I dropped off Saige and told her I would like to see her during the week. Informed her I'll go to my lawyer if I have to. She told me that you two had words." My eyes are on hers. "Now I want to know what fucking words were said, and then I want you to tell me why the fuck you didn't tell me any of this."

"What was there to say?" she fights back with me. "I bumped into her literally on the street. We exchanged pleasantries." I can tell she's lying. "Told me she didn't want me near her daughter."

"You should have told me that," I say, "because I would have called her and told her to go fuck herself."

"And what would that have accomplished, Brock?" she asks, and I know she's right. "It would have pissed you off. You would have called her, and then it would have pissed her off."

"So you sacrificed yourself." She gasps. "She doesn't get to tell me who sees my daughter when my daughter is with me. Just like I don't get into her face when she brings men around. Do I like it? Fuck no, but I try to keep the peace. But that peace ends now." I point at the floor. "I'm going to call my lawyer and talk to him." I close the distance to her. "Then I'm going to go to work, and tonight, me and you are going out." I wrap my arms around her waist. "Then you are spending the night, and we are going to fuck and sleep the whole weekend."

"Is that so?" She puts her hands on my chest. "What if I have plans?"

"We'll fuck around your plans, then." I finally bend my head and kiss her. "You okay with going to the bar tonight?"

"Um, yeah."

"Okay, good. Want to get ready at my place?"

"If I get ready at your place"—she smiles—"we'll never leave."

I put my forehead to hers. "You have a point there. I'll pick you up at eight."

"Sounds good," she agrees, and I let her go, giving her one more kiss before I walk out of the truck and head toward the garage. I'm about to call my lawyer when a text comes in from Karla.

Karla: Fine, you can have her for dinner this week on Wednesday night.

I shake my head but still call my lawyer and leave him a message. Getting home at seven, I rush to take a shower and put on clean sheets before going to pick her up. When I pull up to her house, she's already outside sitting on the steps with a small bag beside her.

She gets up, and I see she's wearing a ruffled orange skirt with white flowers on it. Her hair is over one shoulder, showing me the tight white shirt she is wearing has big straps and falls right above the waist of her skirt.

"Hi." She walks to the truck at the same time that I round it.

"That's a small bag for the weekend." I motion to the little bag she has in her hands, and she smirks at me.

"I thought I was going to be naked all weekend." She holds up the bag. "These are toys."

My cock goes hard as a rock, and I just look at her. "You promised to take me out," she reminds me. "This will be used later." She taps my chest and walks around me to get into the truck. "But I would like to hurry."

I shake my head, getting into the truck and starting it. "What exactly is in that bag?" I ask, and she turns to face me.

"Nothing much, just a cock ring." I stop breathing. "My rose clit sucker, my rabbit vibrator, and I got a couple of anal plugs this week." My hands grip the steering wheel. "Just a couple of things." She winks at me, and I look ahead and make my way to the bar. Pulling up to the garage, I park on the side where it's dark.

Her hand goes to the door handle when I put my hand on her leg, stopping her from moving. "Not so fast," I say, and she looks at me shocked as I reach over and grab the bag that is down by her feet. I open it, seeing more than what she told me, but I can't get into that now. Instead, my hand goes for exactly what I'm looking for, and I turn to look at her. "I want you to put your back against the door," I instruct her, "and then I want you to put one foot here"—I point at the dashboard—"and then the other here." I point at the armrest in the center console.

She doesn't ask any questions; instead, she does what I ask. I move her skirt off her, showing me she's wearing a white lace thong. Her legs spread open for me, and my fingers move it to the side. "Missed you," I say. At the same time, I slide a finger into her, and her head goes back against the glass. "Tell me how many times you played with my pussy this week?"

"Every day," she admits, "in the shower." She pants as I slide another one in her, hooking it on her G-spot. "Before I went to bed." My thumb flicks her clit, and her breath hitches. "In the morning when I woke up."

"Did you finger-fuck yourself like this?" I ask as I pull my fingers out of her and then move them back in.

"Yes." She nods as she looks between her legs. Only the light from the moon is in the truck cab.

"Did you fuck yourself with your vibrator?" I lean over and bend to suck her clit into my mouth, the center console blocking me from really devouring her.

"Yes," she says, "but it wasn't the same." I take the pink silicone that is in my other hand and bring it to her lips.

"Suck this while my fingers fuck you," I instruct her, and she takes it all in her mouth. "I'm going to make you come," I say. "Then you are going to wear this all night." Her pussy gets so wet, my fingers are drenched. "Then when we get home, I'll replace it with my cock." Her pussy spasms around my fingers. I take the anal plug out of her mouth and move it down. "Tilt your hips, baby," I say, my fingers planted all the way inside her as my fingers scissor to play with her G-spot. "Greedy," I tease her as I slide the anal plug inside her. "Even tighter," I say, about to move my fingers.

She grips my wrist to stop me. "You play with me anymore, and I'm going to soak the fucking seat"—I smirk at her—"and you won't get to tease me all night."

"Baby, I really hope you napped today." I pull my fingers out of her and suck her off my fingers. "Because unless you pass out when I'm fucking you, it's going to be a long night."

Thirty-One

EVERLEIGH

HE PUTS MY SKIRT DOWN, covering me before he pulls me forward, making the anal plug go deeper in my ass. "You look so beautiful," he says. I stop breathing, and it's not from the pressure in my ass or the way he just made me come in his car. It's the softness of his voice.

"You aren't so bad yourself." I lean over the middle console and kiss his lips, sweeping my tongue into his mouth.

I get out of the truck and walk to the back, where he waits for me. "How are you doing?" he asks, and I look over at him.

"I feel full." I wink at him. "And fucking horny." He shakes his head as we walk down the sidewalk to the bar. "How long are we staying here?" I ask as I hear music coming from the open door. "Like, are we talking an hour, or are we talking having a drink and then leaving?"

"I'm going to keep you on your toes," he informs me as we walk in, and I spot it's full. "There are too many people here. We should go."

He leans in. "You'll get my cock soon enough," he teases,

walking into the bar, and I follow him. The whole time, my pussy clenches.

We make it to the bar and spot a couple of empty stools. "You want to sit down?" he asks, and I glare at him. "You should sit."

"I think I'll stand," I reply as he pulls out the stool, and the bartender approaches us.

"What can I get you?" he asks, tossing down two coasters.

"I'll have the house blend," Brock orders, then turns to me.

"I'll have the same." He nods at me and walks away.

"So tell me how you feel?" he asks, and I look around, spotting a couple of people I know, including Emmett.

"Like a bitch in heat," I grit out between clenched teeth. Emmett spots us and walks over to us.

"Hey, you two," he greets with a beer in his hand, leaning against the bar with his elbow. "Fancy seeing you two here."

"How fancy?" Brock semi-glares at him, making me roll my lips and Emmett just laughs at him.

"Did you ever check your schedule"—Emmett looks at me—"and see when it's a good time for you to come and take a ride with me?"

"She did." Brock sticks his face into the conversation and puts a hand at my hip, gripping it tight. "It's going to be the day after never." Emmett just grins. "You can schedule her in right now."

"Are you threatening my right-hand man?" Charlie walks up to Brock and slaps his shoulder and then squeezes.

"Who, me?" Brock feigns innocence. "I would never."

"Is Autumn here?" I ask Charlie, and he shakes his head. "She forced me to come out and have a guys' night." He looks around. "I'm going back home in ten minutes and telling her no one was here."

"You do know that she owns this bar." Brock looks over at him. "And she can ask."

"Yeah," Charlie says, leaning on the bar with his elbows, "but by then, it'll be over. She can't get mad at me after the fact."

"Um," Emmett starts, "have you met your wife? She almost kicked you out of the house yesterday."

"She did not." Charlie glares at him. "She just locked the door and refused to open it until I did what she told me to do."

"And what was that?" I ask Charlie.

"Get out of her hair," he deadpans, making us all laugh. He looks over his shoulder at the door, his eyebrows going big.

"Since when did those two start dating?" Charlie looks over at the door, and I turn back to see Caleb walk in with Lilah beside him.

"He asked her out last week," I fill him in. "She came to get a box of donuts for the guys at the barn."

"And left with a fucking date," Emmett snaps and turns back to watch them walk to the table with a group of guys. "Who the fuck is he anyway?"

"What's it to you?" Brock asks him. Emmett turns back, and his eyes are almost in slits. "Word on the street is that you fucking hate her." He pushes off the bar. "Even now, you are scowling at her."

"First of all," he snaps, grabbing his bottle of beer, "I don't fucking hate her. She's young, and she's reckless. Second off, why don't you mind your own business?" He walks away from us and heads to the table where the boys are.

The three of us just watch him pull out the chair and sit down. The scowl never leaves his face as Lilah smiles and looks up at Caleb, introducing him to everyone. Lilah smiles at the bunch, and then when she spots Emmett, she looks down at her hands and avoids looking back at him. Instead, she turns to talk to Caleb, and the two of them walk away to their own table.

"Um." I look over at Charlie. "Is Caleb going to be okay?" Charlie is still looking over his shoulder at Emmett. "He has a couple of days left of work at the bakery, and it's going to be hard for him to do all that with two broken hands, and from the look on Emmett, a broken face."

"He'll be fine," Charlie assures me. "But just in case, I'm going to go and make sure he stays in one piece." He pushes off the bar. "Now I can't leave in ten minutes." He turns to Brock. "Thanks."

"I didn't do anything," he says to Charlie, and it feels like it's old times with the two of them joking. "I just asked a question."

"Oh, didn't you?" Charlie retorts. "You knew what buttons to push."

"Me?" Brock acts like he has no idea what Charlie is talking about. "I just was repeating what I heard around the shop. It's no secret he doesn't like her." He shrugs.

"How much of an asshole were you to Everleigh the first time you walked into the bar and saw her?" Charlie asks him, and Brock just looks at him and grins. "That's how he feels about Lilah."

I gasp and look over at Brock, who is just as shocked as I am. "But he's a horse's ass and as stubborn as a mule. So that is a lot of fun for all of us. We all know she's off-limits to anyone. Caleb just didn't get that memo."

"Well, if he's smart," I chime in, "he'll stop playing games. It's going to be very cold in that bed of his."

I pick up my drink and down it in two gulps, grimacing all the way. "Are we done yet?" I ask Brock.

"Yeah, baby," he confirms, pushing me away from him and getting up before reaching into his back pocket and putting sixty dollars on the bar top.

"Do we have to say goodbye?" I ask, and he shakes his head, walking out of the bar. The whole time we walk back to his truck, he's touching me softly. From his hands grazing mine to his hand holding my neck softly, it feels like his hands are everywhere. He is about to open the door for me when he pushes me against it. I watch as he presses his chest to mine. "I'm going to eat your pussy when we get home." He turns to the side and slides my skirt up, feeling the wetness on the lace panties. "Then I'm going to fuck your pussy with the bigger plug up there." I swear if he touches me now, I would come on him. "Then after that, you are going to get on your hands and knees, and I'm going to fuck that ass of yours." I close my eyes, and I have to put my knees together. "Is that okay with you?"

"When do I get your cock in my mouth?" I ask, and he smirks.

"On the way home," he states as he pushes away from me, opens the door, and waits for me to get in. I bend to tease him, but it's me who gets teased when he pushes the butt plug deeper into me.

He gets into the truck, and my hands are already on the buttons of his jeans. "That's my girl," he praises when I free his cock at the same time as he pulls out of the parking lot. I suck as much of his cock as I can, his jeans restricting it.

"Fuck, I'm going to come down your throat," he informs me when he stops the truck, and his hips jerk up to fuck my mouth. "Suck the cum out of me," he growls. "Take every fucking last drop." I moan on his cock as he shoots his cum to the back of my throat. I swallow it all, and when I let him go, I look around and see we're in his driveway.

"On my bed, spread open," he says, and I grab the bag.

"Fuck eating my pussy," I say as I walk up the steps, my knees almost pushed together. "I need to be fucked."

"Don't tell me what to do with my pussy," he mutters as he devours my mouth, opening the door. His hands frantically grip my tits as my hands go to his zipper. The kiss is all tongue, and when I get to his bedroom, he strips me in two fucking movements, tossing the bag to the side of the bed. "Back now."

I do as he tells me. My whole body feels like it's going to explode when I watch him undress. His cock is semi hard, still shiny from my mouth. He puts one knee on the bed, crawling over to me. "Look at this pussy," he praises, his hand coming down and slapping it, my hips bucking, "and this ass." He uses the loop that is out of my ass as he turns it around in a circle. "It's fucking soaked."

"Fuck me, Brock." I move my hands to grip my own tits, pinching my nipples. "Fuck me good."

He reaches over for the bag, dumping the contents on the bed beside me and grabbing my vibrator. "This is what has been in my pussy?" he asks as he rubs the pink vibrator up and down my slit, putting the tip of the cock inside me, making me pant.

"Get on your hands and knees," he demands, and I roll over, doing as I'm told. My body aches for him. "This is better," he says, slapping one of my ass cheeks before he takes the vibrator and slides the head into me again. I grip the sheets in my hands. "Grab the rose, baby, and stick it to your clit." I can't even see straight right now as my hand moves around beside me. I grab the rose, place it on my clit, and turn it on. The minute it sucks my clit in, I moan. "Hmm," he groans from behind me. "You got my cock so hard right now," he states as his tongue slides into me. "Pussy dripping wet, ass nice and tight." He turns the butt plug. "I'm going to fuck you now." The head of his cock moves into me, the pressure pushing into my ass. "Fuck, you're even tighter," he hisses out as he slides his cock all the way inside me. I swear my eyes roll to the back of my head. "Grip my cock like you want me to come in you," he instructs, and I try to focus. "Your pussy doesn't feel like it wants to get fucked."

"I want to get fucked," I pant. "Show me how much you missed fucking my ass." I look over my shoulder as he pulls his cock out of my pussy. At the same time, I feel the plug start to pull out of my ass, but then he slams his cock into me and the plug in my ass. "Brock," I call out as he moves the plug at the same time as his cock. "I'm going to come," I warn him. "It's going to be a big one." I feel it in my bones, knowing I'm about to come like I don't think I've ever come before. "Don't stop."

He slaps my ass as he pushes me over the edge. The orgasm rips through me as I gush around his cock. My arms almost shake as he pounds me without remorse. "You ready?" he asks. I don't have a chance to answer him because I feel like I'm floating out of my body. The plug is taken out of me. "Going to fuck you now," he says, and his cock enters my ass. My pussy feels empty as it drips to the bed. "Got the head in," he says how it's going, pulling out and then giving me more. "Halfway, baby, you good?"

"Yes," I hiss, the rose still on my clit.

He fucks my ass until he's all the way in. "You have it all," he informs me. "Now fuck yourself."

I look over my shoulder at him, knowing that he lets me do all the work. "Show me how much you like me in your ass." I grip the sheets, moving my body forward and then back. "Yeah, that's it," he urges me on. "You want more?" he asks, and I nod, needing more. "Here." He hands me the vibrator. "Once it's inside you, I'll fuck your ass, and you fuck your pussy." I reach in between, tossing the rose to the side as I turn on the vibrator. His cock is planted in my ass as I move the vibrator into me. He hisses the whole time I slowly put it in me. I shake when the rabbit ears move across my clit. "Baby," he growls between clenched teeth, "if you don't stop fucking around, I'm going to fuck your ass to the point you won't be able to sit until Monday." I smirk at him, and he pulls out and then slams back in. "Move the cock in your pussy."

I move it in and out and then he picks up the speed, matching mine. "I'm so full," I announce, knowing that I'm about to come again. "I think I'm going to come."

"You aren't the only one," he groans, and I frantically push the vibrator in and out of me. The wetness comes out of me, soaking my hand as I close my eyes when I push the vibrator out of me, literally gushing all over his bed. My hips shake but his hands grip me so hard as he thrusts into my ass and roars out my name.

Thirty-Two

EVERLEIGH

I HUNCH DOWN ON MY ELBOWS, looking out of the food truck at my mother who is getting out of her car. Slamming the door shut, she finds my eyes and smiles at me. "Hi," she says almost breathlessly, her smile filling her whole face from ear to ear.

"Hi yourself!" I shout back at her as she walks to me, but her eyes are on the bakery's window.

"You think you're funny?" she asks, pointing at the window I made them put up paper on so she wouldn't be able to see inside.

"You're early," I say, looking at my clock and seeing it's just after one in the afternoon. "I said be here at three."

"I know, I know." She bounces on the tips of her feet. "But come on, you have to show me the space."

I roll my eyes at her. "Two hours isn't going to kill you," I tease her and then look up when another car parks behind my mother. Oliver slides out of the driver's side with a scowl on his face. "Oh, someone is in trouble with Daddy."

My mother whips her head to me. "Don't ever call him Daddy again."

I snort-laugh, pushing up and walking out of the truck at

the same time Oliver gets in front of my mother. "We were supposed to have lunch." He puts his hands on his hips.

"I called and left you a message that I wasn't coming to that," she states. "And I texted; it's not my fault you don't check your things." She folds her arms over her chest. "It's a good thing I wasn't dying. I would have died."

"No!" I snap. "Too soon."

"Okay, fine." She looks up at the sky before turning to look at Oliver. "I'm busy with my daughter. You can go get lunch at the diner." She points at the diner, then turns to me. "Now, you can either go in there with me"—she points over her shoulder at the door—"or I'm going in without you."

"She is so bossy." I look at Oliver. "How long is she supposed to not work for?"

"Would she listen to me anyway?" He glares at her. "I said you could start light work next week."

"I'm not working!" she shrieks. "I'm visiting my daughter."

I put my hand beside my mouth to block it from my mother and aim my words at Oliver. "She glazed some of the donuts this morning."

"You are going to get it," my mother warns with her teeth clenched together.

"The last time she told me that, I was eighteen and I laughed at her," I tell Oliver, "and she took off her shoe and threw it at me."

She doesn't even defend herself; instead, she huffs out as she turns to the bakery and storms into it, but Oliver catches her around her waist. "Let her surprise you."

"No," she barks, "it's time for me to see."

"Fine," I concede. "Such a child." I walk over to the door and look back at her, a smile now on my face. "I'm going to film this for social media," I inform her. "I'm going to go in and then you count to three and then come in." I step in, turning my phone toward the door. As soon as it opens, I tell her, "Welcome to Maddie's." The camera is on her face as she steps in and sees what I did to her shop.

The floors are black-and-white squares, with four white cast-iron tables with matching chairs. The walls are painted a light pink as she walks over to the long white counter with the stainless-steel coffee machine I bought, which is right next to the glass display case. "In the back there"—I point at the built-in shelves I had made that sit behind the counter—"I was thinking we can have some homemade jam or something to sell. There are lots of local vendors that I've reached out to who would love to have some shelf space here." Her hands go to her mouth. "You ready to see the kitchen?"

"I don't know," she says, wiping the tears from her face.

I turn the camera to my face. "I think she likes it," I announce, walking to the back area and turning on the commercial lights we upgraded to. "This is your kitchen," I say and turn the camera back to her. "We put a big stainless-steel island in the middle so you can work on cookies on one side and then donuts on the other." I point at the table. "And we thought everything should be against the walls. You have not one but two fridges, so you can get more prepped." I point at the commercial fridges I splurged on, the four glass doors showing you the empty racks inside. "Then you have your two mixers so you can prep more dough and not do little batches during the day." I point at the two mixers. "Then we got you two ovens because one is just not enough and then four fryers. You will be frying for a very long time," I joke with her as I look back at her marveling in what I did.

"This—" she starts. "Turn that off," she says of the camera, and I raise my eyebrows at her.

"Well, that's it for Maddie. Tune in for the big grand opening next Monday," I tell the camera before turning it off.

"Everleigh, this is all too much." She looks around. "Can we even afford all of this? We haven't even gotten the insurance money yet."

"About that." I take a big inhale and then look over at Oliver, who looks at the ceiling and then braces himself for what is going to come. "The fire chief came in a couple of weeks ago."

"What?" she asks, shocked. "You didn't tell me."

"Well, it wasn't that good of a visit," I admit. "The cause of the fire was arson," I say, and she gasps.

"It's not a surprise," she says, "but hearing it officially takes my breath away." She shakes her head.

"Not only that, he knows we didn't set it, but he can't prove someone else set it either."

"So now what?" she asks. "How did you do all of this?"

"Well." I brace myself for her to totally go off.

"I gave her the money," Oliver finally confesses.

My mother turns to face him, her hair whips her in her own face. "I'm sorry. What?"

"The construction was already underway," he starts, "and to stop it and wait for whatever they were going to say was a waste of time."

"A waste of time," my mother repeats his words. "You paid for this?"

"Not just me"—he points at his chest—"Everleigh took out a loan."

"You what?" My mother turns to me, her voice so loud I squint.

"Okay, before you freak out, can you listen, please?"

"No, you are going to go back to the bank, and we are going to cancel that loan. I'll take a second mortgage on the house if I have to."

"You will not do that," I snap. "This is as much mine as it

is yours." I open my arms to the bakery. "If something happens to you, this, all of this, is my legacy."

"It's not your legacy if you pay for it." She throws her hands up in the air. "A legacy is something that you inherit. Debt is not that."

"Mom, now that you have more space to prepare things, think of the endless possibilities," I say. "You can do breakfast and lunch. I'm not saying for you to start cooking. But you can offer bagels, you have a great recipe." She just stares at me. "You can prepare sandwiches in the morning, and when they sell out, they sell out. There is also the food truck."

"What am I going to do with that?" She points at the food truck.

"Well—" I smile at her. "We can go to county fairs with it. We can do business events. The possibilities are endless. I even spoke with someone about having it at wedding receptions at night, offering donuts and cupcakes."

"I can't do all of that." She looks up. "I'm not equipped for that."

"I know you can't, but I can." I let out a big exhale as her eyes look at me, shocked. "I know, I know, it was supposed to be temporary." I put my hand to my stomach, suddenly nervous that I'm making this declaration out loud instead of just playing with the idea in my head. "But what if I want to make this a permanent thing? What if I want to get a slew of food trucks?" I hold up my hand. "That's not my plan, but who knows. If it takes off, we can have food trucks all over."

"It's the big craze these days," Oliver states with a lightness in his eyes. "I think even one of the big actor guys was caught cooking in the one he bought in New York." He inhales. "I don't know about your mom, but I'd like for you to be closer to home."

My mother looks at him, then back at me. "What about your job?" she asks, and I shrug.

"What if I like doing this more? Creating the donuts was so much fun. Some people might hate working in the food truck, but it was so good to see the same faces over and over again. To ask them how their families were doing. I don't know, it just made me feel settled."

"You used to hate that about living here," she reminds me.

"Yeah, but when you don't have it anymore, you miss it," I say the truth. "It was good not having it, but then when you get it back, you realize how much you missed it."

"Does this have anything to do with Brock?" she asks, and I can answer her with all the certainty in me.

"Part of it, yes." I smile. "The other part is just me wanting to be here."

"Does he know?" she asks, and I shake my head. "You two should give communication classes."

"You are one to talk," I counter back at her. "It took you, what . . . fifty years to declare your love for Oliver."

"I did not declare my love for him." She holds up her finger. "I said I liked him and we were together."

"She loves me." He puts his arm around her shoulders and pulls her to him. "She just has trouble saying the words." That makes us both laugh.

"We are going to pay you back." She looks up at him. "No matter what."

"What difference does it make when we get married? You get half of everything I have anyway." I put my hand in front of my mouth. "Now that you are starting to work and have the energy, you can plan the wedding."

"Oh, snap." I snicker, and my mother just shakes her head, but to everyone's surprise, she doesn't say no. "Now that you've seen the place, you can get out of my hair."

"We need to hire more people," my mother says, and I nod.

"Already have four new ones starting next week," I inform her, and she gasps. "I've been busy," I say, and she smiles.

"Apparently, I haven't been paying attention," my mother notes. I walk out of the bakery and head back to the food truck, leaving her to get used to the new kitchen. I'm about to text Brock when I hear a knock on the side of the truck and look up to see him standing there. "What are you doing here?" I ask him as he steps into the truck with a smile on his face.

"It's nice to see you too," he retorts, and I can't help but laugh as he pulls me to him. It's been five days since Saige went back to her mom. Five days and we've spent every night together. I was surprised I was able to walk on Monday after spending literally all weekend naked. "Don't forget I have dinner with Saige tonight." He bends his head to bury his face in my neck.

"Are you excited?" I ask, and he smiles.

"Do you want to come with us?" he asks again, and I shake my head.

"You haven't seen her all week long," I point out. "Why don't you two have dinner, and then I'll meet you back at your place when you drop her off?"

He looks at me like he has to say something. "Okay." He kisses my lips. "We'll talk tonight." I don't say anything, not liking his tone, but also knowing he has to get back to work. I don't have a chance to say anything to him either when my phone rings. I look down to see it's the local newspaper I called to place a couple of ads this morning. "See you later."

I nod at him as I put the phone to my ear. "Hello," I answer, watching him walk back to the shop.

"Everleigh," the woman says my name. "This is Amy, and I'm calling you from *The Town Chronical.* I'm interested in doing a story about the bakery in the next issue." I look down at my hands. "I'm hoping we could sit down and talk."

"That sounds great," I say, looking over at the bakery door and seeing my mother walk out with a huge smile on her face. "That sounds really good, actually."

Thirty-Three

BROCK

ME: THERE IS A KEY UNDER THE MAT, let yourself in.

I put the phone down as I pull up to Karla's place. The phone beeps, and I look down to see she texted me back already.

Everleigh: Is that safe to have it under the front mat? At least put it in a plant.

I shake my head and look in the back, seeing Saige get out of her seat and open the back door. I get out and hold her hand until the front door, where she turns around and gives me a big hug. "I'll see you in two days," I remind her, and she nods as the front door is pulled open.

"Hey, baby," Karla greets Saige, coming outside and extending her arms to give her a hug. Saige goes into her arms. "Did you have fun?"

"Yeah," Saige replies, "we had steak."

"Sounds yummy," she says. "Go get in the shower." She motions with her head, and I smile at Saige.

"Two days, baby girl," I repeat, and she smiles before skipping into the house.

Karla waits until she's out of earshot before she turns on me. "I got the lawyer's letter."

I nod at her. "I thought we agreed."

"We didn't agree on anything. You said I could have her this week. What about next time? What about when you get a hair up your ass about something and take it out on me?" She doesn't even bother denying it. "I want to make sure that it's on paper."

"Whatever." She turns and starts to walk into the house.

"Karla." I call her name and she turns back to look at me. "Just so we're clear, who I see is none of your business." She spins to face me. "And who I have in my house is, again, none of your business." She starts to say something, but I hold up my hand. "Before you spew any shit, think about it. People who live in glass houses shouldn't throw stones, yeah?" I wait a second. "I'm going to introduce Saige to Everleigh this weekend," I say.

"She already met her," she throws in my face. "Not that you discussed it with me."

"Not that I need to explain myself to you, but she met her as my friend. This weekend, she'll know we're together." I might be getting ahead of myself since I haven't spoken to Everleigh yet, but I want Everleigh to be there with me, and I don't want to hide the way I feel about her.

"Did you even give us a chance?" she asks softly.

"You knew how I felt," I remind her. "I never, ever led you on. You knew I loved Everleigh, and I made it clear to you I didn't think I would love anyone again." She looks down. "You didn't care."

"Well, I guess I made a mistake, thinking I could change you," she says, turning and walking into her house and slamming the door, telling me the conversation is over.

I exhale and make my way over to my house. *One conversation down, one more to go,* I think to myself when I pull up to my house and see the lights on, and I smile knowing she's inside. I walk up the steps and open the front door, listening to her moving around in the house as I kick off my boots.

I find her in the kitchen, putting on the kettle. "Hey," I say, and she looks over her shoulder at me. She's wearing one of my T-shirts, and her hair is wet.

"Hey, I came over and took a shower while I waited for you. I was going to shower when I got home, but I ended up uploading videos to our social media. Then I was making the last-minute things for this Saturday." She turns. "Hope that's okay."

"We need to talk," I say, pulling out the stool and sitting down with the island between us.

"Uh-oh," she reacts, and I can see she's nervous, "that doesn't sound good." I put my hands on the counter. "Did dinner not go well?"

"It went amazing," I say the truth. "Would have liked it if you were there, but next time."

"You guys should have alone time," she says, and it does something to me that she understands that.

"I spoke to Karla tonight," I share, and she walks to the island between us. She puts her hands on the island, and I can see her nervously tapping it. "Told her I was going to introduce you to Saige this weekend."

"I've already met her." She says the same thing Karla said.

"Yes, but she thought you were my friend. I want to tell her you're more than that."

"Isn't that rushing things?" She looks in my eyes, and I feel the crushing on my chest, thinking she's already made up her mind about when she is leaving, and she hasn't told me.

"I don't know, you tell me," I retort. "Soon the bakery is going to be done. It's done already, but soon your mother is going to be back full force. Where does that leave you?"

"Funny you should ask. I had a conversation with my mother today about that," she states, and I hold my breath. I'm bracing for what is to come, bracing for her to say the words she's leaving. Bracing for how I'm going to live without her again, but this time knowing I will never, ever love another woman the way I love her. She's it for me. "We discussed the bakery and how I want to continue with the food truck." I can't even swallow, the lump is growing bigger and bigger in my throat. "And, well, I've decided I'm going to stay." I let out the breath I was holding. "I know this might be a lot for you. That it's too fast and whatever. But you weren't the deciding factor."

"Did you factor me in there at all?"

"Well, of course I did," she says softly. "I just didn't want you to—"

"To what?" I snip. "Hope you were staying for me. For us."

"Brock," she says, and I shake my head.

"I came home tonight and saw the light on, and when I walked in, I heard you in here doing whatever it is you were doing. I've never come home to anyone in this house. When I don't have Saige, the house is dead and quiet. It is eerily quiet, as if the house is standing still. With you in it, it gives it life."

"I'm making tea," she announces.

I smile at her answer, my heart hammering in my chest. "So you are okay with meeting Saige as more than my friend?" I ask, and she snorts. "I'm going to pick her up on Friday and tell her we are having dinner with you. Then I'll tell her I'm in love with you."

She gasps. "That we were in love a long time ago, and I did things that stopped us from being together."

"Don't do that." She shakes her head.

"Tell her what, that I'm in love with you?" She shakes her head again.

"No, about what happened in the past. She's going to be confused enough with sharing you, and then you throw in that you loved me before and everything that happened. I don't want her to ever know, to be honest."

"She's going to know eventually," I say. "The town is small, and the gossip is larger than life."

"Yes, but we don't have to feed into it," she argues.

"Okay, fine." I hold up my hand.

"You love me?" she asks softly, the sound of the kettle whistling behind her.

"I do," I confirm.

"You ever stop loving me?" She doesn't move to the stove.

"Thought I did," I admit, "but I lied to myself."

"Me too," she replies with a soft smile on her face.

"So are you saying you love me?" I ask, and she smirks.

"Maybe."

"You going to get your ass over here right now?" I ask, and she shakes her head. She turns toward the stove, turning it off before she walks over to me. When she is close to me, I yank her to me, picking her up and placing her on the island.

She puts her hands on my face. "You ever stop loving me?" I ask the same question she asked me.

"Sadly, no." She leans down to kiss my lips. "Thought I did."

"I'm sorry. You'll never know how sorry I am."

She rubs my cheek. "Make it up to me," she urges softly. "Every single day, make it up to me."

I grab her around her waist, picking her up off the counter. "Every single day, I plan on doing just that." I walk toward my bedroom. "Starting right now."

Thirty-Four

EVERLEIGH

"HOW DO I LOOK?" I ask my mother when I step out of the bathroom wearing my ruffled baby-pink skirt and a smocked white gauze top with puffy short sleeves that tie in the back. "Mom," I groan. "We're supposed to be dressed the same."

"We are," she counters. "It's literally the same shirt and skirt. I just had to add an extra layer, or else I would forget and bend over and give away the farm." I look around the kitchen, seeing the six people we hired to help us today. "What time is the photographer going to be here?" she asks, looking around, shaking the nerves out of her hands.

"Any minute," I reply, turning and capturing the people working in the back.

"You and that phone," my mother hisses.

"Hey, this phone"—I hold up—"went viral last night." I shake it. "The video of you coming into the bakery was seen over twelve million times in twenty-four hours."

"I don't even know what that means," she admits, smoothing down her skirt. "What if no one comes?"

"To the grand opening?" I roll my eyes. "I made five

hundred donuts. They better fucking show up," I say, and she laughs.

She doesn't have a chance to say anything else because the door opens and the photographer for the local paper comes in. We sit at the table by the window, side by side, with the top of it overflowing with cookies, cupcakes, donuts, and cups of coffee. I look over at my mother, who smiles at me. "Proud of you," I say, and she throws her head back and laughs.

"I'm the one who is supposed to say that," she chides as the photographer tells me to look at him. Two days ago, the reporter called to tell me she wanted to do a story about how the town rallied around us to help rebuild the bakery after it burned down. She asked me a slew of questions, and today, the photographer came out to snap a couple of pictures before our big opening at noon.

He takes what feels like a million pictures before he finally leaves thirty minutes later. I get up and take one look around, seeing the display cases filled to the rim with donuts and cupcakes. The bottom shelf has platters of cookies we are testing out. Five platters of cake sit on top of the display cases, thanks to Harmony. Two platters are cut into slices and then three are full cakes ready to be sold.

I made them add gold hanging lights over the cases just for show, and I have fake white and pink flowers dangling so it looks like a garden. I snap a couple more pictures of the bouquet of balloons beside the front door. "Mom," I call to her, holding up the camera, "what do you want to say about the opening?"

"I want to thank everyone in Montgavin for coming out and volunteering their time for us to be here today. We couldn't have done it without any of them." She smiles. "But most importantly, thank you to my daughter who put aside her life to come back and take care of me and the bakery when I got sick."

She blinks away the tears. "I couldn't and wouldn't want to do this without her." I stop taping her as the door opens, and I look up to see Saige and Brock come into the bakery.

"Ms. Maddie!" Saige shrieks, running over to her, wearing the sundress she picked out last night at dinner to wear today. Her hair is parted in the middle with two tiny braids on each side, tied in the back. "This is so pretty," she says, looking around. My eyes go to Brock, who holds flowers in one hand. He is wearing his gray slacks with a white button-down shirt that is not tucked in, the collar open, and the sleeves rolled up to his elbows.

"Hi." I smile big when I see him.

"Hi, baby." He smiles back as he walks up to me, wrapping his free arm around me and pulling me to him. I think he's going to kiss my cheek, but he bends his head and his lips softly find mine. I open my eyes big, looking over at Saige to see if she saw. We had dinner last night and there was no talk about who I was, at least not when I was there. I've been going since 3:00 a.m. today, so I haven't had a chance to ask him about it. "You look beautiful."

"Hi, Everleigh," Saige greets. "We brought you flowers." She grabs the flowers from Brock's hand, holding them up for me to see the pink peonies. "They are the same color as the walls, so they match."

"These are beautiful," I compliment, grabbing them from her. "Thank you so much."

"Dad says you're sleeping over tonight." My eyes shoot straight to Brock.

"Why don't I go and put those in water?" my mother suggests, taking the flowers from me. "Saige, why don't you come and see the new flavor of donuts that Everleigh made this morning." She looks at her. "She told me you gave her the idea to put jelly inside and peanut butter frosting on top." She puts her hand in Saige's, pulling her to the back.

"You did not tell her that I'm sleeping at your house." I don't even think I wait for them to be in the kitchen before I start on him.

"Baby," he soothes, putting his hands on my hips, "you'll be moving in soon, and she has to be used to you being there."

"I'm sorry, what?" I shake my head.

"Not now, but in the next month, you'll be living with us."

"Brock," I hiss his name, "you didn't tell her that, did you?"

"Of course not." He rolls his eyes. "I said you were working all day and that you'd be tired tonight, so you are going to sleep over so we can make sure you relax."

"She bought that?"

"Probably not with the smirk she gave me, and then she said 'ohh you like her,'" he mimics how Saige must have teased him, making me laugh.

"And then I said, 'no, I love her.'" I gasp. "That's exactly what she did also. But then she said you were pretty." He shrugs. "So I guess she approved."

"I cannot believe you," I say, but then the door opens, and Autumn comes in, her mouth hanging open when she sees it for the first time finished.

"Holy shit," she swears, and Charlie snickers. "This is incredible." Her eyes roam around the room, taking everything in.

"Wow." He shakes his head and looks at Autumn. "You yelled at me this morning because I said you had a fine ass in front of Landon, but you are allowed to say shit?"

"Charlie Barnes, you are getting on my last nerve," she hisses. "Like the last one."

He grabs her around her neck and pulls her to him. "I love you," he declares, and she melts in his arms, "don't forget that."

"How could I?" She wraps her arms around his waist and then looks at their son.

"Welcome," I tell them and then look over to see Harmony and Brady walking in with Wyatt. "Hi." I hold up my hand to welcome them.

I look back down when a hand slides into mine, and my eyes fixate on Brock's fingers laced with mine. My eyes go back up to his as people come in. "I love you," he whispers, and I don't have a chance to answer him when more and more people come in.

I work the room with Mom, thanking everyone for all their help. Every time I look up, I find him looking at me; when I don't, it's because he's right beside me. He doesn't move far from me the whole day. The bakery is filled to the brim. The display cases have been refilled more times than I can count, with people leaving with boxes and boxes of donuts.

I think everyone in town comes in to say hello, and there are lots of new faces from nearby towns because of the viral video. The day flies by, and by the time it hits 5:00 p.m., we have sold out of everything.

"I can't believe we have nothing left," I state, sitting down at the table next to Brock, who puts his arm across the back of my chair. Autumn and Charlie are sitting here also, with my mother beside them.

"Can we have pizza?" Saige asks from the chair beside him, and he looks at her.

"How many donuts did you have today?" he asks, and she shrugs.

"I was taste testing." She looks at me. "That's what Everleigh asked me to do."

I look at Brock, folding my lips together as Oliver comes over and hands me a glass of champagne. He pulls a chair from the other table to sit next to my mother. "I don't know about you guys, but this is what I call a success." He grabs my mother's hand and kisses her fingers.

The door to the bakery opens again, and I'm about to say we're closed when I notice it's one of the deputies. "Hey there," he says, looking at us. "Sorry to intrude."

"Nonsense," my mother says. "I'd offer you a donut, but we're all out."

"That's okay, Ms. Maddie," he replies. "I'm here on official business anyway." I put my glass of champagne down on the table, my mouth going dry as I wait for what he has to say. "We just arrested two men in connection with setting the fire," he announces, and my mother gasps. "We picked them up a couple of hours ago." His eyes go to Brock. "We got a call that they were hanging around your shop." Brock gets up. "Gotta say, they aren't too smart doing it today with all these people here. Someone made a call that they seemed suspicious, gave us the plate number, and we picked them up not long after." His mouth goes tight. "They both turned on each other as soon as we sat down."

"Oh my," my mother murmurs.

"That's not the kicker," he adds. "They worked for the Cartwrights."

Brock's about to jump out of his chair, and I put my hand on his leg to stop him. "Thank you for letting us know," I say, then turn to look over at Brock. "They don't get to have one more second from us." I put my hand on his cheek. "They took too much from us already."

"But they—" I put my finger on his lips.

"We're here," I remind him, "together." I look around the table. "We won."

"She's right," Charlie agrees. "They will get what is coming to them. They have all the rope they need in order to hang themselves."

He nods at Charlie before looking back at me. "You coming home with us?" he asks, and I look at Saige.

"You bet," I confirm, right before he leans over and kisses me in front of everyone, and I kiss him right back.

Thirty-Five

BROCK

"GOOD MORNING," Everleigh says, and I look over my shoulder at Saige, who saunters into the kitchen, rubbing the sleep from her eyes. I see it's past nine thirty as she makes her way around the island toward me.

"Morning, baby girl," I say, pouring two cups of coffee before turning and hugging her around her shoulders and kissing the top of her head. "Did you sleep all right?"

She nods, not saying a word before she moves over to the couch, sitting on it and grabbing the throw blanket from over the back to cover herself.

"I see someone is exactly like their father," Everleigh mumbles from her seat on the stool. I walk over, trying not to laugh as I hand her one of the cups of coffee before bending down to kiss her lips. One of her hands comes up and holds my cheek as she kisses me, smiling at me, and fuck, does it ever feel good. I have never felt so content in my whole life. When we got home last night after the big bakery opening, I threw some steaks on the grill. She and Saige prepared the salad to go with it, and then Everleigh made her broccoli and cheddar rice, which was one of the best things I've ever eaten in my life. It felt like we've been doing it our whole lives. I wasn't overly affectionate with Everleigh, but I didn't shy away from kissing her if I wanted to. Saige has never seen me with a woman before, and I didn't know how she would react. But it's Everleigh—everyone who meets her falls in love with her. Everyone wants to be friends with her, and Saige is one of them. "Exactly like her dad." She runs her fingernails through my beard, making me shiver.

Our eyes are locked on each other, and I marvel in the way hers are light. I hope mine communicate to her how much I love her. "I'm like Dad?" Saige asks from the couch, and I break eye contact with Everleigh before walking over to sit beside Saige and put her feet in my lap. Everleigh faces us, wearing a pair of shorts and matching tank top with the matching sweater she uses for a robe. The ends of her hair are still wet from the shower we took together before Saige got up. It was the only way Everleigh would let me fuck her. She refused to even touch my dick in bed, knowing Saige could get up at any moment. Besides, she was so exhausted from the whole day and being on her feet that she fell asleep almost the minute her head hit the pillow. To be honest, I didn't give a shit as long as both my girls were under my roof. I went to bed and had good fucking dreams. It was even better when I woke up and felt Everleigh beside me.

"Oh, yeah." She nods, not moving from the stool, leaning with her back against the counter before she gets up with her cup of coffee and sits across from us, curling her feet under her. I want her to sit next to me. "He would camp out on the couch until the afternoon if no one told him to get up."

"I did not." I try to defend myself, but she's right. "Not the whole day." She tilts her head to the side, and I know she's going to list each and every time I did it. "What do you want to eat for breakfast?"

"See that, Saige?" She points at me. "That is what he does when he knows I'm right."

Saige laughs when I groan and roll my eyes. "See? That also means I'm right." She takes a sip of her coffee. "I can make some cinnamon roll pancakes," she offers, "or blueberry lemon."

Saige gasps. "You can make cinnamon roll pancakes?" She asks this as if Everleigh just told her she can give her all the answers to the next math quiz.

"I have to see if your dad has all the ingredients, but if not, I'll go to the store today and make sure we have them for tomorrow. I have to go to the bakery this afternoon to prep the dough for tomorrow."

"Can I come and help?" Saige asks, and Everleigh looks at her with glistening eyes.

"If your dad says you can, sure." She smiles.

"Did you finish all your English homework?" I turn my attention to Saige who nods. "And math?"

"Almost." She tosses the cover off her. "I can do it while you make bagels."

"Is that what you want to eat?" I ask, and she nods. "With cream cheese or something else?"

"Cream cheese, please," she answers as she walks out of the living room and toward her bedroom, where I hear her close the door. My eyes move from the hallway, then go back to Everleigh, who is looking at me. "What's that look for?"

She puts her coffee on the table and walks to me, standing between my legs. "I thought I loved you before," she declares as I sit up, putting one hand on her hip and running her hand through my almost dry hair. "But seeing you in dad mode." She looks down at me as I look up at her. "You're a DILF." I throw my head back and laugh at her. "Like hard-core DILF." She leans down and kisses my lips. "I want to do so many dirty things to you."

"Do you?" I extend my hand to put my cup on the table, grabbing her waist and yanking her to me. She yelps as she straddles my hips, sitting right on my cock. "I want to hear all about it." Her head goes back as the room fills with her laughter while my mouth goes to her neck. She raises her shoulder and bends her neck to stop me, giggling even more. "I want to do dirty things to you too," I mumble, pushing her down harder on my cock. "You know what we haven't done?" Her eyes light up, and her eyebrows rise. "I haven't come on your tits yet. Or face-fucked you," I whisper in her ear, my hand roaming up her back.

"I think I'm going to go take another shower," she mumbles, "with a certain pink toy."

"No." I grip her neck in my hand. "You don't touch yourself or your toys unless I'm in the room with you."

"You are not the boss of me," she snaps.

"I may not be the boss of you, but this is mine." I grab her ass with both my hands. "And these are mine." I grab her tits, teasing her nipples. "And this . . ." I move my hand down to her mound, and she jumps off my lap.

"I get the picture," she hisses, "and you have to get bagels in the toaster." I get up, pulling her to me, and her chest crashes into mine as she wraps her arms around my neck.

"I love you, baby." I smile down at her. "More than yesterday and less than tomorrow."

"I love you more," she replies as Saige enters the room.

"I'm done," Saige announces. "Now can we go?"

"Yeah," I say, letting go of Everleigh but bending and kissing her lips. "I'll start the bagels."

"I'll go make the bed, and I might have to stop at home and get a change of clothes."

"Need you to pack a bag," I say, and she looks at me. I know she wants to argue with me, but with Saige in the room, she doesn't dare.

"I'll think about it," she mumbles before walking out of the living room and grabbing her coffee on the way out.

"I'll get the bagels," I offer, grabbing my own cup of coffee and taking a seat. "You get the cream cheese."

She walks to the fridge, pulling out the tub of cream cheese and also the strawberries and blueberries. "Is Everleigh going to sleep here again tonight?" Saige asks me, and I look over at her.

"I was hoping she would," I reply. "Is that okay with you?"

"She's nice," Saige says. "You like her a lot, don't you?"

"I do." I put the bagel in the toaster and then turn to look at her. "I love her." Her eyes go big. "And I want her with me all the time. Just like I want you here with me all the time."

"Mom said you always loved her." Saige shocks me. "Says Everleigh was always the one you were in love with, even with her." I take a deep inhale, wanting to call Karla up and tell her what a fucking moron she is, but I have to take care of this first. "Did you love Mom?"

"I love your mother because she gave me you," I answer her as honestly as I can. "I'll always love her because she's a part of you. And I love you with my whole heart," I explain softly. "Just the way I have loved Everleigh."

"I'm happy she's here with you when I'm not here," she says. "You were always lonely when you called me."

I shake my head. "I'm always happy," I deny. "I wasn't always lonely," I tease her, and she points at me.

"You're lying." She giggles. "Just like Everleigh said."

"I can see the two of you are going to gang up on me," I accuse when the bagel pops out of the toaster.

"Nah." She shakes her head. "I'm always going to be on your side." I look over at her. "You're my dad."

"You bet your ass," I say. She walks over to the sink with the strawberries, opening them and letting the water soak them.

"What are we doing?" Everleigh asks, walking into the kitchen wearing exactly what she was wearing yesterday.

"Dad says you're moving in," Saige announces, and I see Everleigh's mouth hang open. "It's good because he's lonely," she continues, the color in Everleigh's face draining, "and now with you here, he won't be lonely when I'm not here." She turns off the water. "Which he totally lied to me about, but I caught him like you said."

"I wasn't lying." I turn to spread some cream cheese on the bagel.

"He's doing it again," Saige teases. "See?"

"I see." Everleigh walks over to me and puts one hand on my back. "Are you lonely without her?"

I look at her, seeing she's teasing me. "Now that you're moving in"—I turn it back on her—"I'll be less lonely with you here, but I'll still miss Saige."

"I'll still call you every night, Dad," Saige offers. "And when I go away to college, now you'll have Everleigh to take care of you."

"Off to college?" I shriek. "You aren't even in middle school."

"Dad, time flies," she deadpans. Everleigh buries her face in my back, and I can feel her body shaking as she tries to muffle her laughter.

"Eat your breakfast before I turn around, and you're an old lady."

"It's not going that fast," she jokes, taking a bite of her bagel.

I turn and wrap my arms around Everleigh. "So when are you moving in?"

Epilogue One

EVERLEIGH

Two months later

"YOU DIDN'T HAVE TO come with me," I say as we climb the steps to my fourth-floor apartment.

"You think I was going to let you come up here and pack up all by yourself"—he grips my hips, pulling them back to him—"for the whole weekend?" His head buries into my neck. "For the whole weekend." He repeats his words as he takes a deep inhale. "Without you by my side."

"I think you would have survived." I put the key in and turn it, opening the door and stepping into the apartment. "It's two days."

"Two days without you is like a lifetime." His fingers squeeze my hips tighter while I slip the key out of the lock. For the last two months I've been in his bed, even if I didn't want to be. The minute that he told Saige I was moving in, I was in. He helped me pack my bags and then watched me unpack them with a smile on his face. I wish I could say that the past two months have been uneventful but they haven't been.

After discussing everything with Brock about the Cartwrights, we went and got a lawyer. He told the lawyer everything, who then brought all the proof to the sheriff's office and then held a meeting with the safety officials. Just last week, the story ran in the paper and there were now countless lawsuits brought to the Cartwrights as well as criminal charges. From what we've heard, they will be lucky if they have a penny left.

The room is filled with a thickness from being closed all these months. "I need to get a window open in here." I walk over to the living room window, pushing it up and letting some air in.

"You lived here?" Brock snaps at me. I look over at him as he stops in the middle of the room and looks it all over. I have to be honest, never in my wildest dreams did I think he would be standing here. If someone told me that, I would have said you were out of your mind. But now here we are.

"Yup," I say, trying not to be hurt by his words, shrugging. "This is all mine." I immediately correct myself, "This was all mine. Now it's going to be someone else's."

"This place is the size of our bathroom." I roll my eyes at him.

"It is not," I counter, going to the bedroom and also opening the window. "Besides, rent is much more expensive in the city."

"Baby," he says, putting his hands on his hips, and I swear the minute he calls me that, my knees still get weak. It's crazy how much I missed it without admitting it to myself I missed it. "I hate thinking of you living here."

"Well, the good news is that I don't live here anymore." I look around at the tiny space where I made my home, smiling at him. "At least not for much longer. Why don't you start packing the kitchen, and I'll go and pack my bedroom?"

"Sure thing, baby," he agrees, kissing my lips and grabbing my ass in both of his hands. He squeezes me as he passes and grabs a box before walking into the kitchen.

Turning, I make my way to the little bedroom I had. I open the closet and pull out the large suitcase as I slowly start filling it with clothes, making a giveaway pile at the same time I pack the clothes I'm taking with me. I hear slamming coming from the kitchen and smile, knowing the only real reason he is here is because he wants me to be fully moved into his house. He hated knowing that I had an apartment, and I think it was because it was easy for me to leave in his eyes. Little does he know, I've been itching to give up my apartment since he asked me to move in, but I've been doing it in baby steps not to seem like I'm overwhelming him and Saige.

"I'm done in the kitchen," Brock announces, coming in the bedroom and falling on my bed. It's a twin bed, so he's already too big for it. He folds his arm and places his hand on his temple as he watches me move around. "What time are they coming to get all the furniture?" We also discussed putting my stuff in the spare bedroom when I finally gave up my lease. But he has everything, so it would be too cramped. He even offered to get rid of some of his things to make me more comfortable, but I decided it was best to just donate it to a women's shelter. They are going to take everything I have, even my kitchen stuff. It was a huge relief knowing the only thing I had to bring back was my clothes and my linens and towels.

"They said they would be here between two and five," I answer, closing the suitcase once all my clothes are in there. "They will call me thirty minutes before." He watches me as I pull the luggage off the bed, getting up to roll it to the front door.

"I have to do the bathroom and my office, and we're done," I say.

"Why don't I do the bathroom and you do your office?" he suggests. "Then we can go and get something to eat while we wait for them to call you."

"Look at us"—I wrap my arms around his neck—"multitasking." I get on my tippy-toes. "And then, if we have enough time, I might have to pay you back for helping me pack up my things."

"Baby," he says, grinning, "any time you want to drop to your knees, I'm never going to stop you."

"Drop to my knees?" I joke. "I was thinking of you eating me out and making me come on your tongue." He glares. "It would make me happy, and that's all you need, right?"

"Very funny." He shakes his head. "Or you blow me while I eat you, and we're both happy."

"We could do that also." I laugh, walking over to my desk and starting to clear things away. I have organized everything when he comes out of the bathroom, holding on to something in his hand.

"I'm assuming we are taking this with us?" He holds up the pink vibrator in his hand that I keep in the shower.

I can't help but laugh when he turns it on and the sound of vibrating now fills the room. "It's a good one, for sure." I wink at him. "There is a blue box under my bed," I say. "Toss it in there."

He gasps. "You have a treasure chest and didn't pack that first?" He walks over to my bedroom and comes out with the box in one hand, placing it on the coffee table. "After we finish packing, we'll go through that and see."

"Don't promise me a good time, Brock, and not follow through." I point at him. "We won't even have a bed here."

"I booked us a room," he informs me, and now I'm the one gasping.

"I thought you said we would just camp out like we did back in the day."

"Baby, we are both too old to sleep on a wood floor. And we are sleeping in a king-size bed in a hotel. We'll even order room service. It'll be like camping."

I throw my head back and laugh. "That isn't like camping at all."

He puts the pink vibrator in the box and then turns back to the bathroom. "Are there any more toys I should know about?" he asks over his shoulder.

"I'll let you find out," I sing at his retreating back before I go back to cleaning my desk. I put all my documents in my backpack when he comes out with a box with the word "bathroom" on it, and he puts it in the corner of the room next to the luggage.

My phone rings at one thirty, telling me they will be here within the hour. I take a deep inhale when the buzzer rings, walking over and opening the door. Two guys are waiting for me, and two more guys are hanging out on the stairs. Brock tells them he can lend a helping hand to make it go quicker. I point at things as they slowly start to empty my apartment. I thought I would feel a touch sadder, but it's more of a happiness than anything. They carry out the last box at the same time as someone is coming up the stairs. Brock comes out of the apartment, wiping the sweat from his brow. "Hey," Patrick says, giving me a chin up and a sly smirk. "You're back in town." He stops at his door across the way from me.

"Yeah," I reply softly.

"You moving out?" he asks after he opens his door.

"I am," I confirm. He puts his hands on his hips and then takes in Brock, who comes to stand next to me.

"That sucks." He either has a death wish or couldn't care less that Brock is staring daggers at him. "Well, hit me up if you are ever in town."

"Yeah," Brock says, "you wait for that, buddy." He puts his arm around my shoulders and pulls me inside, slamming the door behind me. "Friend of yours?"

"Um." I hesitate, looking up at the ceiling and moving my head side to side. "He was a friend that—"

"You fucked."

"Sort of?" I tell him, and his eyebrows go up. "Okay, fine, we used to hook up from time to time."

"More than once?"

"Sort of." I put my hands on his abs. "It was more of, 'Oh hey, you're home, I'm home.'" I can see his neck get tight. "But obviously not now."

"Obviously," he growls with his teeth clenched.

"Why don't we load up your truck and take off?" I urge him. "You have that whole hotel room waiting, and I have to thank you for today."

"Hmm," he mumbles, walking over to my luggage and picking it up while I go and grab a box of linens. It takes four trips up and down before the apartment is empty. I walk over to the little counter and put my key down on it before turning and walking out, the door locking behind me. Brock puts his hand in mine and ushers me down to his truck.

I get in, taking one more look at my building before he drives out of the parking lot, stopping in the corner near the dumpsters. "What are you doing?"

"Got to toss something," he says, and I think he's going to throw out some of the takeout containers we accumulated on our drive here. I watch him get out and round the front of the truck, opening the back door.

I look over my shoulder, seeing him snatch my treasure chest. He slams the back door closed, and the next thing I see is the chest flying through the air, opening as a couple of my vibrators fly through the air with it and land in the dumpster. I gasp at the same time he opens his door and gets back into the truck. "You did not just do that."

"Oh, baby, I just did that. There is no fucking way that was coming home with us, knowing that you used it with someone else."

"I cleaned them"—I scowl at him—"and I didn't really use all of them with him. Just a few."

He puts the truck in drive and looks over at me. "I can't believe you right now."

"You come into our home and find something from my ex, are we going to keep it?"

"Yes," I snap as he drives down the street, knowing full well I would probably set it on fire. I turn and look out the window, pissed at him.

The truck comes to a stop, and when I look up, we're in the parking lot at the sex shop. "What is this?"

"Got to replace the chest," he declares, "with stuff that only you and I will touch." He opens his door and steps out, looking at me. "You coming, or you going to let me decide what to put in there?" He just stares at me. "I've always wanted to get that paddle."

"You are so fucking lucky that you're hot." I open the door and step down, walking around to his side. "And that I love you and Saige, or else."

He grabs my hips, pulling me to him. "Yeah," he states, "I'm the luckiest guy in the world."

The bells ring on top of the door as soon as I place the donut trays in the display cases. Autumn comes in with Landon in his stroller, clapping as they walk in. "This is an early surprise." I look up and see it's not even eight in the morning.

"Ugh, I know." She pushes the stroller as I round the counter and stop in front of Landon. I squat down and kiss his neck, listening to him giggle. "We got an early phone call from Emmett."

"Oh no," I say, standing in front of her, "is everything okay?"

She looks around, making sure we are both alone. "I'm not sure. He called Charlie this morning. He's headed up north to pick up his daughter."

"Excuse me?" I ask, shocked. "His daughter?"

"Yeah." She nods. "One he didn't know he had."

Epilogue Two

BROCK

One year later

I GRAB THE WORK ORDER on the desk and head back to the garage with it in my hand, at the same time the phone rings in my back pocket. I pull it out, sliding the green button when I see it's Everleigh calling. "Hey, baby." I walk over to my workstation, dropping the work order down on the table and sitting on the stool.

"Hey"—her voice is low and something about it has the hair on the back of my neck standing up—"don't freak out."

I don't know why but I'm already on my feet. "What happened?"

"Nothing," she says. "Okay, so I was driving to go to check out the food truck." I close my eyes and the blood feels like it's draining from my body. "And then I didn't feel right," she adds and I hear car doors slamming in the background, "so I pulled over."

"Where are you?" I rush out the front door and head for my truck.

"I'm fine," she starts to say, "really. I think it's just I haven't eaten anything and maybe my blood sugar went down."

"Everleigh," I grit, my teeth clenched together, starting the truck, "where the fuck are you?"

"Um, so I called Mom and she had the audacity to call Oliver, who called an ambulance."

"Jesus fucking Christ," I swear. "I'll meet you at the hospital."

"I'm fine," she tells me. "It's all for nothing."

"If Oliver sent an ambulance, do you think he thinks it's fine?"

She groans, "He's an overachiever and is begging for me to call him Dad." She tries to joke but I feel like I'm about to rip the steering wheel off and toss it across town.

"He's a cardiologist, for Christ's sake."

"I'm fine," she repeats, not talking to me. "I just need a little apple juice or maybe a cupcake, and I'll be good as new."

"You said you think you passed out," someone says and I hear the rustling of her hand on the phone.

"I have to go. I'm fine. It's all fine. I'm going to kill Oliver, but it's fine," she assures and then she turns to whoever and doesn't click the phone off so I can hear her. "I said, I think I could have blinked and maybe fallen asleep," she hisses out before she finally disconnects.

I speed all the way over to the hospital, barely parking before rushing into the emergency room. I practically smash into the sliding glass door when it takes too long. I run to the woman who is sitting behind a glass divider. "I'm here for Everleigh Bishops." I'm pissed she still doesn't have my name, even though she has my ring on her finger. Something I did as soon as we got back from her apartment and officially moved all her stuff into my house.

I look around to see if Maddie is here, then I look back at the woman who is typing things in her computer. "The ambulance is bringing her in. She called me."

"She is being registered," she tells me like it's not a fucking emergency, and I look over at the sign that says we will not tolerate any abusive behavior. I want to grip the paper in my fist and rip it down. "You'll be able to see her in a little bit."

"Yeah, no," I mumble and pull out my phone and call Oliver, who answers after one ring.

"Where are you?" He doesn't even say hello.

"I'm in the emergency room," I reply, and I hear Everleigh in the background.

"I'm not talking to you," she scolds, "and I mean it this time."

I look over at the two doors that swing open, and Oliver comes out and motions with his head to go to him.

"Where is she?" I ask him as I follow him. "What happened?"

I can hear her voice, and even though I'm freaking out, I somewhat calm down when I hear her say, "I said, I'm fine."

Oliver moves the curtain to the side and I see her in the hospital bed. She's wearing exactly what she was wearing when she kissed me goodbye this morning before rushing out. I walk over to the side of the bed that the nurse isn't standing at, taking her hand in mine and bringing it to my lips. She looks up at me, trying to give me a reassuring look, as she squeezes her hand in mine. The nurse is taking her blood pressure. Her eyes come to me. "I'm fine," she repeats, trying to reassure me.

"Her blood pressure is a little high," the nurse tells Oliver.

"It should be skyrocketing," she barks to the nurse, "and it's all his fault." She points to Oliver and then we hear Maddie walking in.

"What on earth?" I turn to see she's still wearing her apron from the bakery. "What the hell happened?" She rushes over to the side of Everleigh's bed, moving her hair from the side of her face.

"Nothing," Everleigh snaps. "I was feeling fine. Then, the back of my neck started to get hot and my eyes suddenly felt really heavy, so I pulled over to the side of the road, and I made the horrible mistake of calling him"—she points to Oliver—"who blew this whole thing out of proportion."

"You fainted in your car." Oliver puts his hands on his hips. "You are lucky that you pulled over. Can you imagine if you hadn't?" Maddie gasps and I close my eyes.

"Great," Everleigh says. "Now I'll never be allowed to drive by myself."

"She's not wrong," I mumble. "What could have caused this?"

"It could be a whole bunch of things," Oliver says.

"Or it could be nothing," Everleigh snaps and then looks at the nurse. "I would like to get a doctor, please," she says and then side-eyes Oliver. "A real doctor."

"I'm a real doctor," Oliver reminds. "We are going to do some blood work," he tells the nurse, ignoring the hiss that comes out of Everleigh. "Then we'll go from there."

"You are wasting everyone's time," she insists.

"Do it for me," Maddie says. "For my peace of mind." Maddie then looks at me. "And for Brock, who looks like he's about to go Hulk on everyone."

"Fine," she gives in, "but only because after that, I can say I told you so."

"Works for me," Oliver quips, walking out with the nurse as Maddie follows him, leaving the two of us alone.

"I'm fine," she whispers when it's just the two of us. "Brock." I blink, not realizing I am staring at her, not saying anything.

"Do you know how scary that was," I finally say, "when I think of what could have happened?"

"I know." She pulls me down by yanking her hand that is

holding mine. Once I'm close enough, she lifts her other hand and puts it to my cheek. "I'm okay, Brock."

I put my forehead on hers as I breathe in her scent. "I promise I'm going to be okay."

"I can't lose you," I declare in a whisper.

"Honey." Her thumb moves on my cheek.

"We can't lose you." I stare into her eyes. She and Saige are thick as thieves. They spend as much time together as they can. If Everleigh is home, Saige is right by her side and it takes Everleigh a couple days to perk back up when she leaves us to go back to her mother's. Something I know she hates just as much as I do.

"I promise you, if I wasn't okay, I would tell you." She stares into my eyes. "I wouldn't fuck with this. Especially since I just got you back."

"We set a wedding date," I demand of her, "tonight. I want a date and it has to be in the next three months." Her eyes go big. "Consider yourself lucky I'm not forcing you to do it this weekend."

She doesn't say anything to me because the nurse comes back in to take her blood. I pull a chair to sit by her bed, my leg going up and down nervously as we wait for the results. Maddie is sitting in the other chair in the corner. She sits down for five minutes and then starts to pace the room for twenty minutes, or until Everleigh tells her to sit down.

She lies on the bed with her head back on the pillow and her eyes closed, only opening them when Oliver comes into the room with papers in his hands. "Well?" Maddie questions, springing out of her seat, her hand on her mouth and tears already in her eyes. "Is she okay?"

"She's fine." He smiles at Maddie, who goes to him and buries her face in his chest and he wraps his arms around her.

"Then why did she faint?" I stand up and turn to him.

"Well," he hesitates, looking at me and then at Everleigh, "if you want to know the results."

"You're not even my doctor," she snaps at him and all he can do is smile at her.

"She's pregnant," he states and things happen at the same time. Maddie shrieks, Oliver holds his hand over his head, Everleigh's eyes almost come out of her sockets, and I take a step back and my mouth opens in shock.

"I'm sorry, what?" Everleigh finally says, and I sit back down in the chair because my legs feel like they are about to give out on me.

"You're pregnant," he repeats, this time with so much joy in his voice it's like he's screaming. He looks at Maddie. "Your baby is having a baby."

"Are you sure?" Everleigh asks him and he nods his head but doesn't say anything because the nurse comes in with a machine.

"I heard we need an ultrasound," the nurse says. "Are you all staying?" She looks around the room.

"Try to get them out," Everleigh mumbles, "and I'll give you a hundred dollars and donuts for life."

The nurse just laughs at her as Oliver goes and closes the shades and then comes back to stand at my side. "I don't understand how this could happen," Everleigh voices to the nurse as she lifts her shirt halfway. Then the nurse grabs a towel and tucks it in the waistband of her yoga pants, pushing them down, before grabbing a white bottle and squirting blue liquid on her stomach. "I don't know how this could happen," she repeats the words and then looks at me. "How did this happen?"

I can't help but smile at her before bending and kissing her lips. "You need me to tell you how this can happen?" I kiss her again. "You can't keep your hands off of me."

"Well, that's a lie," she huffs.

"Are you ready?" the nurse asks her as she puts the ultrasound transducer on her stomach. "Hopefully, we can catch it with this," she says, moving it around on her lower stomach. "If not, we can go internally."

"Nothing can go internally," I bark at the nurse and she tries to hide her smile.

"It doesn't hurt," she tells me as the sound of swooshing now fills the room.

"What is that?" Everleigh lifts her head and it looks like she's about to slap the nurse's hand away from her stomach.

"That," the nurse says and then turns the monitor for us, "is your baby."

"Oh my goodness," Maddie cries out as I stare at the black-and-white screen. I can see the baby moving around.

"That's," Everleigh whispers, "that's a baby."

"That is a baby," the nurse tells her as Oliver wraps his arm around Maddie's shoulder and pulls her to him. "It looks like you are about ten weeks."

"What?" Everleigh shrieks. "How?" She looks at the nurse. "I haven't skipped a period and I'm on birth control."

"Do you take it regularly?" Oliver asks her.

"Of course I take it regularly," she retorts. "I mean, there was that one time we got a bit drunk and then I forgot but I doubled up the next day."

"That would do it," the nurse says. "Congratulations." She puts the transducer back and then uses the towel to clean the gel off her stomach. "These are for you." She hands her a couple of pictures of the sonogram.

"I need one of those," Oliver says, "for the house, and then I'm going to scan it for my office."

"You haven't said a word." Everleigh looks at me. "Are you okay?"

"No," I say and Oliver stands up straight, "but I will be on Sunday since that is when we are getting married."

"Okay," Maddie says, "that is our cue to leave."

"I'm not leaving," Oliver replies, shaking his head and Maddie laughs as she pushes him out of the room.

"Brock," Everleigh says.

"No," I snap. "I'm not going to listen to anything you say." I put my hand lightly on her stomach. "The first time I was told I was going to be a dad, I was shocked," I start to explain to her, "and a little bit pissed at myself more than anything. I got married because I thought that was the right thing to do. Now I'm about to be a father again, and I'm feeling a little fucking guilty because it's the complete opposite of what I felt when it was Saige, and I have to believe I'm still a decent human for even feeling like that."

"Brock," she says softly, "you are the best freaking dad I know. Minus forcing her to eat all her veggies sometimes because cauliflower can be gross." I stop her from talking when I crash my lips on hers.

"We have to tell Saige," I say when I finally let her go, "and I'm not joking about us getting married."

"It doesn't matter to me."

"But it matters to me." I kiss her lips. "I want you to be fully mine."

"I was yours from the minute you smiled my way," she confirms, blinking away tears. "And now we'll be bonded for life with our child."

"Children," I remind her. "Saige, this one"—I motion to her belly—"and the next five to come."

"Five?" she gasps. "Let's work on one at a time."

"Fine," I pout, "but at least three more."

"Only if you give me a month before we get married," she counters.

"Deal," I agree, smiling and then stop when she winks at me.

"I would have done five and this Sunday." She takes a deep inhale. "Now, I don't know about you, but I'm starving."

"Then let's go." I slip my hand in hers as we walk out of the room. "Thank you," I tell her and she looks up at me, "for loving us like you do." She stops and wraps her arms around me.

"No," she replies, "thank you for making my dreams finally come true."

Exclusive Bonus Chapter

EVERLEIGH

THE ALARM BELLS START RINGING as the sleep starts to leave me, and my eyes flicker open. "Turn it off," I mumble, and then pull the blanket closer to me. "I want it off."

Brock lifts up on one arm and then looks at the door. "It's not mine."

"Brock," I hiss his name, "it's fucking coming from somewhere in this house." I open one eye. "Oh my God." I sit up. "Is that a secret burner phone, and you are having an affair?"

His eyes go into slits. "Or it could be Saige's."

I fall back down on the bed. "Or it could be Saige's," I mumble and turn back on my side. "Why does she have an alarm set for Saturday morning?"

"Um," he starts, and I just close my eyes.

"I don't really care enough," I tell him. "Close the door on your way out."

I feel him over me. "You have to get up also."

"No, I don't. It's my day off, and I just fell asleep." I try to push him off of me, but he pulls me tighter to him. "Brock."

"Baby"—he buries his face in my neck—"you have to get up."

"Brock, I literally have the weekend off. Do you know what that means?" I ask him. "It means I don't have to get up until I want to get up. I'm tired," I huff. "Like between the nausea and you hovering, and then all of a sudden I don't want to sleep at night. I want to sleep until maybe tonight or even tomorrow morning."

"You can't."

"Stop saying that," I tell him, and then hear the sound of Saige's door opening and her running to our side of the house.

"Happy wedding day!" she cheers, throwing her hands in the air with the biggest smile on her face.

"What are you talking about?" I chuckle and ask her, confusion on my face. "That's next month, honey."

"No, it's not." She sings the words, shaking her head side to side. "It's today."

I'm looking at her when the doorbell rings. "I'll get it." She turns and rushes out of the room as Brock tosses the covers off himself and gets up, grabbing a pair of shorts.

He walks to my side of the bed and holds out his hand for me. "You need to get up."

"What is going on right now?" I ask, and hear squealing coming from the front door.

"Is she still sleeping?" I look over my shoulder and see Autumn coming into the bedroom, wearing a baby-blue sweat suit and holding two cups in her hand. "One of these is decaf coffee." I scrunch up my nose at it. "The other is herbal tea."

"I don't want any of that." I shake my head. "What are you doing here?" I ask her, and then Saige runs back into the bedroom wearing almost the identical sweat suit.

"I'm ready." I look over at Brock, who smirks as he goes into the walk-in closet and comes back with a sparkly gold bag with white tissue sticking out of it.

"Why isn't she up already?" Autumn looks at Brock. "You

literally had one job: make sure she was up and ready to go by eight."

"I had more than one job," Brock grunts and then walks back to my side of the bed. "Baby"—he puts the bag down on the bed right next to my hip—"this is for you." I curiously look at him as I pull the tissue out of the bag and see a white sweater with matching pants, the same suit the girls are wearing, but white. "You can change into that, and then you have to go."

"I'm going to need you all to stop talking in code and tell me directly what in the f—" I look at Saige, not ready to swear in front of her. "Flick-flack is going on?"

"Why don't Saige and I wait for you in the kitchen? Brock can explain this to you, and we can get on our way since people are waiting for us." She ushers Saige out the door, closing it behind them.

My eyes go back to Brock. "What the fuck is going on?"

"Well . . ." He sits on the bed in front of me. "Remember at the hospital when I told you we were getting married this weekend? Then it was three months, but then you said you would do it this weekend?"

My mouth hangs open. "Yeah."

"Well, after discussing what kind of wedding you wanted, when you told me you just wanted it to be us and your mom and Oliver—plus Autumn, obviously—I called in a couple of favors, and, well . . . I figured if you were going to marry me this weekend anyway, might as well just do it."

"Are you out of your mind?"

"When it comes to you and you carrying my child, one thousand percent." He leans in and kisses my lips. "You don't have to do anything. All you have to do is put on this." He picks up the clothes in my lap. "Everything else is done. You go and do whatever Autumn set up, and then in four hours, you become my wife."

I look at him, blinking a couple of times. "You just couldn't wait." I toss the cover off myself and get up, throwing up my hands. "Literally said I would marry you in three months."

"I've waited ten years to get you back." He gets up and holds my face in his hands. "I'm not waiting one more fucking day for you to become my wife." His voice goes soft. "We've lost enough time; I'm not wasting more."

"Ugh." I roll my eyes. "When you put it like that"—I hold his wrists in my hand—"I guess we can do it today." The smile fills his face. "I'm going to change, and I'll be right out."

"I'll tell the girls." He turns and walks out of the room, and I pick up the sweater, seeing BROCK'S in capitals across the front and Bride written on the back. I shake my head, put on the sweat suit, and then join them in the kitchen.

"She's dressed," Saige declares. "We have to go." She turns, and I see the back of her sweater says Daughter of the Groom.

"What is on the back of yours?" I ask Autumn, who turns, and I see it says Friend of Brock's Bride. "What?"

"Brock was in charge of getting these, and this is what he got." She points to Brock.

"I went very simple," he explains. "You're welcome."

"Do you get one that says Everleigh's Groom on it?" I ask him.

He smirks. "I guess you'll see."

"Okay, let's get this party started"—Autumn claps her hands—"before he changes his mind and just drags you to the c—"

"Away," Brock cuts her off before she can tell me where we are getting married. "Go." He points to the door. "I'll see you in four hours."

"I don't even have a dress. I have nothing," I remind him. "I love you, you know I do, but these pictures will be displayed in our house for the rest of our lives and—"

"I got that covered," Autumn assures me. "It's all taken care of."

"I got a dress also." Saige jumps up and down, clapping her hands. "It's so pretty."

"You little stinker." I point at her. She's become, hands down, my favorite human ever. The bond we share is one I will cherish forever. "You were plotting this whole time." She smiles, her whole face lighting up with glee as she nods. "I'll get you back. I know what he got you for your birthday." I point at Brock, and she gasps.

"Let's go." Autumn herds us toward the door with Saige gabbing and asking me for hints about her present, but I use my fingers to zip my mouth closed and throw away the key.

I get into the truck and look over at Autumn. "I'm really nervous," I admit to her and put my hand to my stomach, "or that could be nausea. Either way, I think I might actually be sick."

She laughs as she heads toward . . . I don't even know where.

"Should I close my eyes?"

"No." She shakes her head. "This part isn't a secret. We are getting dressed at my house."

I look out the window at the trees passing us by. The same trees I drove past when I got into town, thinking it was going to be temporary, and now knowing I would fight anyone to come back here.

We pull up to her house, and I see my mother on the porch, waving her hand. She's in her own sweat suit. The truck comes to a stop, and we get out, my mother hugging Saige first, always, and kissing the top of her head, then coming to me. "Surprise." She smiles at me, slipping her hand in mine and squeezing it. "I'm"—she turns so I can see the back of her shirt that reads Mother of Brock's Bride. "I think he made sure everyone knew you were his bride." She laughs. "Oliver has one that says Married to Brock's Bride's Mother. Now, I'm under strict orders to make sure you are not stressed and you eat something."

"Shall we?" Autumn says, walking up the steps to her house and through the front door. I follow her, and the minute I step in, I stop in my tracks. Her living room, or what was her living room, is now transformed into a makeshift bridal shop on one side, and on the other side, the makeup and hair squad is waiting for us.

"Dad said I could have a bit of blush on my cheeks and a dusting of eyeshadow." Saige looks at me. "It's a special day."

"It is," I say, putting my hand to my mouth to stop the sob from coming out. "This is just more than I thought it would be." I fan my face with both hands to try to fight off the tears. "I'm getting married"—I look at my mother—"to Brock."

"That's what all the shirts say, so it must be true." Autumn walks over to the rack of dresses. "These are all for you to go through. There are twenty-five here, and that is all we could get with two days' notice."

I walk over to the first dress I see. I touch the spaghetti straps, and my fingers move gingerly down to the bodice that looks like it has little white flowers sewn on, scattered all over the front. "I like this one," I say softly as I pick it up and see how it flows to the floor with a little bit of a train. "It's whimsical." I look over at my mother, who nods. "I think this one."

"You can try them all on if you want," Autumn mentions, coming over to me to hand me a glass of orange juice in a champagne glass. "This is just so we can pretend we are fancy, drinking mimosas, but it's just orange juice, so don't get too excited."

"You need to eat," my mother urges, walking over to the kitchen and bringing me a plate with a couple of breakfast sandwiches. "Then we get you ready."

I nod my head and take a bite of the sandwich.

"Can I have a minute with Saige?" I ask my mother and Autumn. They smile at us and walk out of the room.

Saige is having her hair done exactly like mine. "Today is a big, big day," I start, and she looks at me. "Your dad and I are going to make promises to each other. But I also want to make promises to you."

"You do?"

"Of course I do," I reply, trying not to cry. "I know this is all new to you, but I just want to let you know that I promise to never be in the way of you and your dad."

"You never are," she says quickly.

"I promise I will be your biggest cheerleader and offer you all the support you will ever need." I put my hand on hers. "I love you with my whole heart, Saige."

She gets up. "Thank you for not being an evil stepmother like in the movies." I can't help but laugh at that. "Thank you for always being there when I need you." She hugs me, and I kiss the side of her head. "Dad is going to cry when he sees you," she states, letting me go, "and I'm going to win twenty dollars."

Two hours later, we are all walking out of the house, seeing Charlie standing there beside a truck. "I've been told to get your ass to him now." We all laugh. "Those were his exact words." He opens the back door for me to get in. Saige sits next to me, and my mother next to her, while Autumn sits in the front.

I put my hand in Saige's as we make our way to the wedding. Where? I have no idea, but I'd go to the ends of the earth for this man.

We pull up to the creek, and I see him standing there in a black suit at the end of a makeshift aisle that has little pots of flowers on either side. Oliver stands under a wooden arch adorned with flowers.

The truck stops, and Charlie looks over at us. "It's us first," he says of him and Autumn, "then Saige goes by herself, and then your mom and you."

"Okay," I agree, putting my hand to my stomach as they walk down the aisle holding hands.

"My turn," Saige announces, moving past my mother and getting out. She walks over to the side, grabbing flowers and then coming back. "These are for you from Dad." She hands me the bouquet of wildflowers.

"We should get out there," my mother urges, and all I can do is smile. She gets out first, and then I step out after her. We walk down the aisle, my eyes on Brock's the whole time.

"Hey, baby," he whispers when I get close enough to him. I see the tears in his eyes. "You look beautiful."

My mother kisses my cheek before walking over to the side with Autumn and Saige. Brock takes my hand in his.

"Hey, sweetheart," Oliver says, "you are the most beautiful bride after your mother."

"Hurry up," Brock grunts. "You said you could do this fast."

"We are gathered here today," Oliver starts, "because Brock told us to." Everyone but Brock laughs. "And now to the vows."

"Everleigh," Brock starts, "I think I started writing these vows many years ago." My breath hitches. "Silently, over the past years, I added things to them when I would give myself the grace to think about you. I knew you were the one for me the minute you looked over at me and told me you loved me." I pull up his hand to kiss it. "I knew for sure you were the one for me when I realized what a better person you are than me. Your heart is pure and forgiving, and I'm honored to be standing at your side. I promise you, from this day forward, you will never go a day without knowing how much I love you. I promise to be faithful to you, to respect you, and to communicate to my best ability."

"Good luck with that one," Oliver says, earning him some laughs but a side look from Brock.

"I promise to cherish you and put our family first before anything." He looks at Saige and winks at her. "I promise you that you have all of me, today, tomorrow, and forever."

"That was good," Oliver praises, nodding at him. "Is it her turn?"

"That's going to be tough to follow up on since you took all of my promises from me." He squeezes my hand. "I promise you everything that you promised me, with a couple of modifications. There are no words deep or beautiful enough to describe how I feel about you, but I promise to tell you I love you every single day. Sometimes more than once. I promise to never stop holding your hand, literally and figuratively. One, because you won't let me, and two, because I don't want you to. I vow to be fully committed to you and our family. I vow to express gratitude for all of the beauty you bring into my life. I promise to weather every storm we have by your side, because there is no place else I'd rather be." He lets go of my hands so he can grab my face, right before he kisses me.

"We didn't even do the rings," Oliver jokes, making everyone laugh.

He lets go of me, and he looks over to Charlie holding out his hand. "With this ring," Brock begins, "you are mine. I mean, even without the ring you're mine, but this is—"

"It's like a cement block," I interrupt him as he slips the eternity band on my finger to match my engagement ring. I smile looking down at it. "I hope you got yourself a ring."

"I did," he confirms, "but I don't need it."

"Excuse me?" I cock my hip to the side. "I don't think so. If I have to walk around with this, you need to have one."

"I do," he says, "permanently." He holds up his hand, and I see his ring finger has a tattoo on it. "It's your signature." My mouth hangs open.

"Of course he did," Oliver says. "Is that where you went this morning?"

"Are we married yet?" Brock ignores his questions.

"I guess so." Oliver shakes his head.

"Good," Brock replies, bending to kiss me.

"Ladies and gentleman," Oliver announces, "Mr. and Mrs. Casey."

"About fucking time," Brock says, right before he seals it with a kiss.